Faith and Love

Written by

Cecelia Hopkins-Drewer

ISBN: 978-0-6481160-3-5
Published by CGH Literacy Institute,
Adelaide, South Australia, 2018

ISBN: 978-0-6481160-3-5

Acknowledgements: Cover Photograph by Allan Schultz

Fictional disclaimer:

All characters and events in this work are fictional, and while an effort has been made to recreate the era of the 1980s and incorporate selected aspects of history which are general knowledge; the story was written for entertainment purposes. The characters have no existence outside the imagination of the author and any similarity to persons or events outside the text is the result of coincidence.

CONTENTS

PROLOGUE: AUNT KATHY'S DIARY

Allegra turned to her children, Ellie and Terry: "I know how much you enjoyed me reading you Granny's diary last weekend, so I asked her whether she had kept a diary the next year."

"Oh and had she?" Ellie was instantly interested.

"I'm sorry Ellie," Allegra said, "Grandma said she had not kept her 1985 diary because that was a bad year for her. She suggested I ask Aunt Kathy whether she still had her diary."

"Who is Aunt Kathy?" Terry inquired.

"You know Granny's friend, we sometimes call great Auntie Kay?" Ellie supplied. "The one who gave you Bobo?"

Bobo was a wooden rabbit mounted on wheels. This was not so unusual, as these toys could be purchased in stores - what was special about Bobo was that he was painted lovingly in intricate detail. It was one of Terry's favourite playthings and was surviving his loving ministrations remarkably well.

"Ah Auntie Bobo," Terry murmured.

"The one who paints all the pretty pictures," Ellie said. "Are there pictures in the diary Mummy?"

"I don't know," Allegra said. She opened the diary and flipped the pages. A loose sheet fell out and Ellie caught it. The picture showed a slim angular young man, leaning against a retro-style motorcycle. He was half silhouetted against the sky as he was gazing out over a deep valley.

"Whoever is that?" Ellie asked.

"I don't know, Allegra answered. "Must have been some boy Aunt Kathy knew."

"I wonder why it was a bad year for Grandma," Ellie mused. "Maybe that was the year Great-Gran died. She has been dead forever."

"I'm not sure," Allegra said. "I would have to check. Would you like to hear the story now?"

"Yes please," Ellie cried, curling up comfortably on the sofa next to her mother.

Terry sat down too, although his head was more full of visions of Bobo than curiosity about the past. Allegra began to read the diary out loud:

"My name is Katherine Shipton, and I am sitting here, writing in this journal given to me by my friend Stephanie. Stephanie said that keeping a diary had really helped her last year, so I thought that I would try it for myself.

I have had a rather odd summer. I was looking forward to being home for Christmas and New Year, but my boyfriend Owen basically gave me an ultimatum, saying that he wanted us to either get married, or break up. Getting married would have required me to give up my Primary Teaching course, and that was just too much of a sacrifice for me to make. I figured that if Owen had really loved me, he would have been prepared to wait two years for us to be together forever.

I spent some time with Owen over the long break, but it just wasn't the same anymore. I thought that I would always be special to him, and it hurt to find out that I was no longer the most important person in his life. Owen was feeling disgruntled and wasn't talking to me half of the time, and he had begun to talk to other girls. It used to be assumed that Owen and I would be together at church youth functions, but now, people frequently forgot to even ask me along! By the end of the summer, I suspected Owen was developing a new love interest.

Stephanie wrote to me, and said that there would be guys who were keen to ask me out at university, and I can hardly wait to commence another semester. I also find it hard to believe that I am actually taking relationship advice from Stephanie Lowood, because she was incredibly innocent and rather inhibited at the beginning of last year!

Stephanie had a lot of trouble with Jeffrey Mannington, who was one of last year's graduating class, and also slightly weird in my opinion. Now she is settled with Garrick Morton, who she tells me has actually written to her every week over the long break! That is a pretty big achievement, because it is actually three months from the beginning of December until the end of February. Owen and I were feeling the strain of a long distance relationship after about a month!

So, here I am, taking advice from others, and feeling nervous about dating again. A break-up really knocks one's confidence, but I know deep down inside that I have done the right thing in putting my studies ahead of an unsteady relationship."

CHAPTER ONE: RETURN TO SILVER SPRINGS

The bus dropped Kathy off along the Bruce Highway just outside of Northcoast about three o'clock in the afternoon. She was lucky that the trip from Armidale to Silver Springs University only took about seven hours. Many of the other students had to travel much greater distances, and arrived absolutely exhausted.

Kathy had phoned ahead and booked the university car, so it was waiting on the edge of the road for her. Ever the gentleman, Luke picked up her bags and lifted them into the back of the station wagon.

"How are you Kathy?" he asked.

"I am good thank you Luke," Kathy said. "How are you and your girlfriend Tess?"

"I am well," Luke said, "And Tess is good too. She is waiting back at the dorms. She would have come with me to pick you up, but I have to make a stop off at Northcoast Station for some others, and there mightn't be enough room in the car."

"I am looking forward to seeing her," Kathy said.

"That is nice," Luke said sounding amused. "You seem happy to be back."

"I am," Kathy said confidently. "Second year is looking pretty good."

"Yes," Luke said, "I reckon it will be."

Luke merged onto the freeway, and they reached Northcoast Station in no time. It turned out that the 'others' Luke had to pick up were actually Stephanie and Garry, who had caught the train up from Wollongong.

Stephanie was actually from South Australia, but she had spent the last week of the holidays staying with Garry's family. Kathy was thrilled to see them, and they went through the whole hugging routine.

"Your holiday obviously went well," Kathy exclaimed.

"Yes," Stephanie said, "Garry's parents are pretty easy going."

"That's nice," Kathy said a little pensively. She had always gotten along well with Owen's parents too.

"I can't believe we are back for another year," Stephanie remarked as they settled into the car.

"I can," Kathy said, "I've actually given up a lot to do this course."

Stephanie made a sympathetic noise. "It takes dedication," she murmured.

"And I can probably look forward to bigger and better things," Kathy said cheerfully, and began to talk about neutral things. After all, Garry and Luke were present, and while one could be pretty sure that the boyfriend-of-a-friend had been privately filled in on the gossip, it was a general convention amongst the girls to pretend that the guys were still in complete ignorance.

They arrived at the university, and the boys helped the girls carry their bags up to their rooms. It was one of the few instances when the guys would be allowed to enter the girl's dormitory, as the rules governing male and female interactions were very strict.

Stephanie and Kathy were rooming together, down one end of the wing of the first floor of girl's dorm. Towards the end of previous year, they had discovered that the rooms next to the stairs were slightly bigger that those throughout the rest of the building, and booked one for themselves. Some of the older buildings on campus had been damaged by the hailstorms in January, but Stephanie and Kathy were lucky that having chosen a room in the new wing, their room was fine.

Kathy spent what was left of the afternoon unpacking her suitcases, and arranging everything in the cupboards. Another great feature of the new room was the bed, which was made of wood and had two large drawers built-in underneath. Tea time she dropped by the cafeteria briefly, saying, "Hello," to the many people she knew.

Their neighbour from across the corridor would be Phoebe, who had to travel all the way from Perth, and arrived later that evening. Phoebe started to unpack immediately, and as Kathy was also too excited to sleep, she went into the room Phoebe was sharing with Cara, and talked until two am. Stephanie, who was always a bit more law-abiding than Kathy, was fast asleep when she sneaked back into the room.

Kathy dragged herself out of bed about eight am in the morning, feeling decidedly bleary eyed. She threw some jeans on aimed herself towards the cafeteria, almost bumping into Cara in the corridor.

"Hello Kathy," Cara said. "How are you this morning?"

"Tired," Kathy said. "I hope I will feel better after breakfast."

"I am sure you will," Cara said, "I am heading that way myself, if you want to come along."

"I would love to," Kathy said. "Did you sleep well?"

"Oh yes!" Cara said. "I beat Phoebe to the room yesterday and picked the best bed!"

Kathy laughed: "It sounds like you two will have fun."

"Yes," Cara said, "It makes a lot of sense for us to room together, after all you are rooming with Stephanie."

"That's for sure," Kathy agreed, "Do you know who Joelle is rooming with this year?"

Joelle was Stephanie's former room-mate. They had been good friends for the most part, with the occasional moment of tension because Joelle had accepted an invitation to attend a social with Jeff, the guy that Stephanie had liked. It turned out that Jeff had only been using Joelle to get to Stephanie, and the girls eventually discussed the matter, but the harm had been done.

"Joelle is rooming with Debbie, Tess is rooming with Brenda. Anita is also rooming with Elisabet," Cara said.

"You seem to have caught up with everybody," Kathy remarked, feeling a bit bemused.

"Actually, I checked the floor plan," Cara replied smugly.

"Well, that's one way of finding out," Kathy said.

The girls had reached the cafeteria by now. The room was fairly full, so they collected a bowl of corn-flakes and a glass of orange juice each.

Around ten am, Kathy made her way down to the administration block. She had breakfasted and showered, and filled in all her papers. Standing in line was dull work, so she occupied the time chatting to Debbie and her boyfriend David. They had enjoyed their holidays, and were looking forward to continuing their studies.

There were quite a few first-year students standing around looking disoriented and confused. The returning students looked at them curiously, wondering which of the newcomers would become their friends.

Classes commenced on Wednesday. Kathy was enrolled to do History of Christianity, Education Theory for Teachers, Practice Teaching stage II, and Psychology. Her minor specialty dropped out to be replaced by specialist subjects like Infant Maths and Infant Reading. Her major specialty, Art, continued on and she was very pleased to be able to do pottery for a semester.

Kathy had a full morning, beginning with History of Christianity, which sounded like it would be an absolutely fascinating subject. It covered the progression of the Christian church from the time of the apostles through the Catholic period to the reformation, and even touched on some contemporary issues. The lecturer had done a great deal of research on the subject, and presented even this first lecture in a scholarly and critical manner.

After History of Christianity, they had an hour for general assembly, and then Kathy had Education Theory for Teachers. Education Theory promised to be a fairly dry subject. It seemed like many people had tried to explain the learning process by developing specialist language with which to describe it. However, it was Kathy's opinion that learning involved a bit of a miracle, and she would be surprised if she came across a theory that explained that!

The next afternoon, Kathy had a three hour pottery session. She went across to the studio, absolutely thrilled and full of anticipation, and left frustrated and discouraged. The beautiful smooth pots that she had imagined myself making were further off than ever, because she could not even manage to keep a round lump of clay together on the wheel. No matter how hard Kathy tried, the clay broke up and flew off in all directions.

The instructor, a flamboyant lady also known familiarly as "Ms. Louise", however, was quite pleased with Kathy's efforts. "It takes practice," Ms. Louise said, and showed Kathy how to mix up her own batch of clay. That turned out a bit runny, but all Ms. Louise said to that was, "You're almost there!"

Almost there or not, Kathy felt like a hopeless case, and was glad when she was eventually released to go up to the Cafeteria to drown her sorrows in orange juice.

The next day, Kathy had a full morning with Psychology, Practice Teaching, and Infant Maths. These were all very task oriented subjects and left Kathy feeling tired. She spent the afternoon organising her papers and making folders for all her subjects.

In the evening, about six o'clock, Kathy got a call to the foyer. Pleased to hear that there was a phone call for her, she entered one of the booths and picked up the receiver.

"Katherine Shipton speaking," she said.

"Hello Kathy," a male voice said down the line, and her heart turned over. It was Owen.

"Hello Owen," Kathy said. "How are you?"

"Not so good in fact," Owen said petulantly.

"Whatever has happened?" Kathy asked in concern.

"It didn't work out for me with Isabella," Owen said.

"Oh!" Kathy said. "I don't know what to do about that. It really isn't my business anymore."

"Actually, it is all your fault," Owen said.

"I don't see how it could be," Kathy said in confusion.

"If it hadn't been for you, I wouldn't be looking around for a new girlfriend," Owen said, "And if it wasn't for you, I wouldn't be striking out with all the girls I meet."

"You gave me little choice but to break our relationship off," Kathy said. "And it took the patience of a saint for me to watch you and Bel getting closer all summer."

"Don't get all holier-than-thou on me Kathy," Owen whined. "You know what I mean."

"I don't believe that I do," Kathy said firmly. "I haven't interfered in your new relationship, and I'm not even in Armidale anymore."

"Everyone here still remembers you Kathy," Owen grumbled, "And I remember you too well."

"Are you saying that you would like to get back together with me?" Kathy asked, puzzled.

"No way," Owen said, "I would never get back with you Kathy, you are a shrew."

"I don't know why I ever went out with you Owen," Kathy said in exasperation. "It seemed like a good idea when we were in high-school, but we are adults now. Give yourself some time to get over our break-up before you try to date again, and for mercy's sake leave me alone!"

"Is that all you have to say Kathy?" Owen asked.

"I think so Owen," Kathy said numbly, "It's truly very good advice, and most generous of me, under the circumstances."

Kathy put the phone down firmly, and strode back to her room. Stephanie and Phoebe were there, and they looked at Kathy in concern.

"You don't look good," Stephanie said, "What was the phone call about?"

"Owen is getting moany and silly," Kathy reported dejectedly.

"Oh dear!" Phoebe remarked, "If he keeps it up, you might have to refuse to speak to him."

"I hope that it doesn't come to that," Kathy said solemnly. "I still care about him a bit."

Kathy spent morning in the library and the afternoon catching up with friends. On the whole, everyone seemed happy to be back at university. At the Uniting Church vespers that evening, she saw her friend Lionel, and crossed the floor to speak to him. Kathy expected to find him empathetic as they had often commiserated with each other about the hardships of off-campus romances the previous year.

"How are you Lionel?" Kathy said.

"I am good, Kathy," Lionel said, "Really, really good." He looked very pleased with himself.

"I am glad to hear it," Kathy said. "What has made you this happy?"

"Can I tell you a secret Kathy?" Lionel asked. "Although it's not really a secret anymore because I have told so many people."

"Of course," Kathy said, "Go ahead."

"Well, I am graduating this year, and as Barbara also finishes her Information Technology course at the Queensland Institute of Technology, I have asked her to marry me at the end of the year!" Lionel announced. "And guess what - she said yes!"

"That is wonderful," Kathy exclaimed, trying to be happy for them.

"It is great," Lionel agreed, "I am so happy that we're both completing our degrees - and with a wedding to plan and a honeymoon to look forward to, this year will absolutely fly."

"So it will," Kathy said, "Congratulations and all the best."

"Thank you," Lionel said, and turned to tell his news to some of the others.

Kathy took the opportunity to slip out of the women's assembly area and go back to her room. She didn't want to be mean spirited in any way, but this highlighted her grief and brought all her lost dreams back to her.

If only Owen had been willing to wait a couple of years, it could have been like that for them too.... Kathy cried herself to sleep.

The morning dawned bright and Kathy put on a cotton dress in a tartan print. She usually loved this dress because it was the height of the current fashion, but today she found it's flounces just a touch too cheerful. It seemed as though everyone Kathy knew was paired off, and no one wanted to listen to her. Lionel and Barbara were engaged, Tess was going steady with Luke, Stephanie and Garry were in a stable relationship, Debbie and David were practically co-joined twins, and even Phoebe was on cloud nine since being re-united with her boyfriend, Bradley Parker.

Still, there was the Inter-denominational praise service and Reformed Church service to go to, life went on, and Katherine Shipton was never one to give up hope. By evening she was feeling slightly better. Although coupled, her friends were still her friends, and indeed, Joelle and Cara had not met anyone over the holidays, and were still single like her.

Around mid-evening the students converged in the gymnasium for a rowdy mixer dubbed "The Western Night". Kathy wore her red t-shirt with the tassel trimmed yoke, and her favourite jeans. She fussed around with her hair, finding that it really was too short for any elaborate styles, and finally managed to scrape it back into a diminutive pony tail.

By the time Kathy was ready, Stephanie and Phoebe had been collected by their escorts, and Kathy was left to navigate her way to the gymnasium alone. Luckily for her, the evening had been billed as a sort of fete, and Kathy could feel perfectly comfortable arriving as a single.

Upon entering the gymnasium, Kathy glanced around. Bales of hay had been stacked against the walls, and a select amount of straw was strewn upon the floor. Rough wooden partitions divided the stalls from one another.

Drinks and snacks were available from a trestle table near the main entrance. Up on the stage, several music students were making hill-billy screeching sounds with their guitars. A group of young people in the centre of the room were playing quoits, while another group were making sport with a ball and some wooden skittles.

Attracted by loud laughter, Kathy threaded her way through the crowd to discover that a number of photographs of the lecturers had been attached to a cork board. Students were queuing up to have the privilege of taking three free shots at their subject masters with a dart. Kathy joined them and attempted to avenge myself on her Pottery Instructor for the unsympathetic attitude she displayed, but so poor was her aim that Ms. Louise's portrait escaped relatively unscathed.

A pinging sound next attracted her attention, and Kathy found that a group had gathered around a multi-tiered stand where some of the guys were picking off soft-drink cans with well-aimed pebbles. At the very of the group stood a dark-haired young man, of above average height and wiry build. It was his shots that had accounted for the majority of the fallen cans.

Kathy looked the new boy up and down, and noticing her, he pranced as he mowed down the last of the tin cans. Everyone cheered, and the stall-holder busied himself re-assembling the array.

"That was impressive," Kathy remarked as the crowd dissipated a little.

"Would you like a chocolate frog?" the boy asked, "I've won half a dozen tonight."

Kathy accepted the frog cheerfully. Here was somebody who appeared to be as keen to make new friends as she was. "What is your name?" she asked.

"Rob," he replied shortly with a sparkle in his eye.

"Is Rob short for Robert?" Kathy asked curiously.

"No," he said, "Why don't you guess? I guarantee you will never get it."

"Oh," Kathy said, quite willing to play his game, "Would it be Robson?"

"Wrong!" He said. "Try again."

"Err, Robin or Roberto," Kathy ventured.

"Wrong again," he said. "It is actually Riobard."

"That is unusual!" she exclaimed, "I am just plain Kathy."

"You are not plain at all Kathy," Rob replied quickly.

Kathy laughed, "I bet you say that to all the girls".

"Only the ones who are actually listening," Rob retorted, and Kathy laughed again.

"You are wicked," she said, "Whatever are you doing here at university?"

"Getting my Pilot's Licence if at all possible," Rob replied.

"That is interesting and different," Kathy said.

"And very useful if you happen to hail from the centre of Australia", Rob said.

"Oh yes, it would be essential out there," Kathy said considering.

"Well, introductions and stuff complete, do you want to hang around and let me win you some more chocolate bars?" Rob queried. "I would like to try lassoing that saddle over there."

"I would be flattered," Kathy answered, surprised at the speed this new acquaintance was progressing. However, Rob was so light-hearted she could not accuse him of coming on strong. They spent the evening circulating amongst the stalls in the gymnasium, and Kathy enjoyed herself immensely.

Kathy spent the following morning attending classes, and the afternoon doing some required reading. Weekly reading reports were worth a certain amount of marks for Education Theory, and History of Christianity had a comprehensive textbook, which proved to be surprisingly interesting to read.

Tea time, Kathy ran into Rob in the cafeteria. He was as bright and friendly as he had been Sunday night, and told Kathy that he had spent the entire day out at the air-field. Apparently the Pilot's Licence programme got underway at an unbelievably early hour each morning, and continued on as long as was considered safe for the participants. All in all, it sounded like a pretty intense course.

"What were you doing down there today?" Kathy asked Rob.

"Inspecting the aeroplanes, learning the names of all the parts and going through safety regulations," he replied.

"Oh," Kathy said, "And when do you get to go up in the air?"

"The Instructor will begin taking us up one by one towards the end of the week," Rob answered. "It will be a while before we are allowed to fly the planes on our own."

"On one hand it sounds like a lot of fun, and on the other it seems really scary," Kathy said. "What if something went wrong?"

"That is why we have to learn everything so thoroughly," Rob retorted. "A good pilot is a safe pilot. It is the only thing I ever take seriously."

"Yes, I've noticed," Kathy said, "You have a great sense of humour."

"And I love to have fun," Rob said. "However, I must split now. I'll see you around later."

Kathy had classes in the morning, and in the afternoon Phoebe invited her along to watch Bradley play basketball. Brad was an excellent player, and having played at "A grade" level all last year, he had been asked to captain one of the teams this year.

Phoebe and Kathy entered the gymnasium, and sat down on the bench nearest the court that the A grade teams were using. The players were busy bouncing the ball and generally warming up; but immediately the referee blew his whistle, they assumed their positions. Out of the corner of her eye, Kathy noticed that Tony Dantean jostled one of the other players, but it went unnoticed in the melee.

The referee released the ball into the air, and play commenced. It was a fast game, with Brad and a couple of other high profile players shooting a number of baskets. The points on the board climbed steadily.

Towards half-time, a commotion arose. Brad, finding himself badly placed to shoot a goal, had passed the ball to Tony, who instead of passing it straight back, had begun to run with it. The referee blew his whistle, called out "travel", and awarded the opposing team with a free throw. Tony glared, and roughly tackled the next player who caught the ball. The referee then called "foul" and banished Tony from the court.

Tony stalked across to the bench on the opposite side of the court from where the girls were seated, and sat there trying to look tough. Brad had a talk to him during half time, and he was finally allowed back on the court, where he confined himself sulkily to defence.

After the game finished Brad came across to speak to the girls. "Phew, that was some game," he said, mopping his forehead with a towel.

"I am sorry that you lost," Phoebe said.

Brad shrugged, "We lost by so few points that it hardly counts. We will do better next time, providing Tony behaves himself."

"What has gotten into him?" Kathy queried.

"I think he is trying too hard," Brad said, "He used to be a B grade player last year, and A grade is new to him. At least, I hope that is all it is."

"What will you do if he keeps costing you games?" Kathy asked.

"I guess he could be replaced," Brad mused, "But I wouldn't do that to a guy unless it was strictly necessary."

"We will hope that he adjusts his attitude then," Phoebe said.

"It is early in the season," Kathy remarked, although her experience of university basketball was limited to a few games as a reserve for one of the girls' C grade teams. "Anything could happen."

Kathy's afternoon pottery class proved to be just slightly less frustrating than the one she had the previous week. She mixed her own clay and got it to an acceptable consistency, rolled it up into an appropriate size ball, and placed it on the potter's wheel.

After a couple of practice runs, Kathy managed to hollow out a shallow shape. It was considerably thicker than it ought to be, and the sides were grossly uneven, but the instructor told Kathy that it was quite sound for an early effort.

Kathy set back to work and produced two more pots of somewhat indeterminate shape. She put them up on the shelf to await being fired in the kiln overnight.

After lunch the next day, Kathy went down to the Art Department to collect her pots from the kiln. She ran into Stephanie on the way, and the other girl insisted upon accompanying her.

"I would love to see the Art Department," Stephanie exclaimed, "I do so envy you doing pottery. I love to make things, but can't fit any more subjects into my timetable!"

"Don't get too excited," Kathy said, "My early attempts are pretty rough. I don't even know if they will have survived the firing process."

"Oh, I hope they have," Stephanie said. "Do many pieces break while they are being fired?"

"One breaks every so often," Kathy said, "Or so I am told. These are my first efforts."

Kathy was pleased to find that, although one piece had developed a hairline crack, the other two were intact. They looked nothing like commercially produced pots, but Stephanie praised them for what she called their "rustic charm".

"They are obviously home-made," Stephanie said. "I think that is really great!"

"Yes," Kathy agreed more reservedly, "Well I hope to be making something more like cups and vases by the end of the semester."

"I am sure you will be," Stephanie said blithely, "But these are a start."

"They will look better glazed," Kathy said hopefully, searching around for a suitable cardboard carton in which to pack them. "Some sort of basic brown that will hide a multitude of flaws."

"That sounds great," Stephanie agreed.

After padding the box with a layer of shredded paper, Kathy carefully positioned the pots. "Come on Steph," she said, "Let's go back to our room."

Stephanie opened the door and held it ajar, so Kathy could step through without putting the box down. Kathy said, "Thanks", and they set off towards girl's dorm. They were about half-way across the lawn, when they encountered Andrew Grosvy, who was walking in the opposite direction. Kathy was inclined to pass on by, but Stephanie, who got on very well with Andrew, stopped.

"Hello Stephanie," Andrew said. "How are you?"

"I am well thank you Andrew," Stephanie replied. "How have you been?"

"Pretty good," Andrew said. "And how are you Kathy?"

"I am quite well," Kathy answered, "Thank you for asking."

Andrew glanced towards the box Kathy was carrying. "What are you girls doing?"

"We have just collected Kathy's pots from the Art Department," Stephanie replied. "You should see them, they are very good."

"They are only my first attempts," Kathy said in embarrassment, 'And they are not even glazed yet." Kathy tried to cover the top of the box with her arm, but Andrew stepped forward and gazed earnestly into it.

"Excellent," he pronounced. "We are the clay, and he is the potter - Isaiah 64:8."

"Oh," Kathy murmured.

"I have heard that it is actually very hard to learn pottery," Andrew continued.

"Yes it is," Kathy replied, "You have got that right!"

"I had better go now," Andrew said. "Keep up the good work Kathy...I will see you later Stephanie."

Stephanie and Kathy both said, "Goodbye", and Andrew continued on his way. When he was out of earshot, Kathy turned to Stephanie.

"Is he always like that?" she exclaimed. "Sort of ingenuous?"

"Oh yes!" Stephanie said. "He is a regular walking Bible dictionary. But he is very sweet...."

"Oh no," Kathy said, following her room-mate's drift, "I like outgoing guys. I am sure that Andrew would be far too quiet for me, besides, isn't he preparing to work for the Uniting Church?"

"I guess so," Stephanie agreed. "But you know, there is quite a degree of agreement between some branches of the Evangelical and the Uniting Churches."

"I guess," Kathy said and shrugged. "That doesn't mean I have to marry a minister."

Kathy had a free period mid-morning, and spent it in the dormitory doing her bit for the student work programme. She had been assigned to clean the first floor bathrooms this year. The task sounded very menial, but it actually was quite tolerable, as the toilets were cleaned so regularly that they rarely smelt.

The hardest part of the job had proven to be finding a time when the showers were not in use. When she have such an opportunity, Kathy wiped all the tiles down with a strong bleach solution, and scrubbed everything with a long brush. Kathy found it was advisable to wear something really old when she was doing that sort of work, because she would occasionally spill bleach on her clothes.

Kathy spent the afternoon doing some reading for Education Theory and Infant Reading. Cara visited the room just before the Uniting Church vespers, and they went down to the women's assembly area together, where they were joined by Cara's male friend and Biology classmate, Dylan Perret.

On Saturday, the various churches that supported the campus had designed a lively and inclusive orientation programme, that allowed the returning students to reconnect with their old friends, and also welcome new students on to campus. Participation in the retreat was voluntary, and Kathy attended the activities that interested her the most, including the Taize service and meditation.

CHAPTER TWO: A GOOD BEGINNING

Kathy woke around eight o'clock Sunday morning and took her time getting dressed and having breakfast. She welcomed the chance to take things more slowly on the weekend, and figured that God had known what he was doing when he announced a time to rest. Stephanie had left the room early, presumably to have breakfast in the cafeteria with Garry and attend the Inter-denominational praise service.

Around twenty past nine, Phoebe dropped by the room and invited Kathy to sit with her and Bradley in the Reform Church service. Kathy followed her friend downstairs and across to the meeting hall, where Bradley was saving a couple of seats for them.

"How have you been?" Kathy asked, taking a seat.

"Good," Brad said lightly, "Between reading for English, field trips coming up for Geography, and being the captain of a basketball team, I don't have time to get bored."

Phoebe gave Kathy a wink: "That is an excruciatingly full timetable for an easy-going guy like Brad," she said.

"I know what you mean," Kathy said sympathetically, "My Art practical takes up a lot of my spare time."

"Tell me about it!" Bradley murmured as the praise service commenced and they fell quiet.

After several hymns and preliminaries, a film was screened showing some missionary relief work in Africa. The lesson study was combined, so the students stayed in their seats until the sermon commenced. The reform service was taken by the one of the Theology lecturers and was focused on Paul's advice to young people in the book of Timothy.

When the Reform Church service finished, Brad, Phoebe and Kathy stood up to join the general throng wending their way down the fire-escape stairs towards the cafeteria. Kathy had just reached the ground, when she felt a touch on her shoulder. She turned to see Rob standing there, grinning.

"Hi," he said. "I thought that I would never catch up to you!"

"I am pleased you tried," Kathy said. "I haven't seen anything of you for a couple of days!"

"I've been around," Rob said, "It's you who have been hiding."

Kathy laughed: "Neither of us has been hiding, this is just a very busy place."

"You can say that again!" Rob exclaimed. "Are you on your way in to lunch?"

"Yes I am," Kathy said. "And I can see Phoebe and Bradley waiting for me."

"My mates are over there," Rob said gesturing to the right. "I better catch them up. Why don't you drop by the recreation area this evening? I'll be there, and I'll introduce you to the boys. I know it's only pool and TV, but it helps me unwind."

"I'll remember that," Kathy said, "I don't mind unwinding a bit myself."

Rob left, and Kathy hastened to re-join Bradley and Phoebe.

Bradley was tapping his foot casually. "Who was the guy?" he inquired. "And why didn't you introduce him to us?"

"That was Rob," Kathy explained. "I met him at the Western Night. Thanks for waiting for me."

"Actually I thought you might have wanted us to leave you to it," Phoebe said. "You looked like you were getting along pretty well."

"Rob is just a friend," Kathy said, "He is pleasant company, and he has invited me to the rec room this evening."

"Well, it doesn't look as if you are going to be lonely for long," Phoebe observed.

"Maybe not," Kathy said.

Kathy patted her hair and applied cherry lip-gloss as she prepared to go down the recreation area that evening. Rob had been such easy company at the Western Night, and had driven all her cares away. Playing pool and watching television sounded like fun, but she experienced a fission of nervousness, as she thought about meeting his friends and spending an evening in their company.

"Are you okay Kathy?" Stephanie asked as she prepared for her date with Garry. "You could come with us if you liked, we are only going to the campus snack bar."

"And then onto a moonlight walk and making-out on a park bench," Kathy laughed. "I really wouldn't want to intrude on your date."

"Actually, it's nothing like that," Stephanie retorted. "Some of the guys have set up an IBM computer down there with gaming software. I believe it is called *King's Quest*. Garry has booked us an hour each, which of course we will share. The puzzles are pretty hard to solve."

"That sounds way too nerdy for me," Kathy said. "I think I'll take my chances in the recreation area."

"Have fun then," Stephanie said. "You know where we'll be if you need us."

"Thanks," Kathy squared her shoulders and shut the door. She skipped down the stairs and across campus to the recreation area.

Rob was at a pool table already, holding a cue and waiting for his turn in the game. He turned to wave when he saw Kathy enter, and gestured to a couple of guys.

"There you are Kathy," he said. "You have to meet some of my comrades."

"Sure," Kathy said, "I would be delighted."

"This is Dennis, and this is Hank," Rob said when the guys arrived. "And this is the lovely Kathy that I have been telling you all about."

"It's nice to meet you," Dennis murmured, and Hank nodded in agreement.

"Are you guys both doing your Pilot's Licence?" Kathy asked.

"Yes," Hank replied, "We are classmates of Rob's."

"They survive it somehow," Rob said jovially.

"I am sure they do," Kathy said. "Are you going to let me join the game?"

"Next round," Rob said. "We've already placed our bets on this game."

"Bets?" Kathy exclaimed in surprise. Gambling wasn't allowed on campus.

"Our little joke," Dennis said. "We take it in turns hanging out the laundry. At this rate, Rob will have me as slave for the next week."

"Oh, I see," Kathy laughed. "I don't intend to be anybody's slave."

"You're too pretty to be anybody's slave," Rob said suggestively. "I can think of a few other uses for you."

Kathy blushed. "I'm a good girl, I'll have you know."

"Of course you are," Hank said. "Don't take any notice of Rob, it's just his way."

"I'm a bad boy, I know," Rob laughed. The evening passed in jovial banter and Kathy enjoyed herself immensely. Rob walked her across to the girl's dorm just before lockup.

"I'll see you around," he said. "My timetable is absolutely crazy, so it will be whenever it happens."

"I had fun tonight," Kathy hesitated. Rob didn't seem to be asking her out again, but they had only recently met, and maybe he literally was that casual about his arrangements.

Monday morning after classes had commenced was a good time to give the first floor bathroom a thorough clean, as Kathy had a free period around ten-thirty. It was rare that anyone wanted to take a shower in a hurry around then because most of the girls had left the dormitory.

Kathy finished cleaning around 11:45, and went across to the cafeteria to enjoy a leisurely lunch. This was usually the earliest the cafeteria opened its doors, but when she arrived, Kathy was surprised to see Stephanie and Cara, Dylan and Garry were already part way through their meal. Collecting her savoury, Kathy carried her tray across to the friends and sat down.

"What are you guys doing?" Kathy asked, settling next to Stephanie.

"We have an Ecology field trip this afternoon," Garry answered for the group. "So we had to have lunch early".

"Is this your whole class?" Kathy asked.

"Pretty much," Stephanie said, "The science subjects have a reputation for being tough. It scares some people off."

"We have always enjoyed them though," Dylan said, "Haven't we Cara, my dear?"

"Oh yes," Cara replied, "I wouldn't even consider changing my subjects for a moment, except to get away from you!"

"You don't really want to do that Cara," Dylan returned. "You know that you love me deep down inside."

"Don't worry about them," Stephanie whispered, "They are always like this."

"I have been trying to get Cara to go out with me for ages," Dylan explained, "But she is just too mean tempered."

"That's not it at all," Cara returned, "You can be an idiot sometimes, Dylan."

"I guess you are going to spend all this year turning me down again Cara," Dylan remarked mournfully.

"No, actually," Cara replied provocatively, "I was thinking of asking you to the Reverse Tea."

Dylan looked stunned: "Really? Why would you do that?"

"Because you are a good sport," Cara said, "And I might as well enjoy your company."

"I would be honoured to go with you then," Dylan said, sounding as if he could hardly believe his luck. He had finished his food, so he stood up to leave. "I had better go and get my things. I will see you all down by the science block."

"Goodbye Dylan," Kathy said, "You won't be seeing me at the science block."

"Goodbye Kathy," Dylan said, "It was nice of you to join us." He selected an apple from the fruit bowl, turned and walked out of the cafeteria.

As soon as Dylan was out of ear-shot, Garry turned to Cara. "Have you softened towards Dylan then?" he asked incredulously.

"No," Cara said, "I just don't see why I should have to be mean all the time to keep him from getting the wrong idea."

"I agree," Stephanie said, "That sort of behaviour is completely unnecessary. Dylan is a smart guy, and eventually he will work things out for himself."

"Exactly!" Cara said. "I expect that there is someone special out there for the both of us. We may even be able to meet them at the same time and all be friends."

"Wow," Kathy exclaimed, "You guys are tight!"

"Camping, hiking and field trips together," Stephanie explained. "We used to look out for each other, even before I started to go out with Garry."

"I remember," Kathy mused. "A bit like me and Lionel, but now we don't have anything in common. He has an off-campus fiancé, and I am single."

"You seem to have found someone in that Rob," Stephanie said. "Or there are plenty of other guys."

"I know," Kathy agreed. "It was just easier to advise you last year than take my own advice this year!"

Garry chuckled. "Isn't it always that way? If you do get lonely, I have some other friends, guys who are not quite as crazy as Dylan."

"Thanks Garry," Kathy said pulling a face. "I'm always telling Stephanie to knock off the match-making."

Kathy woke the next morning just in time to grab a quick shower and a hasty bowl of cereal before going to History of Christianity. After History of Christianity, she had Psychology, and then Art. A free period was spent cleaning the showers, and then she headed towards the lecture theatre for Education Theories. After lunch, Kathy went to the library and worked on an essay covering early forms of Art and pottery. It was pretty interesting, and made her wonder if she ought to study a bit of archaeology one day.

Occasionally, her mind wondered onto the next event in the university social calendar, the Reverse Tea. It was a costume event, and usually proved to be a lot of fun. She had considered asking several guys, but her mind kept returning to Rob. He seemed like the ideal companion for a function that wasn't meant to be taken too seriously.

Kathy decided to go to the recreation area after tea and see whether Rob was there. He was playing pool when she arrived, and immediately invited her to grab a cue. The guys shuffled themselves around, and assigned her a place in a team.

"How have you been Kathy?" Rob asked, as they waited for their turns.

"I have been well thanks Rob," Kathy replied, "And what about yourself?"

"Good!" Rob said, "The flying lessons are progressing."

Kathy nodded. "Have you heard about the Reverse Tea?" she inquired discretely.

"That is the function where the girls ask the guys, isn't it?" Rob said. "I haven't been asked by anyone yet. I'm off campus too much and the only girl I've really talked to is you."

"Would you like to go with me then?" Kathy asked.

"I would be delighted," Rob replied. "I wasn't looking forward to missing my meal that night."

Kathy laughed, "That doesn't happen you know. Guys can come across to the cafeteria to eat whether they have been invited or not!"

"Don't you believe it!" Rob said teasingly. "A bloke would have to be super-brave to do that, especially at a function like this one."

"Well, you are out of danger now," Kathy said. "I hope that you like dressing up. The theme is famous couples."

"I'm not too fond of fancy clothes," Rob said, "But I might be persuaded to put on something old and pretend to be a bushranger."

"I don't know if Ned Kelly had a girlfriend," Kathy said, "But I can find something long and floral for myself. Colonial costume sounds like a good idea!"

"That's settled then," Rob said. "It's your shot. Sink as many of those balls as you can for me."

In Infant Maths everyone was talking about the Reverse Tea. Luke and Tess were going as Robin Hood and Maid Marian. Anita had asked Tom 'as a friend', because they shared a lot of classes together. They were planning to go as Romeo and Juliet.

"Do you have a date yet Kathy?" Tess asked.

"Why yes!" Kathy said, "I am going with Rob."

"I am afraid that I do not know him," Anita said, frowning slightly.

"Riobard Watson," Kathy explained, "He is a new guy doing his Pilot's Licence."

"The one you have been talking to a lot lately?" Tess inquired.

"That's the one," Kathy said. "I will introduce you as soon as I get a chance."

"You two sure got together quick," Anita remarked.

"I know!" Kathy said, "I can hardly believe it myself. He is such fun, and I feel as if I have known him for ages already.'

"It sounds sweet," Anita said, "As long as you keep things light at this stage."

"Of course," Kathy said, "We are no-where near being a couple yet."

"A group of us girls are going in to Northcoast this afternoon to buy material for our costumes," Tess said, diplomatically moving the topic along. "You are welcome to join us Kathy."

"I was thinking of going on Thursday," I said.

"Oh no!" Anita said, "You won't have enough time to make a decent costume if you leave it until then."

"Okay," Kathy said, "I would love to join you then. What time are you leaving?"

"Around two," Anita said, "Debbie will be joining us."

After lunch, Kathy made her way around to the back of the girl's hall, where Luke had the university bus waiting for its passengers. Stephanie and Cara had also decided to join the expedition. The group got off the university bus at Northcoast station, and walked across the main street and down some stairs into the fabric store.

"What are you going as?" Kathy asked Cara, as they browsed amongst the rolls of fabric.

"Tarzan and Jane," Cara said. "The costume demands are minimal, and it will suit Dylan's crazy sense of humour." She picked up a large tropical print featuring hibiscus flowers on a background of vine leaves. "Do you think this would do for Jane?"

"I don't know," Kathy replied, "Are there any animal prints?"

"There is some stripy stretch-knit over there," Stephanie said, "It might pass for Zebra."

Debbie was leafing through the Simplicity pattern catalogue and had found a page featuring his and her kaftans. "That is good value," she said, "You only have to buy one envelope, and it contains two patterns in a variety of sizes."

"Are you making David's costume too?" Kathy asked, looking at the garish brown and purple striped fabric Debbie was holding. "Whatever are you going as?"

"Abraham and Sarah of course," Debbie replied.

Kathy laughed. "It might work at that. I take it David is wearing that brown."

"Oh yes," Debbie said, "There is a lovely blue stripe that should suit me."

Tess breezed over to them. "If you buy that pattern, Debbie, I might ask to borrow it. A short version of that kaftan in bright green might do for

Robin Hood."

"What does for Robin will probably do for Romeo, if I make it up in red and black," Anita exclaimed.

"How are you going to get the guys to wear tights?" Kathy exclaimed.

Anita and Tess looked at each other and shrugged: "Track-pants," they said in unison. "The guys are going to buy black for Romeo and Green for Robin."

"Sounds good," Kathy said, and returned to the fabric stands. She eventually selected a navy cotton, printed with pink roses. Kathy planned to make a full length skirt, and hem up a triangular shape as a matching shawl. She would team the ensemble with an old fashioned looking blouse that she already owned.

The other girls were arguing about what women wore in the Fifteenth and Sixteenth Centuries. Eventually, Stephanie, who was by far the best seamstress amongst them, suggested that they bought a milk-maid style pattern. She said she would help lower the neckline and create a series of mid-drift ties for Juliet's costume. Maid Marion could raise the neck, shorten the hem to knee length, and wear a longer length skirt underneath.

Anita chose a rich plum coloured fabric with a pattern woven into it for her Juliet costume, while Tess opted to combine a blue kirtle cotton with a green underskirt. Stephanie selected a Laura Ashley style print, and an additional length of calico. She remarked that it would make a good apron, and could be hemmed and attached at the empire-line.

"Who are you and Garry going as?" Kathy asked curiously.

"General and Mrs. MacArthur," Stephanie replied, "Complete with woolly lamb, if I can find a suitable stuffed toy."

"Are you going to try to make Garry a red suit coat?" Kathy asked.

"No," Stephanie replied, "But I might be able to put together a nice waist-coat for him."

It was almost time for tea when the girls arrived back at Silver Springs University. Stephanie suggested that they assemble in her room after evening assembly, because she was one of the few girls in the dorm who owned a sewing machine.

After History of Christianity finished the next morning, Anita and Kathy hurried up to the meeting hall. Debbie had conscripted them both to support David and Larry, who were making their debut as convocation speakers that morning. Kathy's role was to operate the overhead projector, while Anita was announcing the song service.

Debbie had arrived a few minutes before, and greeted them warmly. "Thanks for coming girls," she said, "I want to make sure that everything goes well."

"We will do our best," Kathy said, and made her way across to where Joelle was setting up on the piano. "Hello Joelle," she said. "I just need to check that we have the same list of songs."

"Here is my list," Joelle replied absently. She appeared to have something else on her mind, so Kathy glanced through the list, and finding that it correlated quite well with the one in her hand, returned it to her.

"That's okay," Kathy said, "I notice that we are skipping two verses out of *Amazing Grace*. I'll try not to put them on-screen by accident."

People were beginning to arrive in the meeting hall, so Kathy walked over to the over-head projector and took her place beside it. A few minutes later, Debbie stood up to introduce David and Larry, and then handed the microphone to Anita.

Kathy placed the first transparency on the projector, and turned it on. She tried very hard to place each subsequent transparency neatly on the display surface, so that the minimal amount of adjustment was required. It was fiddly work, and Kathy was relieved when the song service was over.

David stood up to speak, looking mildly apprehensive. He had been leading worships for his colleagues ever since he started at Silver Springs University, but this was his first convocation service. Kathy was pleased to observe that the audience responded well to both him and Larry.

When the service was finished, Larry approached Kathy with effusive expressions of thanks for her assistance. When Kathy waved him away in embarrassment, he turned to Anita, who looked very pleased. Joelle stood up and joined them, and they were still talking when Kathy left to go to her Art and Education Theories classes.

Kathy spent the time between lectures working on her major project for Infant Reading, which involved designing a curriculum for a junior primary class, and explaining the methods she intended to use to promote literacy. Lunch was already under way when Kathy arrived, so she was pleased to slip into a space beside Stephanie and Garry, who were deep in conversation with Andrew Grosvy.

"Hello everyone," Kathy said, at an appropriate moment.

"Oh hi, Kathy," Stephanie replied. "How are you?"

"Good," Kathy said, "And busy."

Andrew turned to her: "How are the pots going Kathy?"

"Great," Kathy said, 'They look much better now they are glazed."

There was a brief commotion the other side of Andrew, as a couple of students who had finished eating stood up and left. A short plump girl with reddish hair moved in, and took their place.

"Hello Andrew," she said purposefully.

"Oh hello, Damaris," Andrew said. "Kathy, have you met Damaris? She is the lovely lady who has asked me to the Reverse Tea."

"I am pleased to meet you," Kathy said. "Who are you thinking of going as?"

"John Knox and Mary Queen of Scots," Andrew replied.

"Didn't they hate each other?" Garry asked.

Andrew shrugged: "That was a lot of bluster. He was really quite dedicated to saving her soul."

"It is a clever choice," Stephanie commented.

"It is indeed," Damaris remarked. "I get to wear a crown and pearls, and he gets to wander around looking wild and spouting scripture."

"I'm sure Andrew can do that!" Kathy remarked dryly.

Damaris gave her a suspicious look: "You aren't being sarcastic are you?"

"Not at all," Kathy said, "Like Stephanie, I think it is a remarkably clever choice."

"Who are you and your date going as?" Damaris queried in a tone that implied Kathy had better have a date, sitting next to Andrew like Kathy was.

"Ned and Mrs. Kelly," I answered.

"Very Australian," Damaris commented, "You didn't go very far afield for that idea."

"No," Kathy said, "It was Rob's idea. I wanted him to be comfortable with our choice."

"That is nice," Andrew broke in diplomatically. "I have the most exciting news. Have you heard that the Theology Lecturer and his wife are coming? Rumour has it that they intend dressing up as King Xerxes and Esther, and they have the most authentic costumes!"

"Wow!" Kathy exclaimed, "I can hardly wait to see them."

"It is very sporting of them to join in," Stephanie remarked.

"I don't know about that," Damaris said, "It is a university function after all."

"Altogether it sounds like it should be a good night," Garry said. "You will have to excuse us now Damaris, we have finished eating. Goodbye Andrew, I hope we'll see you another time."

Kathy had also had sufficient, so she packed up her tray and hurried after Stephanie and Garry.

"Whatever happened to Damaris?" Kathy exclaimed when they were out of earshot. "Did she swallow a lemon or something?"

"I don't know," Stephanie replied, "But at least Andrew has got someone. He is a bit inclined to get left out of these functions."

"Damaris may improve on acquaintance," Garry observed sanguinely, "But I do have a lot to do this afternoon."

"I'll see you later then Garry," Stephanie said, giving him a kiss on the cheek. "Do you want to work on our costumes now Kathy?"

"Sure," Kathy said. "I haven't been able to do much more because of having pottery all yesterday afternoon."

The girls went inside and up to Stephanie's room. Sewing costumes kept them busy all afternoon.

Kathy had to spend a couple of hours cleaning the upstairs bathroom. She saw Rob at lunch, and he indicated that, as far as he was concerned, everything was organised for their date the following night. Around 2:00 pm, Kathy's tasks for the day were all completed, and she returned to the dormitory room. Joelle and Debbie had arrived before her, and the floor was covered with meters of black cotton.

"Hi," Kathy said, stepping across the floor carefully. "What are you girls doing?"

"Cutting out Joelle's costume," Debbie replied, "She asked if she could use the pattern too."

"Luckily most of us have finished our seams," Stephanie remarked, "Joelle will need the machine this afternoon."

"Who have you asked to be your partner?" Kathy asked Joelle.

Joelle blushed: "I have invited Larry," she said, "And we are going as Katerina Von Bora and Martin Luther."

"I see you are making something pretty plain," I remarked.

"A monkish robe for Larry, and a plain black dress with a white lace collar for me," Joelle said. "I don't think that Kate became very vain, even after leaving the convent."

"And the black and white will suit your colouring very well," Kathy remarked, glancing at Joelle's ash blonde hair and fair skin.

"That too," Joelle agreed.

Kathy settled herself down on the edge of the bed and took out the long skirt she had been making. It required hand finishing around the hem and waistband. "I didn't know you liked Larry," she said.

"I have gotten to know him working on worships and convocations," Joelle said. "There is a group of us who do it regularly."

"It can be fun," Kathy said. "I enjoyed helping the other day. And I used to do that sort of thing back in Armidale for my local Evangelical congregation."

There was a knock at the door and Phoebe appeared. "I have been looking for you Kathy," she said.

"Come in and sit down," Kathy said. "What did you want?"

"Just to know whether you would help me with my hair and make-up tomorrow," Phoebe said. "It's hard to make my hair hold a curl sometimes."

"Sure," Kathy said, "I would be happy to."

"Who are you and Brad going as?"" Debbie inquired.

"Characters out of the 1920's, like Zelda Sayre and F. Scott Fitzgerald," Phoebe required. "I already had a really nice drop waist dress, and all Brad needed was his church suit."

"Cheats," Stephanie remarked teasingly.

"Smart!" Phoebe retorted. "We have had a hundred things to do what with organising basketball. I can tell you one juicy piece of gossip though..."

"Oh, what is that?" Debbie asked.

"Rumour has it that Tony Dantean hasn't been asked by anyone yet," Phoebe reported.

"I would have expected one of the first years to ask him right away," Kathy said. "He is good looking."

"And he used to be one of the trendy crowd," Stephanie observed. "I can't believe he hasn't been snapped up by some adoring basketball fan.'

Phoebe shrugged, "Tony has developed quite a reputation for being temperamental this year. Brad is always having to send him off the basketball court."

"And you think that is putting the girls off of him?" Debbie observed.

"Well, would you want to date someone who is obviously a sore loser?" Phoebe asked. "Or would you rather have someone who can be a good sport?"

"Oh, a good sport for sure," Joelle agreed. "I think most girls are looking for that."

"It might be for the best if no one asks Tony," Stephanie said soberly. "Somebody did like him last year, and it ended unhappily." The girls all looked at Stephanie expectantly, but she refused to go into detail. "I've said too much already," she murmured, and closed her mouth firmly.

"It doesn't matter exactly what happened," Debbie said. "It is good to hear that the majority of girls on campus are able to make wise decisions about what they want."

"Yes," Kathy said, "I think everyone will enjoy the Reverse Tea. I certainly intend to have fun!"

It was raining on the weekend, forcing everyone to dodge carefully between the dormitories and the meeting hall carrying umbrellas. After the Inter-denominational praise service and Reform Church services were finished, a group of students sat in the cafeteria looking glumly out at the rain.

"Would it be a misuse of prayer to pray that it clears up for the Reverse Tea this evening?" Debbie asked wistfully.

"I don't know," David replied, taking the question seriously. "It would be a selfish prayer, but God might not mind us asking."

"We only need a short break to allow us to get across to the cafeteria in one piece," Stephanie said. "I have occasionally asked God to help me get across to my next class, and it might be coincidence, but the rain seemed to lighten at the right time."

"That is an interesting question," Andrew said. "Is God interested in the minutiae of our daily lives?"

"I think he is, when we ask him to be," Kathy said. "Although I don't know how he could possibly find the time."

"Well, he is omnipresent," Garry said. "I guess being able to be everywhere at once would give him an advantage."

"I think that God must be concerned with what we do every day," Phoebe concluded. "Otherwise, he would be judging us by the one or two moments we get a chance to do something noticeable for him."

"After all," said Stephanie, "It is our relationships that we take to heaven with us."

"I always understood that it was our character we got to take to heaven," Andrew retorted, frowning.

"Well isn't our character made up of the way we have interacted with God and our fellow man?" Stephanie reasoned.

The students debated the subject in an amiable manner until it was time to go back to the dormitories. Kathy noticed that the female members of the group were inclined to believe that God was concerned with personal matters, and the male members were inclined to believe him pre-occupied with theological matters. By the time the discussion had finished, the rain had somehow rained itself out.

Rob picked Kathy up for the Reverse Tea at about quarter-past seven in the evening. She couldn't help laughing when she saw him, because he had a cardboard box on his head. He had painted it silver, and cut a square opening in the front to accommodate his mouth and eyes.

"Wow," Kathy said, "You really meant it."

"Oh yes,' Rob replied, his eyes twinkling at her, "You said Ned Kelly was okay."

"I did too," Kathy said. "What do you think of my costume?"

"Superb," Rob said, 'If a little demure." He reached up and teased a lock of hair out of the bun Kathy had painstakingly pinned into place. "That's better. You need to look as though you can like a bad-boy now.'

The couple walked across to the cafeteria and found their way to the assigned table. Kathy had diplomatically arranged for them to be seated between her friends Anita and Tom, and Rob's friend Hank and his date. Rob and Hank joked around a lot, amusing everyone at the table, and ensuring that the time did not drag while they were waiting for the various courses to arrive. Kathy spent most of the evening doubled up with laughter.

Anita and Tom seemed to like Rob too. Tom asked him a few questions about the Pilot's License programme, and Anita laughed nearly as hard as Kathy did at Rob's jokes.

"Your new friend is certainly the life of the party," Anita whispered to Kathy at one stage, after Rob had told a particularly amusing joke. "Is he like this all the time?"

"Pretty much," Kathy whispered back, "I have fun every time I am around him."

After the function was finished, Rob walked Kathy back to the dormitory.

"I enjoyed this evening immensely Kathy," he said. "You are a good sport."

"Thank you Rob," Kathy said, "It is good to be with someone who gets into the spirit of things."

Rob coughed somewhat self-consciously and shuffled his feet. "I would like to keep seeing you," he said.

Kathy tried to keep her reply casual. "Sure," she said, "Look for me at meals and at worships."

"I've been doing that," Rob said, "But you are always surrounded by your friends."

"Just join in," Kathy said, "They are a good crowd. And I'm a second year, so I can't helping knowing more people."

"I'll do that then," Rob said, "See you tomorrow." He turned and swung off into the dark.

Kathy woke up around mid-morning and lay in bed luxuriating for another hour. Then she got up and had a long shower. She had well and truly missed breakfast and her first class, but that did not matter because it was almost time for lunch.

When Kathy arrived in the cafeteria, Stephanie and Phoebe were busy discussing the previous night's function. They were agreed that the costumes had been superlative, and most people seemed to have had a good time.

"Did you and Rob enjoy yourselves, Kathy?" Phoebe asked as Kathy settled herself next to them.

"Oh, yes," Kathy answered, "Rob even asked if he could keep on seeing me!"

"Wow!" Stephanie said, "That puts you two well on the way to becoming a couple."

"It does seem to," Kathy remarked, feeling warm all over. "I am really pleased with the way things are going."

"I saw Rob's costume," Phoebe remarked, "It was quite creative."

"Yes," Kathy agreed, "He did a good job of putting it together on his own."

"And how did things go for you and Andrew last night?" Phoebe inquired of Damaris, who had just arrived at the table.

"I had a nice enough time," Damaris replied, "I was really pleased with my costume, and while the food was a bit slow, it was adequately cooked. Andrew was a tolerable escort, and I expect we will be going out again."

"What does Andrew think about that?" Garry asked gently.

Damaris shrugged: "I don't know, but he does owe me a return invitation."

"One of the other guys could ask you to the next function," Kathy suggested. "You never know."

Damaris gave Kathy a suspicious look. "It could be interesting if something like that happened," she said, "But I don't go out with just anybody. I have my preferences you understand."

"So do we all," Phoebe replied equitably.

Andrew and David chose that moment to arrive, and Brad changed the subject by asking them how their studies were going. Kathy finished eating her food and then went back to the dormitory to clean the bathrooms. She spent the remainder of the afternoon in the library, reading material held on open reserve for Education Theory. Something was niggling at the back of her mind. Despite the easy progression of her relationship with Rob, she was slightly bored. She wondered what other campus activity she could join to spice her life up a little.

CHAPTER THREE: EXPECTED PROGRESS

Kathy saw Rob at tea, and he invited her to come down to the gymnasium in the evening to watch him and Hank play indoor cricket.

"It won't be a match or anything, mind you," Rob said, "We have only just started mucking around down there."

"Okay," Kathy said, "I'll be across about 7:30. I was thinking of tuning in to that new television show called *Neighbours* that Channel Seven has been advertising."

"That show sounds a bit girly," Rob said with a grimace. "And I don't expect it will last. Channel Seven already has *A Country Practice*, which isn't too bad for a soap opera. I'll see you down in the gym later then."

When Kathy arrived at the gymnasium that evening, Hank and Rob were busy hanging a huge net around the section of the floor furthest from the stage. It reached from the floor to the ceiling, and covered at least half of basketball court one.

"I had a terrible time persuading them to let me do this," Rob said. "Although they have all the equipment, it is rarely used."

"Yes," Kathy observed, "Basketball is by far the most popular sport around here."

"Well, I like cricket," Rob said, "And I have booked the court."

When they had finished hanging the net, Rob went and collected the other equipment. There were two sets of stumps, complete with their own little round stands, gloves, protective gear, and a yellow indoor cricket ball, which was slightly softer than a standard cricket ball.

Rob passed a bat to Hank, and said: "Come on Kathy, you can play too."

"Me?" Kathy exclaimed, "I don't play cricket."

"I bet you can field," Rob said.

"Oh yes," Kathy said, "I can fetch and carry."

Kathy was surprised how much fun simply running after a ball could be. She functioned as a fielder until some other guys arrived and decided to join in the game, then sneaked out of the netted area and sat down on a bench.

Indoor cricket appeared to be a fast moving game. If the ball hit the back wall full on, it appeared to count as a 'six', while bouncing or rolling the ball up to the same wall counted as a 'four.' Hitting the side wall counted as a 'one' or a 'two', depending where the ball struck. Runs could also be accrued by the batter completing a round circuit between the two wickets.

The guys packed up after everybody who had decided to join in had been granted a turn being the batsman. There was a lot of laughter, and talk of making a proper team. Rob came over to Kathy and expressed himself exceedingly pleased with the experiment.

"Thanks for joining in," he said.

"You are welcome," Kathy said. "I hope you manage to put a proper team together."

"I reckon it will happen," Rob said, "Some of the guys are really interested."

Kathy was surprised to find a letter from Owen waiting for her when she checked her mail box. She took it back to the room she shared with Stephanie to read in private, and sat down on the bed. Owen commenced by apologising for the things that he said during his last phone call to her, and said that he hoped they could still be friends. Then he launched into a lengthy description of his daily life, work and study at the local technical college. He apparently expected Kathy to still be interested in everything he did, and everyone he saw. Some of the details he gave were a little more personal than they needed to be, and he hinted that he expected reciprocal intimacy from Kathy.

Kathy sat thinking for a while after she had finished reading the letter. It was the sort of thing she would have been thrilled to receive a few months ago, but she had moved on since then. She finally picked up a pen, and selecting some of her nicest white note paper, wrote a careful reply back to him.

Kathy wrote that she would be happy to be friends, but only after things had genuinely cooled down between them; and she was absolutely certain he was not going to attempt to drag her into his personal life. They needed to "give each other space", she wrote, and "develop new non-possessive attitudes towards each other".

Kathy sealed the letter and posted it quickly. She wasn't sure that Owen would understand what she meant, but she had done the best she could to explain her position.

Kathy thoroughly enjoyed her Art practical in the afternoon. She had managed to develop some degree of control over material on the potter's wheel, and amused herself by producing a series of round bowls in three sizes. The edges were still a little uneven, and she had to make the sides quite thick, but the new bowls were a definite improvement upon her earlier attempts.

Kathy thought that the bowls might be quite attractive painted a deep green, and used for storing fruit and nuts. Ms. Louise was very pleased with Kathy's work, and assured her that she was showing a high degree of aptitude for the craft.

Kathy had Infant Maths and Infant Reading in the morning, then went to the curriculum room for an hour to browse amongst the text books and readers stored there. The curriculum room was a specialised collection which functioned independently of the main library. The staff there maintained a good selection of books that teaching students could use as resources when designing lesson plans.

Kathy's last class for the day was Practice Teaching. Her tutorial group visited the Northcoast Child Care Centre, and helped organise simple learning games for the children who were approaching school age. It was an interesting experience, and constituted more of what Kathy considered to be the 'fun' side of Primary Teaching.

Kathy cleaned the bathrooms after lunch, and spent the afternoon reading the text for Education Theory. It was soon time for tea, and then worship. Phoebe and Kathy remained in the women's assembly area for a while after worship, chatting to Joelle, Anita and Debbie, who were helping organise the dormitory meeting program for the year.

The next day, Kathy had a busy morning doing assigned reading, and then spent most of the afternoon cleaning bathrooms. One of the other girls was sick, so she had been asked to clean the second-floor bathroom as well as the first-floor. At one stage Kathy heard her room-mate's name called over the public address system. Knowing that Stephanie was not in class, and would likely be in their room, Kathy ignored the announcement.

However, the announcement was repeated several times. Thinking Stephanie must be over in the library or somewhere, Kathy resolved to take a message for her room-mate. Leaving her cleaning materials, she rinsed her hands and descended to the ground floor. The Student Dean on reception knew that Kathy roomed with Stephanie.

"Hello Kathy," she exclaimed. "There is a call for Stephanie, do you have any idea where she might be?"

Kathy shook her head. "I'm sorry, I don't, but I could take a message," she offered, and the Student Dean handed over the phone.

"Hello", Kathy said into the receiver.

The person on the other end of the telephone seemed to hesitate. "Stephanie?" the deep voice said. It was one of the guys, from their group but Kathy couldn't quite identify them on the telephone.

"No, it's Kathy," Kathy replied.

"Umm, Kathy, it's Bradley here," the male voice said. "I was looking for Stephanie."

"She's not in the dormitory, she must be in the library or somewhere with Garry," Kathy said. "Can I get you Phoebe instead?" She was referring to Bradley's regular girlfriend.

"No, I think she went to Northcoast shopping," Bradley replied. "And I've collected all our English papers, so I thought Stephanie might like hers."

"I will tell her you have got it for her," Kathy said.

"Thanks," Bradley said and hung up. Kathy returned her telephone receiver to the cradle thoughtfully. Brad and Stephanie shared a lot of classes, so there wasn't anything particularly suspicious about Bradley calling Stephanie. Just a little odd.

Later that afternoon, Stephanie returned to their room. Kathy had finished cleaning and was drying her hair.

"Hi," she said. "Where have you been?"

"In the computer room with Garry," Stephanie replied. "Why?"

"I answered a phone call for you," Kathy admitted.

"That's alright," Stephanie said. "What was the news? I hope my family are all okay." Stephanie had lost her Grandmother the year before last. Kathy knew it was an experience she would never forget, and sometimes Stephanie opened messages from home with a slight sense of foreboding.

"Your family are fine as far as I know," Kathy said. "It was Bradley. "He said he had your English paper for you."

"Oh Brads! He collected my papers for me a couple of times last year," Stephanie shrugged. "He would have Phoebe's paper too."

Apparently Stephanie saw nothing out of the ordinary in Bradley's behaviour, but Kathy wasn't completely convinced. "Didn't Bradley like you for a while last year?"

"I think he did," Stephanie said. "But that was before Phoebe."

"How come you didn't go out with him?" Kathy was curious.

"I think I did, just as a friend to some casual event," Stephanie said. "You were around all last year, so you know."

"Yeah," Kathy said. "I meant how come you didn't choose him as your boy-friend?"

"I wasn't over Jeffrey Mannington at the time," Stephanie replied. The previous year Stephanie had a crush on one of the graduating students. He had appeared to return her affections, and had strung her along for most of the year. It was only with the help of her friends that Stephanie had seen through his manipulative behaviour, and chosen a healthy mutual relationship with one of her peers.

"Are you fully over Jeffrey Mannington now?" Kathy enquired.

"Most of the time," Stephanie sighed. "Sometimes I remember and feel a sharp pang that I never feel around Garry. I don't like to talk like this. I wouldn't lose Garry for the world."

"Of course not," Kathy was thoughtful.

"How would you like it if I turned the tables and asked you whether you are over Owen?" Stephanie returned.

Kathy sighed. "I know I'm not over Owen," she admitted. "I don't know what stage I'm in, but I know I'm still grieving."

"Where does this leave the new guy?" Stephanie asked.

"He makes me laugh," Kathy said. "He is my medicine."

"Your rebound guy?" Stephanie suggested.

"I hope not," Kathy said. "I would like to think I was more mature than that."

"You have always been one of the most mature of our group," Stephanie observed.

"Part of that came from having been in a long-term relationship," Kathy said. "Now the shoe is on the other foot."

After tea, Kathy showered and changed into a neat navy skirt and cream silk shirt for vespers. When she arrived at the women's assembly area, Kathy could not see Phoebe, so she sat with Stephanie and Garry, Cara, Dylan and Tom. Rob arrived just before the song service was due to commence, and asked whether he could sit with them. Feeling a little self-conscious, Kathy introduced him all around.

"This is my friend Rob," Kathy said. "Rob, I would like you to meet my friends. You met Tom at the Reverse Tea, so the others are Cara, Dylan, Garry and Stephanie."

The boys shook Rob by the hand and asked which course he was doing, and the girls said that they were pleased to meet him.

"Kathy has told us a bit about you," Cara said, and Rob laughed.

"My ears should be burning," he said, "But they are not, so I guess Kathy has made me out to be better than I am."

Rob took the seat beside Kathy, and worship commenced. The devotion for the evening was presented by a visiting minister who had considerable experience in the mission field. He recounted several amusing stories about his attempts to communicate the Bible story to those of a foreign culture.

Apparently people whose cultures were not imbued with the Latin-European heritage could interpret things quite differently than Anglo-Americans or Australians did. One Indigenous culture that admired cunning, was even inclined to perceive Judas as the hero of the New Testament, until the minister managed to find something in Christ's ministry that appealed to them.

When vespers finished, Kathy turned to Rob and asked him whether he had had a chance to play any more indoor cricket.

"No," Rob said, "I have been busy, and the net takes a fair bit of setting up. However, I intend to play again next week."

"Where have you been playing indoor cricket?" asked Dylan, who had overheard the conversation.

"In the gym after worship," Rob replied. "It's a bit tough getting the basketball players off of court one for a while, but it is worth doing. I hope to get a team together pretty soon."

"Would you be having proper matches?" Garry inquired.

"Sure," Rob replied, "If I can get the numbers."

"I would be interested for one," Dylan said.

"And so would I," Garry exclaimed.

"You would be welcome," Rob said, "But don't you guys play basketball?"

"We both play B grade," Dylan replied, "But we are not fanatical enough to pass up on other sports if they are on offer."

"Well, drop by the gym on Monday evening then," Rob said, "I would be glad to see you."

"I would like to come along too," Tom said, "And I think Luke might be interested if I told him about it."

"Wow!" Rob said. "That is half a team already."

"You will need at least two teams for a competition," Cara remarked.

"We will spread the word around a bit further," Dylan said enthusiastically. "You never know who will want to join us."

"Girls can play too," Rob remarked. "Kathy has already had a go. Would you be interested in joining us Cara?"

"I don't know, I will think about it," Cara said, but she looked pleased. Cara was quite sporty. She was a member of the university Adventure Club and played A grade basketball.

Rob looked at Stephanie and she shook her head: "I might come along and watch," she said, "But I don't think I will be playing."

"I hope to persuade you to have a go someday," Rob said equitably.

"Maybe," Stephanie said. She looked amused.

The boys continued talking about cricket for quite some time. Kathy sat back and listened. She was very pleased that Rob had proved to be a hit with all her friends.

Kathy woke up early enough to accompany her room-mate Stephanie to the Inter-denominational praise service. Then the Reform Church service passed by very pleasantly. Kathy had dressed in a brown skirt with a floral print, and a fawn blouse. The blouse had a scoop neck and decorative lace collar, but was still quite modest.

Rob joined the group at lunch, and they arranged to go for a walk with Anita and Joelle, Tom, Larry, Luke and Tess. Stephanie and Garry were invited, but had already planned to wander off somewhere on their own.

It was a pleasant afternoon, but inclined to be a little humid as the rain had ceased, and the sun was drying the moisture off the ground. Kathy was glad of her low heeled sandals, as she picked her way along the bush path, and did not object when Rob took her hand to help her along. Tom remained with them, talking to Rob about engines and aeroplanes and other guy-things.

Joelle and Larry drew ahead with Anita. They all three appeared to be deep in discussion of hymns and tunes for worship. Some of their conversation drifted back to Kathy. Joelle, who studied the piano, was making the most suggestions, and Anita who was on the worship committee, was attempting to have some input. Larry appeared to be collecting ideas from both of the girls.

Luke and Tess, who were quite absorbed in each other, brought up the rear. The group walked all the way along men's walk, and along University Drive to the main road. Then they turned around and re-traced their steps with a detour down to the suspension bridge. It was almost time for tea when they returned, so they sat in the lounge and waited until the cafeteria opened.

Later that week, Kathy had suffered through her classes, and was settling down to some reading in her room, when Joelle dropped by for a visit.

"Hello Kathy," she said, "Can I talk to you for a while?"

"Sure," Kathy said, "How are your studies going?"

"Pretty good," Joelle replied. "I love Music, and History is interesting even though it is a lot of work."

"What are you doing in History this year?" Kathy asked curiously.

"Medieval studies," Joelle replied.

"Oh," Kathy said, "I do miss it a bit, you know. I have to do Infant Reading and Infant Maths instead this year."

"Are those good?" Joelle asked.

"Sort of interesting," Kathy said. "A bit like Practice-Teaching."

"Oh," Joelle said, "That sounds like a bit too much of the same thing."

"I know," Kathy said. "I've been thinking about finding another extra-curricular activity to give myself some variety. I guess, it's just Rob and all his recreational activities that's holding me back."

Joelle frowned, "You have barely met Rob. He is obviously very lively and good company, but you mustn't re-arrange your life for him. Especially if he is only going to be on campus for a short while."

Kathy was startled, "Err what?"

"Do you know how long the Pilot's Licence program lasts?" Joelle said. "It is about a semester. A few core units and 60-150 hours flying time, depending on how serous a license he wants."

"How come you know this?" Kathy exclaimed.

"A cousin of mine did the programme a few years back," Joelle reported. "That's why we rarely see the pilot guys on campus, and they don't generally stay around long enough, for us to get to know them."

"And yet I met Rob," Kathy mused.

"It may have been meant to be," Joelle suggested.

"Or I was lonely while the rest of you were hitched up," Kathy speculated.

Joelle blushed. "I'm single again this year, in case you haven't noticed. "That was something about that I wanted to have a chat about."

"I'm sorry," Kathy murmured. "Go ahead."

"I guess you have noticed that I have been spending a fair bit of time with Larry lately," Joelle said. "The trouble is, I cannot tell whether he really likes me, or is just being friendly."

"He went to the Reverse Tea with you didn't he?" Kathy asked. "How did the date go?"

"Larry was very polite," Joelle said, "And we talked about our studies."

"What sort of things have you done together since?" Kathy asked.

"Mostly organise worships," Joelle said, "And stuff in groups."

"I see the problem," Kathy said, "That could mean anything."

"Exactly!" Joelle exclaimed.

"You appeared to be quite friendly yesterday," I said. "Why don't you ask Larry how he feels?"

"I am scared to," Joelle said. "While I don't know, I can keep on hoping he is interested."

"It might be better to know," Kathy said slowly. "If Larry is not interested, you could look at other guys."

"Would you ask a guy how he felt about you?" Joelle inquired.

"I don't know," Kathy said. "I might if it were really bothering me not to know. However, I have never been in that situation. I usually go out with guys who have no problem chasing me. I'm sorry if I can't be any more help."

Soon after that, Stephanie returned from her afternoon activities and the conversation moved onto more general topics. Eventually Joelle left and went to her own room, and the room-mates settled down to study.

After class the next day, Kathy began to put together a cheap set of shelves she had bought in Northcoast. The shelves came flat-packed and were assembled using a hex key. The instructions were confusing, so after studying them for a while, Kathy did what she usually did with her projects, and worked from what the pieces told her to do. When she was finished, the shelves reached about to her chest in height.

Stephanie returned to the room and exclaimed in surprise. "Wow! Are you planning to buy a lot more books?"

"No," Kathy laughed. "These are for the pots I made in pottery."

"Of course," Stephanie said. "I think your pots will look wonderful there."

"You don't mind my using the space?" Kathy enquired.

"Of course not," Stephanie said. "That side wall was pretty blank, and it's over on your side of the room anyway."

"Thank you!" Kathy said.

"I love the things you make," Stephanie said. "If only I could fit some Art units into my degree!"

Kathy laughed. "You are practically taking an over-load as it is," she said. "If it weren't for Garry, you would have no fun."

"Lucky I have Garry then!" Stephanie joked. "I have been meaning to ask you – what is that *Neighbours* show you started watching like?"

"It is a bit puzzling really," Kathy said. "Among the young ones, almost no one has a real job, and very few are studying either."

"I guess the unemployment rate is a bit high," Stephanie observed.

"The show is made in Melbourne, so everybody from Victoria loves it," Kathy said. "I'm not sure whether people from New South Wales and Queensland can relate so well."

"Garry and I have been thinking of checking it out," Stephanie said. "It's something to do."

"I know you are fussy and prefer the classics," Kathy murmured.

"I want to see Australian film and television develop as well," Stephanie declared. "Even a soap has its part to play if it becomes popular."

Friday after class, Kathy spent the afternoon cleaning the bathrooms. One of the other cleaners had dropped out and Kathy was still carrying two floors worth of cleaning. She would rather be spending the time on an extra-curricular activity, but at least cleaning gave her time to think. And the money helped a little with her fees. When she returned to her room, Kathy found Joelle had slipped a note under her door.

"I need to talk." The other girl had written.

Concerned, Kathy hurried across to the room Joelle shared with Debbie and knocked softly.

"Who is it?" Joelle's voice came cautiously through the door.

"It's me, Kathy," Kathy called out.

Joelle opened the door and ushered Kathy into the room. Debbie was not there because she was out with her Theology student boyfriend David.

"Are you okay?" Kathy asked. The normally calm and self-possessed Joelle had unusually red eyes and puffy eye-lids.

Joelle shook her head. "No," she murmured. "I tried to talk to Larry after rehearsal today."

"And?" Kathy enquired.

"I don't think he is interested in me," Joelle whispered.

"Exactly how clear were you?" Kathy asked.

"Well," Joelle said, "We were packing up the song-books, and I said to him: 'Larry, I've been wanting to talk to you'."

The Musician paused for breath.

"Go on," Kathy said, "What next?"

"And then I said," Joelle continued, "We have been spending a lot of time together lately organising services and practicing the hymns, and I would like you to know that I think of you as a friend, not just another team member."

"What did Larry say to that?" Kathy asked.

"He said: 'Thank you Joelle, that is really sweet! I would like you to know I think of you as a friend too. If you ever need any help or advice, or even someone to talk to, I would like to think you could come to me'," Joelle reported.

"He offered you help as if he were already a minister and you were part of his congregation?" Kathy exclaimed.

"Yes, something like that," Joelle confirmed.

"What was his tone like?" Kathy asked. "Do you think Larry is one of those guys who offers to help when he really wants to get a girl's attention?"

"No," Joelle said. "He sounded honest, as if that was exactly the way he meant it."

"You only said 'friend', so perhaps that is all he thought you meant," Kathy suggested. "Otherwise his response sounds patronising."

"I certainly hope that's it," Joelle said. "Because then the internal phone rang, and when he answered it, his tone was very different. Almost tender. I think there is someone else."

"Could it have been his mother on the line?" Kathy inquired.

"It could have been," Joelle admitted, "But I doubt it. Very few mothers would know how to ring through to the Music Department."

"So where does that leave you?" Kathy asked.

"I don't know," Joelle said. "All I know is that I have to play for vespers this evening as if nothing had happened. I have to look normal and make no mistakes."

"Tough call," Kathy sympathised. "Is there anyone who could fill in for you?"

"Not really," Joelle said. "And what would I say – I suddenly came down sick in the few hours between practice and vespers? I'm a professional musician, or training to be one. I have to carry on."

"That does sound like the Joelle I know," Kathy said. "Just make sure you take some you-time as well. Hang out with Rob and me if you like, I'm not sure what we will be doing, but it will be something. Probably going to the beach night!"

"I can't possibly impose," Joelle said. "You are a new couple. Debbie will understand if I hang out with her and David. Just so long as David doesn't want to hang with Larry, the guys are friends."

The beach night was a casual event which proved highly popular with the students. It would also be the last official social event before the mid-semester break. Several busses had been booked to transport the students to a sandy beach slightly north of Noosa. The beach offered reasonable waves for surfing and long expanses of shoreline for romantic walks.

Kathy and Rob caught the same bus as Phoebe and Bradley, and Stephanie and Garry. Always prepared, Stephanie and Garry had brought a checked picnic along to sit on. Phoebe and Brad both had huge towels that they spread out alongside the picnic rug. Kathy blushed a little as she brought out her average sized bath towel to lay down, but Rob caught her eye and gestured to her to wait. Reaching into his back-pack, the trainee pilot brought out a grey wool camping rug and laid down against the cheery picnic rug.

"I'm a good boy scout," he said.

"I'm impressed," Garry exclaimed.

"Actually I'm not a scout at all," Rob admitted, "But I am a survivalist."

"It would be a handy skill to have as a pilot," Bradley observed.

"What else is in your pack?" Stephanie enquired curiously. "A parachute?"

"No but I do have a good multipurpose tool," Rob said. He pulled the tool out of his pocket and showed the group. It was shaped like a set of pliers, but other attachments, including can openers, screwdriver heads and a non-lethal blade could unfold from the main hand grip. The other boys admired the multi-purpose tool with its handy attachments immensely.

"It's legal," Garry said, "It's not a flick knife."

"I carry it for work purposes," Rob said. "If a light plane

crashes, the pilot may well need to cut himself and his passengers loose of the debris, unscrew panels and any number of things."

"It's nifty, but do you really need it at the beach?" Phoebe remarked disapprovingly.

"You never know," Bradley remarked. "What if the Café Proprietor had forgotten to pack a can opener and we couldn't get into those huge tins of pineapple juice over there?"

"Luckily he hasn't forgotten anything," Stephanie remarked, observing the buckets of punch that were being mixed up.

"Is anyone thirsty yet? Can I get you a drink?" Bradley offered impulsively and Phoebe glared at him.

"We are going for a walk first," she declared.

"Hang on Phoebes, I was only suggesting…" Bradley began, but Phoebe took him firmly by the hand and began to drag him towards the cliffs.

"I want to climb up and admire the view before sunset," she cried.

Bradley, being of a generally easy going nature, docilely began to follow.

Stephanie and Garry linked hands, and followed a few paces behind Phoebe and Bradley. It appeared neither couple wanted to over-crowd the other.

"Let's go too shall we?" Rob suggested, holding out his hand to Kathy.

"Yeah," Kathy took his hand and scrambled to her feet. By mutual consent, they lagged well behind the other two couples.

When they reached the summit of the cliff, Rob halted and pulled Kathy towards him.

"I feel like I'm on top of the world with you," he whispered.

Kathy gazed deep into his eyes. "You rise higher when flying," she whispered.

"But I'm alone then," Rob murmured. "I love flying, but it's much like driving. And I'm responsible for the safety of the plane."

"I wouldn't know," Kathy murmured.

"I will take you one day," Rob said. "Once I have my full license. Students aren't allowed to carry passengers."

Rob wasn't an incredibly tall guy, just above average, but Kathy was still shorter, so he had to bend to kiss her. Kathy submitted quietly, trying to gauge how she felt. This was her first kiss since breaking up with Owen. It was pleasant. She wasn't sure about fireworks – but pleasant was good. After a few minutes she called a halt.

"What about the others?" she whispered.

"I don't think they will notice," Rob remarked wryly. Glancing around, Kathy saw that Stephanie and Garry had retreated to their own piece of clifftop, and were snuggled in an embrace. Phoebe and Bradley were strolling hand-in-hand some distance away. They stopped, and Bradley said something that made Phoebe laugh. He gave her a quick peck on the lips.

"Naughty, naughty, mustn't watch," Rob jested. "If you are feeling shy, let's go back down to the beach and grab some food."

Half an hour or so later, when Kathy and Rob were enjoying the delicious home-made hamburgers the university cafeteria had provided, the other couples meandered back to join them.

"Did you know those cliffs were dangerous?" Garry enquired conversationally. "The Biology Master says fishermen have been washed off them at high tide."

"Yeah they looked pretty dangerous to us," Rob snickered suggestively.

Phoebe gave Rob a suspicious look, and Stephanie and Garry had the grace to blush.

"Living in a fish-bowl-like campus," Stephanie explained, "You learn to grab your moments when you can."

"Ah yes, I must learn that," Rob agreed with mock earnestness and it was Kathy's turn to go red in the dusk.

Later that evening, when they were sitting on the woollen blanket listening to the strains of someone's radio, which was tuned to some orchestral concert, Rob slid his arm around Kathy's shoulder.

"You are my steady girl aren't you?" he whispered close to her ear.

Kathy nodded in the dark, secure in the knowledge he could only feel the movement of her head. Then some campus official spoilt the mood slightly by going around switching on battery operated lanterns.

Local government elections did not usually interest the students at Silver Springs University greatly, but the election of Sally-Anne Atkinson as Brisbane's first female Lord Mayor was one of the topics of conversation at the breakfast the next morning.

There was a degree of disagreement regarding the significance of the appointment. The male students thought it was a significant step towards the inclusion of women in politics, while the female students were inclined to think it was a well-deserved, and somewhat belated appointment, given all the talented women in Australia.

Kathy yawned. She was only up that early because it was Andrew Grosvy's preaching debut, and Stephanie insisted they support their class-mate by attending.

Andrew led the Inter-denominational praise service, and made a great deal of it being Palm Sunday. He also expressed his wish to see world peace. True, Jesus said he did not bring peace, but a sword. Jesus death was a sword that would cut through sin, challenge his followers and revolutionise the world.

The spread of the gospel on occasion brought conflict, but its message promised ultimate peace. God's kingdom would one day be restored, and there would be peace, he argued. The normally reticent Theology student grew earnest and waxed eloquent. Even Rob was impressed.

The following days were full of classes, and Kathy also had to clean the bathrooms. She was beginning to tire of carrying the extra cleaning and hoped the Deans would soon find someone for the ground floor area. After her chores were completed and she had enjoyed a quick tea in the cafeteria, Kathy went down to the gymnasium to watch Rob play cricket.

His idea was growing in popularity, and the indoor cricket program now attracted a number of guys and girls. Even Arthur and Michael, who used to hang with the popular crowd the previous year, had asked to join the team.

Tuesday evening, Rob and Cathy went down to the gymnasium, with Phoebe and Stephanie, to watch Garry play in a B grade basketball match. Garry played very well, and so did the rest of his team. It appeared that both teams were evenly matched, and the advantage passed back and forth between the teams, each time one managed to score a goal.

Finally, Garry's team pulled ahead, scoring two goals in a row. The opposing team became desperate and knocked the ball out of bounds. Garry's team gained another goal when the ball was returned to play after the free throw, and they emerged the winners.

After the B teams had played, Bradley was due to play in an A grade match. The A grade matches attracted the most spectators, with the B grade players lingering to watch the outcome. Garry slipped onto the bench, and slid his arm around Stephanie's shoulders.

"Hello babe," he said.

"Well played," Stephanie murmured. "Well played indeed."

"I'm happy," Garry said. "Now let's see how Bradley's team

goes."

It so happened that evening, that Bradley's team was up against a team of seasoned players - boys who were mostly third and fourth year students. Every attempt had been made to create even teams, but a little shuffling had occurred due to timetabling and friendships. This meant that the opposing team had a slight edge upon Bradley's team, and outscored them heavily in the first half.

The teams took a small break at half-time and congregated to talk strategy. When play recommenced, Bradley who was a good all-rounder, had been placed in offense because of his height, and it was clear that his team was depending upon him.

Stephanie gasped with tension as the ball was passed to Brad and he approached the goal. Garry tightened his hold on her hand in sympathy, and when Bradley scored his team's first goal for the game, they both broke out cheering and clapping. Phoebe clapped enthusiastically for Brad too, but Kathy noticed her glance towards Stephanie. There was something in her expression, that hinted at a shade of darkness.

Bradley was run off his feet as the opposition tried to surround him, and diminish his advantage of height with their skill. Stephanie forgot she was holding hands with Garry, and clasped her fingers tightly together in her lap. Her eyes were shining and she began to get teary-eyed with the suspense.

Phoebe was no longer watching Bradley play. She was frowning at Stephanie instead. "It appears as though you barrack harder for my boy-friend than you do for your own," she remarked coldly.

Stephanie was clearly stunned. She turned her gaze from the players toward Phoebe. "Err, what?" she gasped.

Garry's arm was protective around Stephanie's shoulders. "It is a different sort of game," he said. "Much more intense. Even I can tell that, although I was pretty involved when I was playing my match."

"Garry played a good game," Stephanie said. "But he wasn't almost losing – like this!"

"Go Brad, go!" Garry and Rob both shouted, ignoring the disagreement between the girls, as the intensity of the final moments became over-whelming. Kathy added her cheers to the cries of the crowd. Bradley threw a final basket, bringing the two teams to an even score. The referee blew his whistle and time was up.

Brad looked exhausted. He accepted congratulations from Zach, the opposing captain, and then headed out the back door of the gymnasium towards the drinking fountains. Phoebe tried to follow him, but she found he was surrounded by his team-mates. She returned to her friends.

"Do you want us to wait?" Garry asked, and Phoebe shook her head. "I'm walking Stephanie back to the dorm then," Garry announced. "See you tomorrow, everyone."

"Night mate," Rob said.

"I think we'll wait a bit longer with Phoebe," Kathy said. "I'll see you back in the room Stephanie."

It was a few minutes before Bradley returned and then he

flopped on the bench. Rob and Kathy sat and waited.

"I'm beat," Brad announced. "For a while there, they were all after me. It might not be manly to admit, but I was mildly afraid of a foul or two."

"You did good man," Rob said.

"I was proud of you Brad," Phoebe ventured.

"Thanks Phoebe," Bradley said. "I am really tired, and I don't want you walking back to the dorms alone. Would it be okay if Rob took both you and Kathy back?"

"Of course," Phoebe said, but she looked hesitant. "Are you sure you don't want me to walk you back to the men's hall?"

"Nah," Bradley said. "There are a few of the guys around here still. I'll swing home with them."

The next morning Kathy opened a sleepy eye and gazed quizzically across the room at Stephanie. "Do you have any idea what that was about last night with Phoebe?" she asked.

"Not really," Stephanie said. She had been to the shower and was almost dressed for breakfast. "Perhaps she wanted to be Brad's biggest cheer-leader. That is all I can think."

"Phoebe said she wanted to meet with us today after classes," Kathy said. "I suggested straight after lunch, because I have Art at 2:30. I hope that's all right by you."

"Sure," Stephanie said. "Our room or hers?"

"The girl's lounge actually," Kathy said.

"Okay, I'll be there," Stephanie said thoughtfully. "I'm off to breakfast now."

Kathy climbed out of bed and headed for the shower. The only drawback with those few extra minutes of sleep she loved, was that she had to rush her showers and occasionally skip breakfast.

Classes were uneventful and the girls gathered in the downstairs lounge soon after lunch. The room was quite full, as Phoebe appeared to have invited as many girls as she knew, including Cara, Joelle, Debbie, and Tess. Looking further into the room, Kathy could also see Anita, Elisabet, Brenda and Damaris. The girls were all twittering and talking in an animated fashion when Phoebe arrived.

"Hello girls," Phoebe said immediately. "I guess you are wondering what this is all about?"

"Yes, we are," a few of the girl's chorused.

"I have decided that I am tired of us girls just watching the boys play sport down in the gymnasium," Phoebe announced with unexpected firmness.

A few girls gasped.

"I know I have been one of the most devoted basketball girl-friends," Phoebe continued. "However, I got to thinking lately about how much time I waste watching Bradley, instead of doing anything for myself. I bet all you other girlfriends can relate if you are strictly honest with yourselves."

"There's girls' basketball," Cara objected.

Phoebe dismissed that with a sweep of her hand. "I sometimes fear that is treated like the poor relation of boys' basketball."

Cara shrugged: "You may be right, but some of us take it seriously."

"I know," Phoebe said, and she glanced in Kathy's direction. "I also know you are just dying to bring up how Rob allows girls, as well as guys, to play indoor cricket, Kathy."

"I was now you mention it," Kathy concurred.

"That's very nice, but it still isn't anything especially for us girls," Phoebe exclaimed.

"I once tried to get badminton going," Stephanie ventured.

"We've got tennis outdoors for anyone who wants," Phoebe remarked, somewhat dismissively. "I have been having a talk to the Deans, and they have agreed to us launching our own Aerobics program! They have even offered to make Aerobics worth one credit point for anyone who enrols and takes it seriously."

"Oh wow!" a few girls breathed.

Questions were thrown at Phoebe hard and fast:

"Where would we hold the class?" Debbie cried.

"What music would we be using?" Joelle queried.

"Who would teach us all the moves?" Stephanie asked.

"All in good time girls," Phoebe declared. "We will be commencing when we return from the Ester break. I have asked one of the final year Physical Education major girls to lead the class. We can use one of the side-rooms in the gymnasium so the boys playing basketball won't ever interrupt us."

"As to music," Phoebe continued, "I am asking you all to bring your favourite cassettes back after the break. We will go through them and choose songs that are suitable. Unfortunately all songs will have to be approved by the Deans to make sure they aren't too sexual, refer to drugs or contain swear words."

"How exciting," Kathy exclaimed. "Our own Aerobics programme. I just hope it won't be at 7 am."

Phoebe laughed. "Posters will be going up all round the dorms after Easter. We are thinking of organising it for 7:30 pm. That is after the evening meeting, and I know some of you still watch *Neighbours*, so it is also after that."

A small twitter ran around the room.

"I have to go to Art now," Kathy exclaimed, looking at her watch. "You will have to excuse me. I must be the only person to have a late class before the break! Goodbye if I don't see some of you again before you leave – have a great time."

Some of girls had made travel arrangements commencing soon after their last as their last class finished, so they also shouted their goodbyes as Kathy exited the room.

Rob accompanied to Northcoast station the next day. It was a pain to be travelling on Maundy Thursday when everything was over-booked and rushed, but Kathy had not been able to help it. By the time Art was finished, it was far too late to be commencing interstate travel. Rob of course, was always happy to hang around Northcoast air-strip and get a few more hours on his flight log.

In fact, he was only going home for the public holiday period and would be back early to continue his flying. He suggested to Kathy they could spend some time together if she came back a day or two earlier. They hugged and kissed before Kathy boarded her bus to Armidale, and Rob boarded the train to Brisbane.

CHAPTER FOUR: CHANGES IN THE AIR

The Easter break passed uneventfully. Kathy ran into Owen once at church, where they exchanged brief stilted greetings and one-line descriptions of their activities since the beginning of the year. Kathy did not feel the need to advertise the fact that she was in a new relationship, because she felt that her manner made it clear she had moved on.

Rob had called twice during the holidays, despite the long distance charges. He had chatted jovially to her parents on the phone and they thoroughly approved of what they knew of him so far. Time at home with her parents was very precious, so Kathy did not take Rob's request that she return to campus early very seriously. Hence she arrived on the Sunday afternoon, the day before classes were due to commence.

Rob met her bus at Northcoast station and gathered her into his arms for a big sloppy kiss that left her gasping for breath, and secretly wiping her mouth.

"It's so good to see you again," Rob exclaimed. "It's been very quiet around here, but the dorm is beginning to fill up again."

"I missed you," Kathy exclaimed. A funny thing she had noticed about travel was that once you got to your destination, life at the other end seemed vague and unreal. Now she was back at Silver Springs, Rob, her studies and university friends were her whole world.

The couple bought tea in Northcoast, because the university cafeteria would not be serving until breakfast the next morning. It was fun and more like being on a "real date" than the average campus social function.

Stephanie was back later that evening and the two room-mates hugged effusively. They spent the evening after night-fall unpacking and chatting. In the morning, Kathy woke uncharacteristically early, and accompanied Stephanie to the cafeteria for breakfast. Garry was already sitting there with Bradley, and Rob joined them soon afterward. Kathy greeted Garry and Bradley, and asked them how their holidays had been. Then she asked Bradley whether Phoebe was back yet.

Bradley stirred uncomfortably. "Thank you for your concern," he said. "But there is something you girls ought to know. Phoebe and I have broken up!"

"When did this happen?" Stephanie asked curiously.

"She told me during the holidays," Bradley said. "She seemed to think it made it easier then."

Kathy nodded: "Holidays and special occasions seem to trigger these things. Did she say why?"

Brad shrugged. "No, just that we weren't suited anymore."

The girls exchanged glances. This would explain Phoebe growing tired of spending her time watching basketball for one thing. "We won't have to choose between friends will we?" Kathy cried in alarm.

"Choice already made," Rob asserted. "Bradley's my man. I dunno much about the girl."

"I'm afraid I'm in a similar position," Garry declared. "Bradley is a good mate."

"Phoebe and I have agreed we will both still be part of the group," Bradley said. "The split is amicable, if inexplicable."

"Here she comes now," Stephanie murmured as Phoebe entered the cafeteria.

Phoebe collected her tray and a bowl of cereal, and sat down at the opposite end of the table to Bradley. "Hello everyone," she said.

"Hello Phoebe," various murmurs arose around the table.

"Girls are you ready for Aerobics to start?" Phoebe asked. "I thought tomorrow, as it is worth credit and we had no sessions in the first half of the semester."

"That sounds fine Phoebe," Stephanie said.

"See you all in class then," Phoebe said, and got up having barely finished her cereal. She placed her tray on the dish-washing rack and stalked out of the cafeteria. The other girls followed more slowly.

The girl that Phoebe had organised to facilitate the Aerobics group was called "Annie". Annie was a fourth year Physical Education major, whom Kathy had seen around campus, but never really got to talk to. As a fourth year, Annie had shared no classes with the second years this year, or the year before, and due to her intense involvement in competitive sport, rarely attended university social functions, unless they were related to sport. Rumour also had it that Annie had no boy-friend, but was hoping to find someone, before the year was up, and she graduated.

Annie had already obtained a disk of musical hits from the previous year, and had a few of them vetted by the Deans. She greeted the girls, and explained a few safety procedures, before the session commenced. Although it was their university campus and gymnasium, not all the girls were aware of the location of the girls' toilets and changing rooms.

Then Annie led the group through a gentle stretching session. These exercises were accompanied by the wistful tones of John Waite singing "*Missing You*", followed by a warm-up to Paul McCartney and Michael Jackson's livelier duet, "*Say Say Say*." Then some light hand weight work was performed to "*What's Love Got to Do with It*" by Tina Turner.

The intense heart-warming full body exercise segment was accompanied by "*Jump For My Love*" by the Pointer Sisters, "*Girls Just Want to Have Fun*" by Cyndi Lauper, and "*Let's Hear it for the Boy*" by Deniece Williams. The strenuous exercise was followed by slower cool down exercises, accompanied by Phil Collins singing "*Take a Look at Me Now*". By the end of the session, all the girls were hot and sweaty, and some were seriously puffed. Kathy knew that she would be stiff the next day, because she had used her muscles in a totally different way than that to which she was accustomed!

"Be sure to sign the enrolment form and initial the roll before you go," Phoebe urged all the girls.

"I think it was a bit strenuous for me," Damaris remarked. "I'm on my feet all day doing hospitality as it is."

"I'm not sure I'll be able to make it every week during basketball season," Cara said. "But I'm happy to attend if you are taking casual attendees."

"That will be not-for credit, but you can still sign up," Phoebe said. "What about you Stephanie – too busy watching Garry and Bradley play basketball?"

"Actually I would love to keep going at Aerobics and even earn the credit point," Stephanie observed coolly.

"I think it is just the missing element I was looking for," Kathy added. "How clever of you to realise us girls needed something for ourselves, Phoebe."

"Thanks Kathy," Phoebe grunted.

"I'm in too," Debbie said. "It will be my girl's night without David."

"Cool," Phoebe said. "What about you, Joelle and Anita?"

"Sign me on as casual," Joelle said. "I have so many practices for worship services."

"About the same here," Anita said. "I would love to come along when I can."

"Tess?" Phoebe enquired. "Elisabet and Danielle?"

"I'm in," Tess replied enthusiastically.

"You can count on us," Elisabet said.

"It was sorta fun," Danielle added.

"I will be promoting the program more with the third and fourth year girls," Annie said. "I'm glad Phoebe had the idea and we could all benefit. Who's going to recruit amongst the first years?"

"I will," Cara said. "My sister Bede has started studying teaching this year, and she tells me a few girls in her class need encouragement to get involved."

"Thank you Cara," Phoebe said. "Don't wait for me girls, Annie and I still have a bit of work to do here."

Kathy and Stephanie threw their towels over their shoulders and turned to cross campus to the girl's dormitory. Their leggings were a bit revealing, but both were wearing long shirts, so they didn't care.

"I say," Stephanie mused thoughtfully. "Have you noticed Phoebe seems to be stirring me a bit? Almost like she doesn't want me in the class? What would that be about?"

"If I was a polite friend, I would say you were imagining things," Kathy remarked. "But, I'm inclined to be painfully honest, so I will agree with you. I think Phoebe may be carrying some bad business, because of her break-up with Bradley."

"And this is because Garry and Bradley are good friends?" Stephanie speculated.

"I think it's more because you and Bradley are good friends," Kathy suggested.

"I had nothing to do with their break-up," Stephanie snorted.

"I know you didn't," Kathy assured her room-mate.

"Well, she's out of luck," Stephanie said. "I like the Aerobics idea and I'm sticking to the class. And I still consider Phoebe a friend, so I'll be seeing her around too."

"I'm sure it will blow over," Kathy said.

The next morning Kathy attended her classes, and then did her cleaning work in the bathrooms. She was pleased to find that the Deans had re-assigned the ground floor for the second half of the semester, and she subsequently only had the first floor to clean. The extra time would come in handy for completing assignments, building her art portfolio and studying for exams.

When she arrived at lunch, Kathy found the boys were all talking excitedly.

"You will never guess what?" Rob shouted to her immediately.

"I wouldn't?" Kathy returned puzzled.

"Brad has bought himself a bike!" Garry exclaimed.

"I see," Kathy exclaimed, visions of a bicycle riding through her head. "That's nice. A mountain bike?"

"No silly," Rob said following her train of thought. "A real bike!"

"What do you mean?" Kathy was bewildered.

"He means a motor-bike," Dylan reported.

"It's a 1978 Honda CB 550 K3," Bradley explained proudly.

"Oh!" Kathy exclaimed. "Really?"

"Yes really," David agreed. He might be studying Theology, but he was as keen on vehicles as the next guy.

"Four cylinders, 5 speed manual transmission," Brad said. "Cruises like a dream."

"I'll bet," Larry was keen as well.

"As soon as we have finished eating we will go out to the student parking and look at it," Brad announced. "I've got a spare helmet, so I can take one of you guys for a spin."

The girlfriends were all looking somewhat amused at the boys' enthusiasm for the new toy. All except Phoebe, who was frowning from some distance away.

The boys were obviously impatient to go and look at the bike. Kathy gulped down the last of her food. "Okay I'm ready," she announced.

Rob grabbed her by the hand and they followed Brad out onto University Drive, and into the parking lot reserved for residential students. The cars here mostly belonged to third and fourth year senior students. Brad's road bike was parked in pride of place under a small shelter.

"What sort of brakes does it have?" Garry enquired.

"Single disk on the front and expanding on the rear," Brad explained.

"Yeah," the guys leaned in close to inspect.

"I like the red and black colour," Kathy ventured, feeling obliged to say something.

"I like all the shiny chrome," Rob said. "It's a beast Brad."

Bradley looked proud. He picked up a pair of helmets he had left strapped to the chassis. "So who's coming for a ride?"

"I have to go to Art now," Kathy said. "You can go Rob, I know you want to!"

Rob gave her a quick peck on the cheek goodbye, and then returned his attention to the bike. Kathy hurried towards the pottery studio. Time was passing, and she had been keen to paint everything that had survived its first firing in the kiln. She was glad to be able to say her efforts had improved massively, and she could now fashion a curved bowl and shaped vase.

Kathy woke the next morning with a slight headache and furry throat. Fearing she might be catching a cold, she drank orange juice at breakfast and lunch. The day passed quickly and uneventfully, but in the evening, she was surprised to find Stephanie sitting in their room looking glum.

"What's up?" Kathy enquired, wondering why her room-mate appeared to be lacking her usual fire.

Stephanie sighed. "I'm not sure yet," she replied. "Garry told me his mother was not well when he went home for the Easter holidays."

"I'm sorry to hear that," Kathy responded. "Did he say what was wrong?"

"She found a lump in her breast," Stephanie replied. "They are waiting on test results to find out whether it is anything serious."

"I hope it's not cancer," Kathy murmured. Both girls were quiet for a moment. Of all the cancers that could kill, breast cancer seemed somehow the most frightening.

"I really liked Garry's mum when I met her," Stephanie whispered.

"I know," Kathy acknowledged. "And what is this going to do to Garry?"

"I don't know," Stephanie said. "I know he adores his mother."

"Do you want to pray about it?" Kathy asked.

Stephanie nodded. "I have been praying all I can. It is the only thing that helps, because of course I cannot do anything."

"I will pray too then," Kathy promised. "What about the others – did Garry say you could tell them?"

"No," Stephanie said. "Please keep it between ourselves. I'm sure Garry will tell his friends when he feels ready."

"Okay," Kathy said. She hugged her room-mate tightly. "I will pray the tests come back clear."

"Thank you,' Stephanie said. "Perhaps the weight of both our prayers will help."

Kathy sighed and pulled out her text books. "No matter what's happening in the real world, our Education reading won't wait," she said.

"I know," Stephanie agreed. "I had better study too. But it's been so hard to concentrate."

The younger girl pulled her notes out of her folder and fiddled with them restlessly. She was usually such a studious person too. Kathy thought about suggesting they read to each other, and then decided that might be pushing too hard.

Friday Kathy handed her weekly Education reading report in before going to clean the bathrooms before the weekend. She was busy scrubbing the floors when Joelle sought her out.

"Ah there you are," the lively musician said. "Stephanie said you would be in here."

"Yeah," Kathy said. Her hair was in her eyes, but she didn't dare push it out because she was wearing gloves, and they were covered in bleach. "How can I help you?"

"Debbie and David, Larry and I are organising the music for vespers this afternoon," Joelle began. "I was wondering if you thought it would be a good time for me to drop a hint about the Champagne Breakfast."

The Champagne Breakfast was a traditional Silver Spring University social event where the students dressed up, and ate a gourmet meal early in the morning. It was also a prestigious dating occasion for couples and would-be-couples.

"Drop a hint with who?" Kathy was puzzled.

"Larry of course," Joelle whispered.

"I thought you had given up on that one," Kathy remarked. "Weren't you suspicious there was someone else?"

"I might have been mistaken," Joelle said. "He hasn't been hanging out with anyone in particular since. Just us on the worship committee."

"Be careful," Kathy advised. "Don't be so obvious you embarrass yourself."

"Of course not," Joelle flipped her blonde head. "If he doesn't take a simple hint, like over-hearing me ask Debbie what she is wearing to the function, I will back off."

"Good," Kathy said. "Because in my experience, guys who are interested can do their own asking."

"What about you and Rob?" Joelle said.

Kathy laughed. "I might have to remind him, as he probably doesn't know what the Champagne Breakfast is all about – but we are going steady. I am allowed to do that."

"Lucky girl," Joelle mused. "I'll leave you to your cleaning. Sorry for interrupting."

"That's alright," Kathy said. "I might have to re-spray the bleach because it's dried on, but that won't hurt."

The door closed softly behind Joelle as she left.

The Uniting Church vespers programme that evening was conducted by David and Larry. Joelle accompanied the song service on the piano looking slightly tight lipped. It was only something one would notice if they were very clever, and knew the musician well as Kathy did. Debbie had been scheduled to operate the over-head projector, but somehow she had been replaced by Anita, who fumbled slightly with the sheets, because she was not so well rehearsed.

Debbie slid into the pew beside Kathy and Rob. "Hello," she said.

"You're solo tonight, that's different!" Kathy exclaimed.

Debby laughed. "Don't worry about me," she said. "I'm more worried about Joelle," Debbie continued in a whisper. "She kept asking me what I was wearing to the Champagne Breakfast...and I haven't made my mind up yet."

"We really ought to go shopping in Northcoast," Kathy suggested. "I could do with a new dress."

"Yeah me too," Debbie agreed. "And then Joelle asked David what time he was picking me up. David was a bit surprised, because he will just come over to the girl's dorm a quarter of an hours before it starts. He thought she was worried about being alone, so he invited Joelle to accompany us."

"Good old David," Kathy laughed. "Always trying to make everybody happy!"

"Joelle said she would think about it, and Larry was very, very quiet," Debbie continued. "A few minutes later, Larry told me Anita had volunteered to do the over-head projector, so I could have a night off. I said 'thanks' of course, but now I'm wondering, whatever is going on with them?"

"Nothing that I know of," Kathy returned. "Joelle does like Larry, but I think they are just good friends."

"I see," Debbie said. The ceiling lights were dimmed and the projector burst into light. Anita put the words to the first song of the evening on the screen.

"Not to be rude," Rob murmured discretely on Kathy's other side, "But I was wondering what you two were talking about."

"Oh," Kathy explained. "There is a social function called the Champagne Breakfast coming soon. You are going to take me of course."

"I am?" Rob exclaimed. "What if I don't want a fancy breakfast?"

"You always eat breakfast," Kathy said.

"Yeah and then I rush off to the airfield, to start my flying lesson," Rob said. "You would know that Kathy, if you weren't always so late in the morning yourself."

"Please Rob," Kathy plastered an appealing smile on her face.

"Okay on one condition," Rob said. "You come to Northcoast Airfield tomorrow, I have booked the university car to take us. I've been dying to show you the planes."

"It's a deal," Kathy laughed. People around them were trying to sing, and Kathy received a few sharp looks for talking during the programme, but she was too happy to notice.

Kathy woke up the next day and showered and dressed before sharing a leisurely breakfast in the cafeteria with Rob. The university car had been booked for 9:30, so the couple walked down to the parking area to meet Luke, who was the regular driver. A few minutes later they were on their way to the Northcoast airstrip, which was not situated in the centre of the township, but some distance away to allow for the runways required by even light planes.

It was there that Kathy met what Rob referred to as the "other love of his life", the Cessna. The Cessna 150 was red with a white stripe and aerodynamic lines. It was a compact machine. Rob explained that although it had been remodelled slightly, the Cessna 150 had been on sale since 1959. It was a light aluminium two seater plane, which was used for pilot training, aeroplane racing and stunts.

The airfield was also very proud to own a late model Cessna 152 manufactured in 1983, but the trainee pilots were not allowed to touch it until their licenses were almost completed. The other notable aircraft parked at the airfield were several Cessna 188, which Rob explained were also known as "ag-wagons". These light single seater planes were designed for crop dusting and aerial seeding. Pilots who already had their Private Pilot license could take these out, to learn how to handle them under working conditions.

Rob reported proudly that he was only a few flight hours off gaining his Private Pilot license certification. Once he had his hours, his log-book would be inspected and he would be required to answer a number of rigorous safety questions, before taking an instructor for a test flight. During the second half of the semester, Rob would be working on accumulating the hours required to become a Commercial Pilot, so that he could carry passengers or freight for a fee.

"And then I can fly one of these," Rob said with a longing sigh. He led Kathy across the small tarmac to a Cessna 172. "It is a single-engine, fixed-wing aircraft that can carry up to four people."

"Very nice," Kathy said.

"Technically I can fly one with just a Private Pilot license, and that would allow me to practise," Rob said. "However, I can't be hired as a pilot without my full Commercial Pilot license so that is what I really need to achieve."

"I am sure you will," Kathy said. She was very impressed, and not a little awestruck by the line-up of planes and the realisation that Rob really did take at least the Cessna 150 up in the air.

They greeted one of the instructors who was doing paperwork in the office area. "Hello Rob," The flight instructor said. "Are you still going to do an hour this morning?"

Rob turned to Kathy. "Would it be alright?" he asked. "I ought to have got my hours before Easter really, but I got distracted and spent too much time on campus with you."

Kathy knew they would not have been able to access the air-field if no one had been in attendance, and suspected this had been Rob's plan all along. Luckily she had slipped her Psychology text into her bag.

"I'm sorry," the Instructor said. "Rob doesn't have his Private Pilot license yet, so he can't take a passenger. There are tea and coffee facilities here in the office. Feel free to help yourself, but don't touch anything else."

"Please Kathy," Rob begged. "I want you to watch me take-off and land."

"Yeah sure," Kathy said. She settled down on one of the saggy lounge chairs in the shed, and watched as Rob and the Instructor kitted up for the flight. Then they walked to the foremost Cessna 150 parked on the runway. Kathy's heart moved into her mouth as she watched them climb in, check and adjust everything, and then begin to taxi.

The Cessna lifted slowly into the air, and Kathy breathed a sigh of relief. Flying was relatively safe except when taking off or landing. There was also very little to see once Rob was in the air. She boiled the kettle and brewed herself a cup of coffee, even though she didn't really like the strong taste. She opened her Psychology textbook.

Rob must have forgotten her, or got carried away with his love of flying, because it was more like two hours before the aeroplane circled back to the run-way. Kathy put a marker in her text when she heard the throb of the engine, and watched as her boyfriend skilfully set the plane down. He leapt out and shook hands with the instructor. Then he raced across to Kathy and greeted her with shining eyes.

"Guess what babe? Next time I go out it will be my license flight!" he cried.

"I'm thrilled," Kathy exclaimed. It was almost worth the dull couple of hours with the textbook to see the joy on Rob's face. She would do well in her next test as a bonus anyway. "I'm glad I was here for this milestone."

"When can I do my test?" Rob asked the Instructor, who had joined them more sedately.

"As soon as I can book an hour with an independent instructor," the man replied. He picked up the telephone and made a few calls. "You're in luck!" He said: "I can get someone from Mackay on Monday. Be here and be well prepared boy."

"Thanks," Rob said. They used the office phone to call for the university car to come and pick them up. There would be a wait of around half an hour, as Luke required a bit of notice, so they sat down to relax.

"I hope you don't mind," Rob apologised to Kathy. "When the instructor said I could make my hours today if we stayed up there, I just had too."

"I understand," Kathy said. "It's a bit like when I'm making a pot, I can't run off and leave it half moulded on the wheel."

"I'm glad you understand," Rob said.

Privately Kathy thought she would not be coming across to the airfield very often. It was too clearly a place of business and instruction, and Rob was wholly absorbed once he arrived there. They had even missed lunch, and the fruit they grabbed from the cafeteria, when they arrived back on campus, barely carried Kathy through to the afternoon. Still it was quite exciting tell all the students at tea that Rob had made his hours, and would be getting his license on Monday all being well!

Sunday after the various church services, Kathy was sitting with her friends enjoying lunch, when Damaris came and slid into the seat next to Andrew Grosvy.

"What is this I hear about a Champagne Breakfast?" The red head asked.

"It is the next event on the college social calendar," Stephanie explained patiently.

Damaris looked around the group, "Are you all going with your boy-friends?" she asked.

"Pretty much," Kathy said. "The Reverse Tea was about the girls asking the guys, but the Champagne Breakfast is about the guys asking the girls."

"Ooh!" Damaris' eyes were large. She turned to Andrew. "It would be gracious then, as I asked you to the Reverse Tea, for you to ask me to the Champagne Breakfast."

Andrew looked slightly troubled. "It doesn't really work that way around here," he said. "Are you sure you don't want to get to know someone new?"

Damaris shrugged. "Why would I, when I can get to know you?"

"I would be honoured to take you to the Champagne Breakfast then," Andrew said with a sigh.

"I would love to go!" Damaris exclaimed. "Thank you for asking me Andrew."

"Your welcome," Andrew began to look amused. Damaris finished her lunch and then rushed off to be with her first year friends.

"You have a fan there," Stephanie remarked.

"I know," Andrew said. "I really don't want to hurt her feelings, but I would like to see her mix more."

"I think the Hospitality course is very demanding," Rob remarked. "It could be a bit isolating – like the Pilot's program."

"I know," Andrew said. "And that's one reason..." The young Theology student stopped himself. "A gentleman doesn't talk about his lady friends."

"There aren't any gentlemen in the men's room at the gymnasium then," Dylan remarked and the whole table began to laugh.

"Good one Dylan," Garry remarked.

"I go in there occasionally too," Bradley observed as the mirth died down slightly. "And I like to keep my personal life to myself."

"You must be the exception to the rule then," Rob said.

"I expect I am," Bradley agreed. "And I've got plenty to talk about with my new bike."

"We all love you Bradley," Kathy said.

Kathy was busy with classes and cleaning all Monday morning, and did not hear how Rob's test flight had gone until mid-afternoon, when he returned from the air-field. He had passed comfortably, and was bristling with excitement about commencing his hours for the Commercial Pilot license.

That evening after tea, Kathy was watching Rob playing indoor cricket. Occasionally she joined a team when the numbers were uneven, but the activity had proven so popular her participation was rarely required. Most of the boys from their friendship group played, and today Lionel and Craig, who had not played before, had elected to join the game. There were still a few regular female participants, including the ever-active Cara, and Annie their Aerobics instructor, who had heard about the activity from Cara and decided to join.

Stephanie arrived about half-way through, and slid onto the bench beside Kathy. Although they roomed together, both girls had been so busy that had not had a chat for a couple of days. Moreover, watching Garry play cricket reminded Kathy of his mother.

"Have you had a good day?" she asked.

"Pretty much," Stephanie said. "I have just completed another essay."

"You are so good," Kathy observed. "Even when I begin research early, I usually have to finish the paper at the last minute."

Stephanie shuddered. "The thing is," she said. "I cannot work that way. If I did that, I would have very few ideas and make a lot of mistakes. Or I would fall asleep and never get it finished at all."

"Maybe," Kathy was amused. She knew that Stephanie took her timetable very seriously. "Have you heard anything more about Garry's mother?"

"Yes," Stephanie returned. "Garry told me the biopsy came back containing abnormal cells."

"What happens now?" Kathy was saddened.

"Garry says they will be attempting to remove the lump, while leaving as much of the normal tissue as possible," Stephanie said. "Then there may be some radiotherapy required. It all depends on the first operation going well. If the doctors get it all she may be all-right."

"I do hope so," Kathy murmured. "What is Garry planning to do?"

"He is applying to Wollongong University, so that he can be closer to his mother next semester," Stephanie said. "I am supporting him in this, even though I am worried..."

"About what happens to couples when they are separated for a considerable period of time," Kathy finished the sentence for her room-mate.

"Exactly," Stephanie agreed. "Garry is taking next semester off whether he gets into Wollongong University or not. So he won't be with us either way."

"I'm sorry," Kathy said. "Your Ecology class is going to be small isn't it? How many are in the class now?"

"There are four of us," Stephanie said. "Dylan and Garry, Cara and me. Without Garry, there will be three – and the lecturer. It doesn't bear thinking about."

"Could you go down to the University of Wollongong too?" Kathy suggested.

Stephanie shook her head. "No," she said. "My parents are far too strict to allow me to change universities." She exhaled slowly. "I will just have to hope for the best."

"Enjoy the rest of this semester while you can," Kathy advised.

Stephanie smiled. "I intend to," she whispered.

The girl's Aerobics ran smoothly the next day, because the participants were more familiar with the format. Annie introduced one or two more exercises and varied the music selection slightly. Phoebe looked very proud because this was her project and it looked like it would succeed.

The programme made the boys curious however. Any males practising in the gymnasium at the right time saw a stream of girls entering one of the smaller rooms and then heard the contemporary music playing for an hour. They could not enter because the girls had voted for the activity to be female only. This seemed like discrimination, but most people thought it was fair because so many things on campus were male oriented in practice if not in theory.

Lunch time, Rob and Garry were asking how the Aerobics program was going, and what really happened behind the closed doors. The boys' heads were full of images of Jane Fonda in a skimpy leotard.

Cara laughed. "Except for the music, it is much like the stretch and conditioning parts of basketball training without the 'sport specific' segment," the sporty girl explained, trying to use imagery the boys would understand.

"Aerobics does have its own sport specific moves, and the Association of National Aerobic Championships has run competitions since 1983,"

Phoebe added, "But Annie will be introducing the more complex movements slowly."

"It's a bit like dance isn't it?" Bradley ventured.

"Don't say that around here," Kathy murmured. "The Reform Church doesn't allow dance."

"I didn't mean the silly stuff," Bradley said apologetically. "More like ballet – which is quite disciplined."

"Also very exclusive," Phoebe added. It was one of the rare times the group had seen her speak to Bradley since their break-up. "I promoted the program to the Deans more on the strength of Kenneth Cooper's research on fitness."

"I think it's great," Stephanie exclaimed. "I'm really enjoying classes. However, I wish Annie would not use *"What's Love got to do with it?"* all the time. The rhythm is all right to exercise to, but the words are so ugly."

"What do you mean ugly?" Bradley asked.

"Doesn't Tina say 'what is love but a second-hand emotion'?" Stephanie extrapolated. "Shouldn't love be at the foundation of everything?"

"She doesn't mean Christian love as we perceive it," Andrew said. He adopted one of his earnest looks as he continued. "The story I heard, Tina was being beaten up by her husband Ike. She is probably on the bitter side now she has escaped from him."

"Oh," Stephanie's eyes were big. Despite having a boyfriend, Stephanie was still very innocent. "So she doesn't believe in love anymore?"

"I think that's the general idea," Andrew replied.

"If you don't have love, all you have is lust," Stephanie said blushing. "That's what I thought she was talking about."

"Perhaps," Andrew said, "But if you don't have love – you might have NOTHING. That's another way of looking at it. And some ladies have been treated so bad, they would rather choose nothing than a relationship. Its peaceful and they can rebuild their self-respect."

"But how could she mistake being beaten up for a relationship?" Stephanie was still puzzled. "Most girls would get smart to what works and what doesn't work after the first few months of dating. I know I did last year!"

"They were married," Garry suggested. "And maybe he was nice at first."

"How long were they married?" Stephanie asked.

"About fifteen years, and then she escaped," Andrew said. "She had to rebuild her career and everything, all the time being in fear of Ike."

"Wow," Kathy breathed. "What a brave lady."

The girls from the group were sitting together at tea time when Damaris came up and sat down beside Stephanie.

"Hi guys," the first year girl said.

"Hello Damaris," Kathy said.

"I'm afraid I have some bad news for Andrew," Damaris said. "Where is he?"

"He should be along any moment," Stephanie said. "Look, there he is with David and Larry."

"Thanks," Damaris replied.

Andrew caught sight of the girls sitting together and came across to the table with a quizzical look on his face. Larry slid in between Anita and Cara. David put his tray down beside Debbie. Rob and Garry, who were following close behind, took their places beside Kathy and Stephanie. Andrew had no choice but to take the next spare seat, which was beside Damaris.

"How are you?" he inquired. "You look like something is the matter."

"I'm good," Damaris said. "But I do have something to tell you Andrew."

"Yes?" Andrew was patient.

"I have just found out that as part of my course, I have to work as a waitress at the Champagne Breakfast," Damaris said. "I do hope you are not too disappointed, we cannot go together after all."

"I am sorry to hear that of course," Andrew said diplomatically. "But if it is part of your course to serve at functions...I guess you must do it."

"Yes, I have to," Damaris said. "Waitressing is a skill I need marked off, along with catering, serving beverages and baking."

"Let us know when you have been practicing baking," David remarked somewhat cheekily.

"Whatever we make usually gets served to everybody," Damaris said. "But if you would like to know specifically when I made the food, I would be happy to tell you."

"We would be very interested to know," Andrew said. "To be honest, I don't know a lot about the Hospitality course."

"I would be happy to tell you more," Damaris looked flattered.

Andrew pinned the earnest look he usually reserved for Theological topics on his face, and spent the next few minutes deep in conversation with Damaris. At last she excused herself and moved in the direction of the dishwashing area. Apparently cleaning chores were part of the course as well. Andrew turned to his friends with a relieved look on his face.

"Damaris' course suddenly became very interesting when it was the cause of your separation mate," Rob remarked somewhat cynically.

Andrew frowned. "None of that sort of talk please," he said. "Damaris isn't far away.

"Just telling it like it is," Rob observed, but he subsided gracefully.

"She really is a nice young girl," Andrew said, "And I didn't want to hurt her, but I'm glad things worked out the way they have."

"Don't let yourself get caught again man," David said. "It isn't always so easy to get to of things gracefully."

"Now who are you going to ask to the Champagne Breakfast?" Stephanie asked curiously and Andrew smiled secretively.

"I have a few ideas," he said. "You will know soon enough if anyone says 'yes' to me."

"Would you believe that?" Stephanie whispered after the girls had left the cafeteria, "Poor Andrew was stuck because he couldn't say 'no' to Damaris."

"Actually, I thought it was rather sweet," Cara, who had been relatively quiet that afternoon, said.

"So did I," Kathy agreed.

"What happened to your preference for assertive men?" Stephanie asked Kathy.

"Nothing," Kathy said. "I'm just re-assessing Andrew. I think he is beginning to assert himself in his own way."

"I've always seen a little of that in him," Stephanie said. "You just have to be patient to see it."

Kathy devoted some extra time to her pottery that afternoon. She required a variety of articles, and even a matching set for her portfolio assessment. When Kathy returned to the dormitory, the girls reminded her that she had promised to go dress shopping in Northcoast with them.

Stephanie was still in her Ecology laboratory when they left. She had given Kathy some money, a Butterick pattern number, and a request for two-and-a-half meters of cream taffeta. The clever girl was going to make her own dress in the few days left before the function.

The university car arrived for them at four pm, and Debbie, Joelle, Phoebe, and Kathy climbed inside. It had been a while since any of them had hung out off campus, and they would be missing tea in the cafeteria, so they planned to get takeaway food while they were in Northcoast.

The clothing stores in Northcoast included a department store, the teen-shop that Stephanie had always loved, and an import store where you could get tie-die and batik print and other quite hippy style clothes as well as a variety of gifts. Kathy reflected that Stephanie had always loved that store too. And of course the fabric store, where girls who could sew loved to shop.

They went to the department store first. Debbie's' eye immediately lit on a drop waisted dress. It was glamourous without being revealing, sporting a large bow on the hip and full skirt below the straight bodice. It was a rich purple colour and looked just right for the girlfriend of a Theology student.

"I'm thinking about a suit," Joelle said. "Not a work-a-day suit, but something like that!" She lifted a two piece outfit from off the rack. It had a loose jacket that was more like a large shirt with collars and cuffs, and it topped a slim-line skirt. There was a huge leather belt to clinch around the waist. The colour was a bold red and the fabric was not exactly satin, but something else shiny. The ensemble was very 1980's!

"That looks nice," Phoebe said, pointing to a pale blue dress with a lace collar. It was distinguished from every-day styles by its fine silky fabric.

The three girls took their selections to the changing rooms and Kathy looked around with a sigh. She couldn't afford the price tags she saw on the clothes in this store, even with the discount offered this week. Clothes were an investment for Joelle because she was a performer, and was on public view playing her music so often. Debbie had recently received birthday money from her parents, and Phoebe's Grandmother sent her the occasional cheque. It was nowhere near Kathy's birthday, so she was on the tightest budget.

"Let's go to the teen store," Kathy said when the other girls all returned pleased with their selections. They passed through the checkout, and crossed the street. Kathy was in luck because the teen store was having a sale. She immediately fell in love with a royal blue satin dress. It had a sweetheart neckline and shoestring straps. The bodice crossed over at the front and the skirt opened into a split just above the knee.

"It's nice," Debbie said. "If a bit revealing…"

"Very playful," Joelle remarked. "Sexy, but not too short."

"I think it would suit you Kathy," Phoebe added.

Thus encouraged, Kathy tried the dress on, and once she was satisfied with the fit, purchased it. Then the girls went to the fabric store to buy Stephanie's taffeta. Stephanie had given Kathy a sample to match and the girls found the fabric easily. Joelle remarked it was more of a beige than a cream, but Kathy was sure that the noticeable tint was what Stephanie wanted.

Their business accomplished, the girls retired to the Northcoast snack bar for ice-creams, pies and milkshakes. They were all young and slim, and could afford the calories.

CHAPTER FIVE: FIRST GIRL ON BRADLEY'S BIKE

Friday morning Kathy attended her classes and in the early afternoon she concentrated on her cleaning for the weekend. Later that afternoon, she had agreed to go for a walk with Debbie, Joelle and Phoebe. David was included because Debbie was going, and Larry accompanied him. Kathy thought that Larry hesitated slightly when he saw Joelle was part of the group, but the well-mannered Theology student recovered quickly and greeted the girls politely.

Rob had promised to join the expedition if he was finished at the airfield, but there was no sign of him at the rendezvous point. Kathy assumed he was busily clocking up more air hours, an activity which seemed to be a constant concern for all the young pilots.

"This is so refreshing," Joelle exclaimed as they set out along University Drive. "Normally we would be practicing all afternoon, but with the group from Hillsong visiting on the weekend, worship has been taken care of for us."

"It is nice to have a holiday," Larry agreed. "Andrew and Anita are still busy however, because someone has to show the visitors around."

"How exciting," Kathy exclaimed. "They must feel privileged."

"I met the Hillsong people last year," Larry said. "In fact I went down there and gained some experience in their church in Balkham Hills, when I did my practical."

"What was it like?" Phoebe asked curiously.

"Very large," Larry said. "And very noisy. They offer worship that appeals to youth. I'm not sure about all their Theology."

"They have a lot of music don't they?" Joelle inquired. She stepped forward so she was standing between Phoebe and Larry.

Kathy noticed the musician stayed as close to Larry as was possible, without being totally indecorous for the rest of the walk. Kathy suspected Joelle was still hoping that Larry would ask her to the Champagne Breakfast. However, it was Kathy's opinion Larry would have asked Joelle by now if he had been planning to do so. Joelle risking being labeled a "Theol chaser" if she continued to be so obvious. This was the term used contemptuously on campus to describe girls who made it obvious they were seeking to marry a minister.

The group walked the length of University Drive, and then turned right. About half an hour along the track, they came across the footpath that led down to the river. They followed this and crossed over the suspension bridge, marveling how the water had dropped since the rainy season had concluded.

"It was up to here when we came in March," David said, gesturing to the board walk. "The bridge was not safe at all!"

"I'm glad it is safe today," Kathy said, or else we would have to go all the way back along University Drive."

"Yeah, I think that is longer," Phoebe agreed. "And we pass the rose gardens on the way back this way too."

Unlike the normal vespers, the students had been required to purchase tickets to the Hillsong concert that evening. The programme ran for about an hour, and cost $10 to attend. Most students had been interested enough to buy tickets and some were even making a special date out of it.

Rob picked Kathy up at the girls' dormitory, and they headed into the meeting hall, which had been chosen as the venue for the evening. This was due to the building being larger than the women's assembly area. It also had a proper stage and enough room for a band to set up.

The music was original and different. Kathy wasn't quite sure what to think. The style wasn't like the hymns she was used to, but was much more modern. It was rhythmic, but not as pulsating as rock music. Instead of sitting in their seats, the students were encouraged to stand up sway and wave their arms around. It was something of a shock to everyone who was used to a seated service.

The next day, which was Saturday, was the gala Hillsong concert. It was held in the gymnasium because that was the only building large enough to hold all the students, plus local Christians and community members who had bought tickets. Tickets to this event were $25 each, because the concert ran for two-and-a-half hours.

Kathy had not bought herself a ticket to the gala concert, because she had signed up to be an usherette at the event. This meant that she would be assisting on the door, checking tickets and showing people where they could find a space to sit. In this way, she would earn her entrance, although her enjoyment of the concert would be interrupted by a few duties. Kathy had thought the savings well worth the effort, and Rob had been keener on going across to the airfield and making his hours than attending another concert.

The whirr of the sewing machine greeted Kathy as she returned to her room. Like many of the students on a strict budget, Stephanie had chosen to only attend the cheaper Friday night concert. Moreover, her boyfriend Garry had flown to Wollongong for the weekend to see his mother.

Kathy pulled her psychology textbook out. Of all the students she knew, only Stephanie was so disgustingly ahead on her studies that she was making her own Champagne Breakfast outfit.

"That's pretty," Kathy remarked.

Coming to the end of a seam, Stephanie snipped a thread and held the dress up. "It is beginning to take shape," she said. "I have to thank you for getting just the right shade of taffeta."

"And the pattern is very 1985 meets the twelfth century," Kathy observed. "Or it will be when you have finished it."

"I must admit I have a thing for peasant styling," Stephanie said. "How was the concert?"

"Okay, I guess," Kathy said. "I'm glad I didn't pay for it."

"Yeah," Stephanie said. "I went to the campus book-store and tried to listen to a tape of their music."

"Some of the songs were alright," Kathy said. "The ones where you could hear the words clearly...and recognize as Christian songs."

"Exactly," Stephanie said. "If the words are, 'I love you – I love you so', how do we know they are singing to God and not a boyfriend or girlfriend?"

Just then Kathy's name sounder over the public address system. "That will be Rob," she exclaimed. "Finally back from the airfield! We are going to the canteen for ice-cream if you want to join us."

"No I better finish this, the Champagne Breakfast is not that far away," Stephanie replied. "Have fun you two."

The Hillsong group had remained to sing at the Sunday praise service free of charge. The service was held in the women's assembly area, and the Hillsong people mingled their voices with the university musicians. While the event was less spectacular than the concerts, it was more inclusive.

After all the excitement and religiosity of the past few days, the Reform Church service seemed tame, and Kathy suspected it would be poorly attended. Whether her suspicions were true, she could not say because she was one of the non-attendees. David and Debbie, who did attend, confirmed her suspicion with their observations that participation was low.

Sunday library hours were limited, but in the afternoon Kathy was forced to go across to the repository of knowledge, and seek out a few books on a social issue for her Psychology essay. As she passed through the reference section, Kathy thought shew saw Cara deep in conversation with Andrew Grosvy. When Kathy returned to borrow her selection of books, Cara was still there, surrounded by mighty ecology tomes, but Andrew was no-where to be seen.

"Was that Andrew I saw here before?" Kathy asked curiously.

Cara blushed slightly. "Yes, he asked me to the Champagne Breakfast."

"He's not your usual sort of guy," Kathy remarked.

"You mean he's not Dylan," Cara observed dryly.

"Something like that," Kathy agreed.

"That's so not happening," Cara pronounced. "And Andrew is very sweet."

"So you said 'yes' then?" Kathy asked.

"Of course," Cara tried to look very matter of fact. "I have a nice dress and everything. Might as well go on a date. Well I better get back to my study, a weekly practical report, it really stinks."

"Hmm," Kathy was suddenly very glad she only had to make her pots. Not analyze them to the nth degree. Of course there was some theory involved in art. Projects and stuff, but no laboratory reports.

Classes and cleaning kept Kathy busy all Monday morning, so she was mildly surprised when Anita and Larry walked into the cafeteria at lunch time holding hands. Anita explained that Larry had asked her to the Champagne Breakfast and they were coming out as a couple.

"It has taken us a while, because Larry was afraid of hurting someone else, who is a good friend," Anita continued in a low voice. "But the longer we left it, the worse the situation seemed to get."

"Oh?" Kathy murmured.

Some of the boys were right out of the loop of campus gossip, and didn't know who Anita meant. However, most of the friends either knew or could guess.

Joelle entered the cafeteria just then. Her head was held high and her posture was stiff. She collected her lunch, and stalked to a place on the table, as far away from Anita and Larry as possible. She ate without speaking, aside from a muttered, "Hello," when greeted by the others.

Anita and Larry finished their meals and said, "Goodbye." They placed their trays on the dishwasher trolley and left the cafeteria. As they exited, their hands slid together and clasped. David and Debbie threw the group apologetic smiles, and followed the other couple.

"Poor Joelle," Stephanie whispered, "What can we do?"

"There's nothing you can do," Joelle returned bleakly. "We were all such good friends, and all spent so much time together, it was impossible to tell. The only thing that would have helped, would have been if he had told me earlier."

"It would seem like the right thing to do," Stephanie observed.

Cara turned to Dylan. "Dyls, I want you to ask Joelle to the Champagne Breakfast please, so she has someone to go with."

Dylan sighed. "Cara when will you learn I am not your performing puppet? You can go with Andrew Grosvy if you wish, but you cannot tell me who to ask. In fact, I was thinking of asking that Annie who leads your Aerobics class. She seems like a nice girl."

"Since when were you into older women?" Cara asked in scorn.

"She is about one year older, that is all," Dylan said. "Of course, I'll be here as a friend if Joelle needs me."

"We all will be," Garry added.

"This really isn't necessary guys," Joelle muttered in distress. "So I couldn't read which way the wind was blowing, I'll recover." Her voice trembled slightly. "Eventually."

The easy-going Bradley rose to his feet and extended his hand to Joelle. "Come on Joelle," he said, "I think this calls for a ride on my bike."

Usually Joelle would have been too cautious to consider getting on the back of Bradley's motorbike, but today it looked like a lifeline. She rose from the table and took Bradley's hand.

"Thanks Brad," Joelle murmured.

"We will go up the mountains," Bradley said. "There are some magnificent windy tracks up there. Just right for blowing away the cobwebs. Don't worry, I'll ride safely."

Joelle and Bradley departed the cafeteria with new horizons on their minds, while Garry, who had returned from his trip to Wollongong, thoughtfully stowed their trays in the dishwasher trolley.

"The first girl on Bradley's bike," Kathy exclaimed. "Lucky Joelle!"

"How chivalrous of him," Stephanie said. "Although I remember Bradley was good to me last year too."

Of their current group, Phoebe was the only one dateless for the coming Champagne Breakfast. The girl had been fiercely independent since her break-up from Bradley. However, Tuesday after lunch, she dropped by Kathy and Stephanie's room. Kathy was just finishing her Education reading report when Phoebe arrived. Stephanie was hemming her new dress.

"Hey girls," Phoebe remarked cheerfully after knocking on the door.

"Hi Phoebe," Kathy said. "How are you?"

"I'm good," Phoebe said. "You two?"

"I'm good," Stephanie said. "What have you been up to since English?" Stephanie and Phoebe saw a lot of each other because they shared the same major.

"Not much," Phoebe said. "I thought I might write my paper on Dorothy Hewett. We hear a lot less about the female poets."

"I wrote about the Ern Malley hoax," Stephanie said. "A poet who is made up as a joke, and then becomes popular years after he had been unmasked....interesting."

"I thought about that," Phoebe said. "But it sounded like a lot of work."

"That's not a problem if you start early," Stephanie rejoined.

"Yeah," Phoebe said. "I presume you have heard Bradley asked Joelle to the Champagne Breakfast?"

"He said something in Australian Literature," Stephanie said.

"I sort of guessed after the other day," Kathy said. "Are you all right with it?"

"Yeah sure," Phoebe said. "I have been spending a lot of time with Rob's friend Hank, to tell the truth. I owe it all to you Kathy, if you and Rob had not connected, our two groups would not have coincided and I would never have met Hank."

"That's cool," Kathy exclaimed.

"I've even been out to the airfield with him," Phoebe said. "It is a fascinating place isn't it?"

"Err, did he leave you on the ground, and go up in a plane for two hours while you were there?" Kathy inquired.

"Of course not," Phoebe looked puzzled. "Hank's not like that." The penny dropped, and she looked understanding. "Did Rob do that to you?" Kathy laughed. "He did. He was desperate to make his hours."

"Rob's a bit thoughtless," Phoebe observed. "Hank is much more organized."

"To tell the truth," Kathy said. "I only see Rob's friends when they play cricket with him. Hank always seems very nice though."

"I think he is," Phoebe said. "I mean, it's nothing major, I only parted with Bradley a few weeks ago. But Hank seems a very straight forward and practical sort of guy. We've talked about keeping in contact after he leaves campus. You know it's only six weeks until the Pilots finish?"

Stephanie sighed. "It seems like all our guys are leaving in June."

"Garry too?" Phoebe was surprised, although the news had filtered through most of the group.

"Yes," Stephanie said. "He has applied to Wollongong University because his mother is ill. He should hear back from them sometime in May regarding their mid-year intake."

"I try not to think about next semester," Kathy said. "Enjoy the present, and the future will take care of itself."

Wednesday morning saw a flurry of unaccustomed activity around the dormitory, as the girls rose early to do their hair and make-up and dress in festive attire for the Champagne Breakfast. There was an unprecedented rush for the showers, and intense competition for power-points as hairdryers and curling wands were employed frantically.

A slight mist of hairspray lingered in the corridors, as multiple girls pasted their uplifted curls into position. Added to this, the incense of several hundred perfumes and deodorants rose through the building.

Stephanie sneezed and reached for her hay-fever medication. "How do I look?" she said, smoothing the lace at her neckline, and tying the huge home-made sash around her waist.

"Perfect," Kathy said. "You just need some flowers in your hair to be a bride. Were you hoping to trigger Garry proposing?"

"I don't think he is that suggestible," Stephanie said, scrabbling under the bed for some light coloured shoes. "Although it would be one solution to our problem."

"Don't wish that sort of pressure on yourself," Kathy said. "I know, I've been through it."

"Yeah," Stephanie murmured, "And it wouldn't make his mother any better..."

Kathy's name sounded over the public address system, and she hugged her room-mate. "That's me," she exclaimed. "I'm so excited!"

Kathy hurried down the stairs, falling into step with Phoebe on the way. Hank and Rob had chosen a place on the plan for them to sit together in the cafeteria. Kathy greeted Rob with a kiss, while Hank self-consciously extended a hand to Phoebe. As Phoebe had said, it was early days yet for them, but on a special occasion like that morning, she accepted his hand.

"You look stunning," Hank said. Phoebe was wearing a green satin sheath dress. Its lines and style were time-less, and its neckline was lower than many of the frothy eighties concoctions.

"You look gorgeous too," Rob said to Kathy. "I do love a girl in blue."

Kathy nodded. She had been pretty sure the playful lines of her dress would appeal to her boyfriend. "You look smart in your suit," she said.

The quartet traversed the short distance between the girl's dormitory and the cafeteria. They could hear music playing, and light was streaming from isolated points in the cafeteria.

"Candles," breathed Kathy. "How romantic."

"Eating in the dark," Rob teased. "How messy."

"You are incorrigible," Hank said. "Just imagine watching the sun come up through all the windows along the side."

"I didn't know you were so poetic," Phoebe murmured.

"Having the right girl by his side can turn a man into a poet," Hank said.

When they arrived at the cafeteria, the attendees were shown their way to their assigned tables by members of the Hospitality class. The Hospitality students also looked very smart in their professional white uniforms. They saw Damaris standing proudly by the interior door to the cafeteria, and waved. Kathy wasn't sure whether Damaris saw them in the crowd and soft light.

The first course was a delicate pumpkin soup with herb bread. This was one of Kathy's all-time favourite dishes. This was followed by skewers on which small chunks of vegetable had been threaded, interlaced with juicy pineapple and lightly grilled. The main course was fettuccini verdi, which Kathy was told was spinach pasta in a creamy sauce. The fettuccini was available in vegetarian and light meat options. Desert was a scrumptious sticky-date pudding covered in sweet sauce and topped with ice-cream. Anyone with special needs such as coeliac disease or lactose intolerance had been required to fill in a special form so the Hospitality students could modify the recipes appropriately.

Kathy had always considered Hank pleasant, but light company. However, now he was going out with Phoebe, she found herself learning many interesting things about the trainee pilot. He was a year or two older than they were, as he had completed a full mechanical apprenticeship, before enrolling at Silver Springs University. He also had a car. It was an older car, a 1970 Fairlane 500 automatic, which he serviced himself. This explained how Hank managed to get between campus and the airfield more easily than Rob, and clock up his hours for the Pilot's License faster.

Rob had warned Kathy he would be in a hurry to leave for the airfield, but at least he stayed for desert, and the couple watched the sun rise above the trees through the balcony window. Then he offered to walk her back to girl's dormitory, stopping behind a handy clump of shrubs to kiss her 'good morning'.

"I have to go now," Rob whispered. "Hank is giving me a lift to the airfield."

"One more little kiss," Kathy murmured.

"I think I can do that," Rob responded. He held her for a couple of minutes and kissed her, then he released her. "Have a good day, Kathy."

"You too Rob," Kathy whispered, but he was already gone, heading down the path towards University Drive. The rest of her day was lost in a whir of classes, cleaning and her Art practical. In the evening she had to study for the coming Psychology test.

Thursday morning, the majority of the second year students had to sit a test for their psychology subject. This test was worth around a third of their grades, with the essay being worth another third, and final exam being worth 40%. Kathy was confident she passed, but not sure how high her score would be. There had been so many terms and names involved!

Friday straight after lunch, the girls met in Kathy's room to talk about the Champagne Breakfast. The girls with 'regular' boyfriends said they had a great time as usual, while Phoebe blushingly admitted to the others that she and Hank would be seeing each other regularly from that point onwards.

"Do you think there is any bad feeling between Hank and Bradley?" Kathy asked curiously.

Joelle shook her head. "No," she said. "That's not the guys' way.

When Brad and I were coming back from our ride, we passed Hank in the student car park. The guys started talking about 8 cylinders and 302s, and something about the gears. I believe Bradley has more gears on his bike than Hank has on his car, or something strange like that."

"And what about you and Bradley?" Debbie asked curiously. "Still riding his bike?"

"Brad has promised to take me off campus whenever I need a break," Joelle admitted. "But really, he is just being a good friend."

"Are you sure about that?" Tess asked. "Good friends can become good boyfriends. That's exactly how it was with me and Luke."

"I'm pretty sure," Joelle said. "Brad's a bit unreachable that way."

"I know what you mean," Phoebe said, opening up to the other girls at last. "Bradley and I were girlfriend and boyfriend and everything, but his demeanor was too easy going, and he laughed my attempts to get serious off."

"Sounds a bit like Dylan," Cara volunteered.

"Perhaps you didn't give him enough time," Debbie suggested mildly. "You only went out for around six months."

"I don't think that was it," Phoebe said. "Anyway, Hank seems much more mature."

"To be fair, Hank is several years older, and has already completed one qualification," Kathy added.

"Yeah," Phoebe, "I didn't mean to be negative about Bradley, I know he is friends with most of you."

"No problem," Tess said. She turned to Cara. "And how about you and the noble Andrew?"

"Andrew was very nice," Cara said. "He behaved like the perfect gentleman, and he was even interesting to talk too. He is very widely read and he notices a lot."

"So are you seeing him again?" Stephanie asked.

"He did say something about the weekend," Cara said. "But I got the impression he was more inviting me to a discussion group he belongs to, than out on a date. These Theology students can be very hard to read."

Joelle and Debbie, who had both been out with Theology students, nodded. "You have to wait until he makes himself clear," Debbie said. "I made David work to get me."

"And I got it wrong with Larry," Joelle murmured.

"I'm sorry," Cara said, "I didn't mean to remind you of that."

"You are being very quiet," Tess said, turning to Stephanie.

"Yeah I'm sorry," Stephanie said. "I'm just not sure how many of the weekends Garry is going to be here. He can't afford to go to Wollongong every week, but in some ways, it's like he's already left."

"I have to go and do my cleaning," Kathy announced. "Friday afternoon waits for no-one."

"I have to practice," Joelle said. "With Larry and Anita too, I'm so not looking forward to it!"

"I'll come along if you like," Debbie said. "My presence should take the edge off the awkwardness."

"Me too," Tess said. "Luke is busy driving the university car, so I may as well keep you company."

"I've got things to do," Phoebe announced. "I'll see you all later."

There was a chorus of goodbyes and most of the girls went their separate ways. As Kathy closed the door behind her, she could hear Cara speaking gently to Stephanie.

Kathy had agreed to go out to the airfield with Rob again on Saturday. She had an Education test to study for, but past experience had taught her that she would get time to herself while Rob was flying. He now had his

Private Pilot License, but the flight school was incredibly strict to ensure there were no accidents, and also to maintain their accreditation.

That morning, Rob elected to take up one of the single person ag-machines. The instructor stood on the ground supervising the take-off, and then he retreated to the office where Kathy was seated reading her text-book. When Rob was due to land again, the instructor went outside to supervise the landing, sign Rob's log book and de-brief him from the flight.

His hour logged, Rob turned to Kathy. "Let's go for a walk," he said.

"Alright," Kathy said, not really sure where they could walk around the air-field.

Rob stowed Kathy's text-book into his backpack and the couple set off towards Northcoast. The airfield was about three kilometers out of Northcoast, which represented almost an hour's walk for two fit young people. However, Rob led the way along a dirt track between some trees.

"Is this a shortcut?" Kathy asked.

"I'm not sure if it is shorter, but it does get us there," Rob said. Kathy guessed they were about half-way along the dirt track, when they came to a small shelter. During the week, school children took refuge under the roof from the rain, while waiting for their bus pick-up. However, on the weekend, there was no school bus and very little traffic along the unsealed road.

The roof of the shelter extended a little way on the roadside and back in the opposite direction as well, creating a private nook around the rear. Rob stopped and pulled his wool picnic blanket out of his back-pack, and spread it across the rough bench at the rear of the shelter.

"Do you feel like taking a break?" he asked.

Kathy figured they were already late for lunch at the cafeteria, so she sat down. She was not surprised when Rob put his arm around her and bent his head for a kiss. They had been a couple for a few weeks now, and she had to admit they had not explored the physical side of the relationship very far. The kisses were very nice and very pleasurable, but Kathy tensed up when Rob began to unbutton her blouse.

"Shh," he whispered. "We only have a month left and if I am going to be flying in and out to see you later, I need more."

"What exactly do you need?" Kathy asked in sudden fright.

"I just need to know you are really into me," Rob whispered.

"Can't we have a little more time to get to know each other?" Kathy whispered.

"We have the time we have," Rob said. "I don't know how to make more time. I've always told you I was keen to work in the outback."

"I was enjoying your company so much, I didn't think about it," Kathy murmured.

"It doesn't have to be today," Rob said. "Don't get all tied up about that."

"What about the July holidays?" Kathy pleaded.

"I have to look for work," Rob said. "This was a very expensive course Kathy, with no student allowance to support me."

"You never talked like this before," Kathy cried.

"I don't like to be serious all the time," Rob said.

"What about writing – talking on the telephone – and spending Christmas together? Kathy whispered.

"I will do all of those things if I'm sure this relationship is going somewhere," Rob returned sturdily.

This is sounding a little like the Owen thing, Kathy reflected, and Rob wasn't even proposing. She sure knew how to pick them, all fun and games at first, and pressure later. Never truly in there for the long haul.

"I'll give you what assurance I can," Kathy said and kissed Rob deeply. Perhaps she was misjudging him. Boys must have their insecurities too.

After making out, Rob and Kathy rose, and folded the blanket back into Rob's backpack. Then they walked the rest of the way into Northcoast, and used a public telephone to call for the university car. While they waited for their transport, Rob bought Kathy some hot chips to compensate for missing lunch at the cafeteria.

Sunday Kathy slept in and then attended the Reform Church service. While this service was generally less appealing than the Inter-denominational praise service, it was timetabled better. Rob was also looking a bit bleary eyed when he met her at the door. He explained that some of the guys had smuggled a television into boy's dormitory and set it up in an area where the Deans rarely checked.

This television was not programmed to turn off at ten-thirty like all the sanctioned televisions on campus. Thus the boys had spent the night watching horror movies. He began describing *Alien*, which Kathy thought most repulsive. She shushed him so they could listen to the service.

Dylan and Annie joined them on the seat. Kathy was mildly surprised, because Cara and Dylan were usually back at their sparring, soon after dating other people. She concluded that the Physical Education major must have really taken Dylan's interest this time.

Cara did not even attempt to join them as she was two rows behind, sitting with Stephanie and Garry, Andrew Grosvy, Debbie and David. Kathy noticed that Cara was not seated directly beside Andrew. It did not appear anything other than friendship was developing there.

After the service the friends shared lunch in the cafeteria. Then all the second year students who were completing Teaching degrees retreated to their various study stations to cram for a significant Education test. Kathy retired to the room she shared with Stephanie. She was alone in the room all afternoon because Stephanie had chosen to study in the library with

Garry.

Monday dawned cool and fine. Kathy hurried to the shower, and ate a medium size breakfast in the cafeteria. They say that too much, and too little food, both affect intellectual performance and she needed all the help she could get. Another hour and she was sitting in the lecture theatre, her pencil poised over the test sheet. Ten multiple choice, five true or false bamboozlers, and three short answer questions. That did not sound too hard, but the period was only one hour long, and the results went straight into their grade. Kathy did the best she could.

After her classes finished, Kathy went down to the cafeteria for lunch. The dining area was full of second year Education students moaning and groaning about the test.

"At least it's over now," Kathy mused, sliding into place at the table next to Phoebe.

"Oh yeah," Phoebe agreed. "On to the next thing. I've got a History essay coming up."

"I miss History," Kathy said. "I get to do it again next year though."

"History is a lot of work," Phoebe said. "I sometimes think I was mad to sign up for it."

"Art is a lot of work too," Kathy said. "But at least it's creative and satisfying."

"Hank should be here any minute," Phoebe said. "He called the dormitory, and said he was about to drive back from the airfield. I expect he will have given Rob a lift too."

"Here they are!" Kathy exclaimed as the guys stepped through the door.

"Hi guys," Phoebe exclaimed. "How did it go today?"

"Fine," Hank said as the boys passed the table. "Tell you all about it when we have collected our food."

In the evening, Kathy found herself watching Rob's cricket, and talking to Annie who had arrived after the first match, then sat down on the bench. The older girl professed herself tired, because she had also played basketball that evening.

"I have seen you hanging out with Dylan a bit," Kathy ventured.

"Ah yes," Annie said. "I like Dylan. He is sporty and funny. He is even smart. His Biology minor contains some of the same stuff I study in Sports Physiology. In fact, I think I might pick up a Biology unit as an elective second semester."

"Would that put you in Dylan's class?" Kathy inquired.

"It might," Annie said. "Depends what I pick."

"My room-mate will be glad," Kathy said. "Their class was looking pretty small for second semester."

It was on the tip of Kathy's tongue to tell Annie about Dylan and Cara, but she managed to restrain herself. If Dylan had really changed allegiance it was irrelevant. All three together in a very small class sounded like an explosive combination, however.

CHAPTER SIX: TOGETHER OR NOT AT ALL

Tuesday Kathy had classes all morning. After a brief chat with friends in the cafeteria at lunch, she returned to the girl's dormitory to clean the first floor bathroom. Someone had left their make-up bag in one of the showers, and Kathy placed it on the shelf under the mirror in a prominent position. Surely the owner would come looking for it! Then she turned to bleaching the tiles.

Kathy was busy scrubbing toilets, when she heard the door open. "Be careful, the floor is wet," she called out, from her inelegant position with her head nearly in a bowl.

"I think I left something in here this morning," the husky voice sounded like Damaris.

"Over underneath the mirror," Kathy called.

"Ah there it is," Damaris said. "It's you Kathy is it? How are you?"

"Err yeah, it's me, and I'm busy," Kathy returned.

"I see that," Damaris said. "Do you still make those pots? Andrew used to talk about them all the time."

"I do," Kathy replied. "It's a subject I'm doing this semester."

"I thought some of your pots were ugly, when I saw them in your room," Damaris said.

Kathy tried to laugh. "Those were early attempts," she said. "Pottery really isn't easy."

"Yeah, some of the new ones are better," Damaris conceded.

"Thanks, I think," Kathy said dryly. "I thought you and Andrew weren't seeing each other anymore?"

"We are still friends," Damaris said. "Just because I had to cater for the Champagne Breakfast instead of attend, doesn't change that."

"Oh of course not," Kathy emerged from the final toilet and straightened up to stretch her back.

"I hope your friend Cara remembers that," Damaris remarked somewhat sharply.

"I think Cara and Andrew are just friends," Kathy observed.

"I don't see Cara with Dylan much anymore," Damaris said.

"That's a different story," Kathy extrapolated patiently. "Well I have finished my cleaning, and you have found your cosmetic bag, so let's go. I have to pack up the buckets and I will be out of here."

"Goodbye then," Damaris said. "I'll see you around."

"Goodbye," Kathy murmured.

Kathy's project to make a matching set of pots had gone quite well. After extensive practice, she mastered the art of shaping items sufficiently to make a set of large coffee mugs, with sturdy handles. They were glazed a blue-green in colour, and the glaze had crept into every crease emphasizing the home-made quality of the pottery, and giving it rustic character. She had also made a set of low saucers to go with the mugs. Saucers weren't strictly necessary with mugs, but they could double as snack plates.

Another requirement of the subject, had been to create something that was as ornamental, as it was functional. Kathy had chosen to fulfill this by making a flat platter in the shape of a fish. The scales and eyes were hand etched into the pottery. She had found herself thinking about Andrew Grosvy as she had created the masterpiece – how he would view it, and say it reminded him of the miracle of the loaves and the fishes. Kathy chided herself mildly for thinking about Andrew, while she was going out with

Rob, but Rob had never shown the slightest interest in her pottery.

Her latest project was her most romantic to date. Kathy had heard somewhere, that in the Victorian era, brides were given a large basin, and a matching pitcher which stood inside the bowl. This was their washing set, as many houses lacked plumbing, and the lady of the house would want to perform her bathing routine in the privacy of the bedroom. Designs varied, but a bridal set was usually identified by its voluptuously curved jug, with generous lipped spout. Even modern re-creations of these sets were worth quite a bit of money, and Kathy had decided to glaze hers a glossy pink. Pink wasn't everybody's favourite colour, but it seemed so incredibly 'Victorian'.

Although she had created a bridal set, it did not mean that Kathy had marriage on her mind. Her boyfriend, Rob was fluctuating between spending all his time at the airfield, and asking Kathy to go on walks after dark. There were a few nooks on campus, where the security cameras did not reach, and students rarely ventured. Serious couple learned about these places where they could go and express their affection towards one another, and Rob appeared to have heard about them all.

Kathy quite enjoyed the hugging and kissing, but it worried her that Rob wanted more. One day he would run out of patience and what would she say then? Rob was being longsuffering by his high-flying standards, and "I'm not ready yet", would not be accepted as an answer for very much longer.

Lunch time Thursday, Dylan was in a serious mood, which was most uncharacteristic of him. He was sitting alone at a table when Kathy and Stephanie entered the cafeteria, despite Cara and another of their friends already being at lunch.

Stephanie collected her food on a tray and headed towards Dylan. Kathy glanced between groups of friends and then followed her room-mate.

"What's up Dyl?" Stephanie asked as she sat down.

Dylan glanced around and ascertained their table was relatively unpopulated and mildly private. "Annie told me not to waste her time, if I was still hung up on Cara," Dylan said.

"It's not nice to be strung along," Stephanie said. "I can see why Annie might be worried."

"Nevertheless, I don't like ultimatums," Kathy observed.

"She didn't give me an ultimatum exactly," Dylan said. "Just asked to be clear where we stand. This is her last year, and she views her time as precious."

"Do you like her?" Stephanie asked.

"Yeah," Dylan said. "But I wish no one had told her about Cara."

"It wasn't me," Kathy was happy to be able to say.

"I think it's common knowledge you used to chase Cara," Stephanie said. "Annie would be very dim if she didn't work it out."

"How would I prove I was over Cara?" Dylan asked.

"Genuinely giving your attention to Annie," Stephanie said. "A girl knows."

"I don't think you need to drop Cara," Kathy said, "As you aren't exactly going out with her."

"Can I still talk to her in class do you think?" Dylan asked.

"Of course," Stephanie said. "It's all about whether you would be secretly longing to drop Annie, and resume chasing Cara."

"I don't think I'm like that," Dylan said. "I reckon I've wasted enough time on Cara, for all the response she has given me. And it would be nice to have a real girlfriend at last."

"So if you are sure," Stephanie advised, "Ask Annie to go steady."

"Ah right," Dylan said. Garry came up and joined them just then, followed by Rob. The conversation turned to other topics.

Later that afternoon, the talk of the campus was a small scene that had occurred between Cara and Damaris at the other table; while Kathy, Dylan and Stephanie had been busy talking. According to Phoebe, Damaris had deliberately sat down beside Cara, and informed the older girl that Andrew did not really like her and had only asked her to the Champagne Breakfast because Damaris was waitressing that night. To her credit, Cara had kept her temper well, explaining to the younger girl she ought not to read too much into isolated university social events.

"A lot of people go to events just as friends," Cara had responded. "It doesn't always turn into a relationship. And many stay friend afterwards as well. Andrew and I are simply friends."

"Are you saying Andrew and I are also just good friends?" Damaris demanded.

Cara admirably retained her temper. "I'm sure you and Andrew are very good friends," she said. "However, if you want to know exactly where you stand, I think you should take the matter up with Andrew. It's not for me to say."

When Andrew was told later, he blushed a fiery red.

"After all my attempts to be nice, but clear towards Damaris!" the gentle Theology student exclaimed in mortification. "And to behave so towards Cara, who is such a lady." He cheered up momentarily. "Are you absolutely sure that is what Damaris said?"

"Pretty much," Phoebe confirmed. "Give or take an impression of my own."

It was Friday lunch time when Kathy saw Andrew speak to Damaris. The second year friends were sitting at one table and some of the first years had joined them. Andrew walked past his friends and sat down amongst the first years, right next to Damaris, who initially looked pleased.

"I heard about what you said to Cara yesterday," the Theology student said. "I just want to be fair, and make sure the gossip reported to me was true."

"I did have a chat with Cara yesterday," Damaris admitted sulkily.

"And did you tell her I didn't like her?" Andrew demanded sternly.

"I didn't mean that you did not like her at all," Damaris said. "I see how that would have sounded rude if it was reported to you."

Andrew sighed deeply. "Never mind how it was reported to me Damaris! Speaking to Cara like that was not appropriate or acceptable. I want you to promise you will never do anything like that again."

Damaris looked shocked. "I promise if it means that much to you Andrew."

"Rest assured it does mean a lot to me," Andrew said.

"So do you like Cara better than me then?" Damaris fluttered her eyelashes, and looked ready to cry.

Andrew struggled with his determination to remain stern. "How can I put this? I like you and Cara exactly the same amount."

"Oh," Damaris said. "That is so confusing."

"No, it is not," Andrew continued firmly. "Let me explain this thing. You are a nice young lady, so I went to the Reverse Tea with you. Cara is another nice young lady, so I asked her to the Champagne Breakfast with me. Next social event, I may ask another nice young lady to go with me...until I find the nice young lady who is destined to be my wife. Then I will ask her to go steady with me!"

Damaris' false tears were real this time. "When you put it like that, I can't even be angry about it."

"It works both ways," Andrew said. "You have to go on dates, when your course allows, until you find the nice young man meant for you too. I am sure there is someone."

"Yeah," Damaris was still misty eyed, and Andrew could hardly bear it.

"Excuse me please, now I must go and sit with my other friends," the Theology student said, and made a break for freedom.

"Sit here mate," Garry said, indicating a seat conveniently located between him and David.

"Oh man," Andrew said, depositing his tray and sliding down into the chair. "I don't think I can show my face here again for a month!"

"Actually, I think your stock just rose with three-quarters of the girls in here," Stephanie said. "You won't be lacking in dates for the rest of the year."

"How come?" Andrew was genuinely puzzled.

"Girls like assertive guys," Kathy explained. "You just joined the club."

Andrew looked alarmed. "Was I assertive?" he asked. "I was trying to be polite."

"You did just right!" Stephanie assured him.

On Saturday Kathy considered going to the airfield with Rob, but knowing she would likely be left alone on the ground, she chose to work on her Practice Teaching presentation. The lesson she was due to plan had to be suitable for reception children. After some thought, she settled on learning the alphabet using pictures of fruit and went across campus to the library to try to find a fruit picture for each letter of the alphabet.

Some letters such as "A", "B" and "C" were easy, as she had a choice of fruit that started with that letter. "E" was a little tricky, but she decided to go with elderberry. "H" was for honeydew, a species of melon. "X" stood for xigua, or Chinese watermelon. When doing "Y", she decided to cheat and talk about a yellow pear.

The letter "V", she debated covering with valencia orange or vanilla bean. She finally decided that children might be familiar with vanilla as a flavor, and it was better to reserve orange for "O". A lot of lists cheated and used zucchini for "Z". Even if zucchini was technically a fruit, like tomato, Kathy decided that children would not associate it with the fruit list and went with the Asian fruit, zhe.

In the afternoon, after Hank and Rob had returned from the airfield, Phoebe invited Kathy on a group date to the movies in Northcoast. This was Kathy's first trip in Hank's Fairlane. The car seated three across the front, if Phoebe snuggled up close to Hank's arm. Cara and Andrew had been invited to come with them, but they did not mind being separated, with one sitting in the front, and one sitting in the back. Kathy was seated in the centre of the back seat, between Rob and Andrew.

"*Witness*", starring Harrison Ford, was being screened at the institute as a fund-raiser for local charity projects. Due to the restrictions imposed on campus by the Reform Church, the Silver Springs University students were able to identify with the Amish community in the film, and also appreciate the humour in the situation. On top of this, the film had action, suspense and romance.

On the way back to campus, Kathy was half asleep when she found herself dreamily comparing Rob and Andrew. Rob was so dear and outgoing, and funny, while Andrew was so gentle and earnest, and thoughtful. She didn't know why she was making comparisons, and tried to pull her mind back from that territory. Rob was her steady boyfriend and he wanted to be even more in the near future.

On Sunday at the Reform Church service, Rob and Kathy were seated just behind Dylan and Annie. While trying to concentrate on the service, Kathy could not help notice Dylan reach his arm out, and slide it along the back of the pew, finally coming to rest upon Annie's shoulders. It appeared that Dylan had made his decision, and asked Annie to go steady.

In the afternoon, Kathy continued to work on her practice teaching presentation. She had decided to use her art skills and draw each fruit onto small rectangles of paper. She then carefully scripted the letter and name onto the card. Finally, she went across to the library, where students could use the laminator for a fee. The finished product was a set of laminated, fruit themed flash cards. Kathy still had to design the lesson plan to go along with them, but she was very proud of her work so far.

Monday was a routine day with classes in the morning, and in the afternoon she worked on the lesson plan to accompany her practice teaching presentation, which was due the following day. By evening Kathy was tired of study, and treated herself to a half-hour of television viewing *Neighbours*. The show was developing rather predictably, into a combination of soap opera and situation comedy.

After *Neighbours* Kathy hurried towards the gymnasium to watch Rob play cricket. She knew he felt she was putting her studies before their relationship now assignments were due, and was eager to make amends. However, when she arrived, Rob appeared too busy managing his team, to take any notice of her.

Kathy sat down on the bench, and after half-an-hour passed without a single glance, nod, wave, or even request that she field a ball; she began to feel that she was the one being neglected. Still, she resolved to patiently wait the game out.

The game over, and even a few final casual bowls finished, the participants began to pack up the cricket equipment. Dylan and Annie said, "Hello," to Kathy as if nothing was wrong, and so did a few of the others. Rob remained silent, although Kathy thought she saw a slight frown upon his face. It wasn't anything he was revealing to his sports teams, however.

After every bat and bail was packed away, Rob turned to Kathy: "You were late," he said.

"I watched *Neighbours,*" Kathy said. "It's never been an issue before."

"You can't spend time with me because of assignments, but you can watch *Neighbours?*" Rob was incredulous.

"I needed a break," Kathy cried. "Why is this an issue suddenly?"

"Between my time on the airfield, and your time doing assignments, we never get to see each other," Rob frowned.

"There are two of us involved in that problem," Kathy said. "And what about the movie on the weekend?"

"The movie was amusing enough," Rob admitted. "But that was another thing – why a group date? Are you going off this relationship?"

"Hank has a car, and he's your friend too," Kathy said.

"You have been avoiding being alone with me," Rob said. "And I don't buy your line about needing more time."

"Why not?" Kathy was puzzled.

"Don't you know Kathy?" Rob said. "I fell in love with you at first sight when we met on the Western Night. You have never had to doubt my feelings, and yet I have to wait and worry about yours."

"I like you very much," Kathy stumbled.

"Like, not love," Rob retorted. "You will have to do better than that, Kathy."

Kathy's mind was racing. Could Rob be right in saying that she felt less for him than he felt for her? And what exactly had that warm feeling been that passed between them the evening they met?

"I think I may have felt love at first sight too," she whispered.

"That's my girl!" Rob exclaimed. "Now you are talking. So what's happened since – have you gone off me?"

"No," Kathy said. Although a small part of her mind was warning her that might be true.

Hadn't she noticed a few things about Rob, since laughing and joking together was no longer enough? Wasn't he a little impatient, maybe a fraction careless, and prone to leaving her wait for him when he was fulfilling his dream to fly?

"I'm cautious with words," she stammered. "And I think we need more than love at first sight."

"I believe we need more too," Rob said. He suddenly looked pleased and keen. He gathered her into his arms despite the fact they were still in the lighted gymnasium, and kissed her deeply. "At last we agree on that. I will walk you back to the girls' dormitory."

Rob kept Kathy outside girls' dorm, kissing until after curfew, and she had to use her swipe card to gain entrance. She crept to her room, half-fearing that the Deans would catch and reprimand her. Surely they would not be too harsh on a first-time offender?

The next day Kathy presented her fruit based flash cards, and accompanying lesson in tutorial session, and received a good mark. Everyone loved the colourful hand-made cards, as well as the child-friendly concept. Kathy returned to the dormitory in a happy mood.

As Kathy passed through reception, the Dean looked out of her office.

"Oh there you are Kathy," she said. "I noticed according to the log that you got in a bit late last night."

"I helped pack up the gymnasium last night and it did get late," Kathy excused herself, using half of the truth.

The Dean looked knowing. "Sometimes these things happen," she said. "But what about that young man of yours? He isn't putting too much pressure on you is he?"

Kathy blushed. "A bit," she murmured.

"Try to remember you have your whole life before you and your own studies to complete," the Dean advised, although she looked sympathetic.

"Thank you," Kathy said. "I will." She hurried back to her room and threw her books on the bed.

"What's up?" exclaimed Stephanie, her room-mate.

"The Dean noticed I was out late last night," Kathy reported.

"Oh dear, I have been wondering a bit about your late nights myself, you must barely make it through the security system," Stephanie observed.

"Last night I had to use my keycard," Kathy admitted.

"I hope you are having fun at least," Stephanie said.

"Is something wrong with me?" Kathy burst out. "First Owen and then Rob. Together they seem to be saying I can't commit my feelings."

"Men can be impatient," Stephanie suggested. "And Rob doesn't have much longer on campus. He essentially graduates in June doesn't he?"

"There is no ceremony," Kathy frowned.

"The Pilots take their certificates and leave," Stephanie said. "I guess if they wish they can return and parade with the other graduands in November?"

"Maybe," Kathy was still frowning. "And he wants to work outback, as far outback as he can go."

"Then what?" Stephanie said. "Would he come back to civilization to settle down with you? Do you share his passion for helping in the outback?

Have you asked him what it is he likes – the land, the people – or just flying?"

"We don't talk about those things much," Kathy said. "But I think Rob mostly likes flying – and being himself. He is most himself out there."

"What do you want?" Stephanie asked.

"I want to have more time to get to know each other," Kathy breathed. "But Rob says he will only fly-in and fly-out to see me after he completes his licenses, if I give him more."

"More what?" Stephanie asked sharply. "With guys that is often a code for more physical."

"I think that is exactly what he means," Kathy admitted. "But he says it would prove that I am into him, and we would last."

"And if fly-in-fly-out proved too troublesome to maintain after all that, you would have a broken heart," Stephanie warned. "Be careful Kathy."

"I know," Kathy sighed. "Say, do you think Annie and Phoebe would mind if I missed Aerobics tonight? I'm tired after last night."

"Phoebe said at the beginning that if we wanted the credit point we would need to make 100% attendance," Stephanie remarked. "To make up for the programme commencing mid-semester."

"You are right," Kathy groaned. "Maybe I could fall asleep during the stretches."

The next day Kathy worked on her art all afternoon. The Victorian bridal basin and pitcher had nice clean lines, and had survived their first firing in the kiln. The pink she had selected to paint them was slightly lighter than rose, but darker than pastel and had a slight sparkle to it.

Her next project had to fit the category of a mass-producible small marketable item. After searching through pottery books for hours, Kathy had decided to create small disks, suitable for threading on leather and marketing as necklaces. Knowing the Reform Church's restrictions on jewellery, however, she would take the precaution of presenting the disks as keyrings.

Thursday afternoon, Rob suggested they take the university car to Northcoast for late night shopping. He said that although he wasn't a great one for shopping, he needed some new shoes, and they could indulge in some fast food in one of the snack-bars. He was grinning when he picked Kathy up from the front of girl's dormitory and walked her around to the university car's staging point.

"What are you happy about," Kathy enquired, slipping her hand through his.

"I've added up my hours and I am about three-quarters of the way to Commercial Pilot," he announced. "That's another reason I suggested we go out."

Kathy giggled in relief. Rob was always happiest when his flying was going well. "I'm so glad for you," she said.

There wasn't much choice in men's shoes in Northcoast, so they headed straight toward the department store. Rob needed sturdy boots suitable for wearing around the airfield, and his foot was an average size, so he was fitted easily. Then they fell to considering their food options, finally deciding to order a pizza to share between them.

"What do you like best about flying?" Kathy asked in an effort to keep things light, and also to understand him that little bit better.

"I dunno really," Rob said. "I've always wanted to fly. I think it's the challenge. That's why I am aiming for what some people call 'bush flying'. It involves taking off and landing on small, and even temporary runways. The flights are never routine and the majority of them are not very long."

"Are long flights tiring?" Kathy asked.

"I don't think so," Rob said. "I meant they are more likely to get boring. On an international flight the pilot would just sit there for hours."

"I see," Kathy said. "And in the future, where do you see us heading?"

"You have got another year-and-half of your course," Robb said. "I guess I fly in to see you during that time. Then you go to teach somewhere, and I fly to see you wherever you go. I am pretty flexible."

"Do you see us ever getting married?" Kathy asked curiously. The picture Rob was painting involved a great deal of flexibility, but not much security.

"Girls don't really like marrying pilots," Rob said. "The profession is too risky."

"I expect hundreds of pilots get married," Kathy returned. "Army, Airforce, Navy, missionary pilots, airline pilots…"

"It works when they have steady jobs and routine schedules," Rob said. "But it takes a long time for a guy to establish that in the field."

"Sure," Kathy murmured, her eyes downcast. She didn't want to be perceived as having proposed to Rob, or prompting him to propose to her.

"I live for today then," Rob said. "And I thought when we met, that you did too."

"I think it is a good philosophy," Kathy admitted. She had been talking that way, and thinking that way too, until a few short days ago. Now she wondered. How much of her getting together with Rob had been on the rebound from her long term relationship?

"Well let's go catch the university car back to campus," Rob suggested when the pizza was finished. He did not attempt to keep her out late again that night, as his mind was on getting to the airfield early on Friday to continue earning hours.

Kathy had classes in the morning and spent the afternoon cleaning. When Rob came to pick her up for vespers that evening, she was wearing a white drop shoulder shirt with lacy shawl collar, and a knee length skirt.

"You look pretty," Rob said twirling her around. "In fact, so pretty, I wondered whether you would like to skip vespers and go for a walk with me?"

Kathy knew what a walk in the dark with Rob might lead to. However, she hesitated. He was her boyfriend and she could manage him, couldn't she?

"Just let me change my shoes," she said.

"Yeah, sure," Rob agreed. He put his hands in his pockets and turned to read the notice board, appearing nonchalant.

Kathy ran up the stairs to her room, and changed her delicate heels for some low heeled, slip-on court shoes. She considered changing her shirt and skirt into something more serviceable, but decided she still wanted to look pretty for Friday night. Running back down the stairs, she greeted Rob again. He took her by the hand and led her outside into the dark.

"I thought we would visit the rose garden," Rob said.

"I would like that," Kathy agreed. The roses were sweet and fragrant in the early evening, and the garden was not one of the isolated spots on campus sought by desperate lovers.

"How did your flight go today?" she asked as they settled down on one of the park benches there.

"Very well," Rob said. "I can see my Commercial Pilot's license beckoning to me. It is so close now."

"How many more hours do you need?" Kathy inquired.

"About 35 hours," Rob said. "That is at least one hour for every day left in the semester, including your exams. Some days we do not go up in the air at all. Other days our flights are only limited by fatigue laws."

"Ah right," Kathy responded. She was keeping the topic on safe areas such as Rob's flying.

"Kathy, I have been thinking," Rob said. "If I ignore distractions and make my hours as fast as possible, I may be able to leave campus, go home early and make a start on job hunting. Doesn't that sound like a good idea?"

"It sort of does," Kathy said. "But it gives us even less time together."

Rob kissed her softly. "I've got the keys to the gymnasium here so I can set up for cricket on Monday. If you want what I want, we could sneak in there and make ourselves comfortable on a foam mat. I'll make you very happy."

Rob's hand was warm on the thin skirt over her thigh. Kathy felt a brief thrill and then found she just did not want to go with him, after all.

"I'm scared Rob," she whispered.

"Don't be, I will take care of you," Rob promised.

"If someone caught us, I would be expelled," Kathy said. "They always blame the girl."

"The Philistines," Rob said. "That's so unfair. I wouldn't let it happen. I would put the foam mat behind the stage curtains. No one goes there."

"There are cameras all over campus, they might see us enter the doors," Kathy objected.

"But they couldn't prove we were doing anything wrong," Rob said. "I'm beginning to think you have other reasons."

Kathy began to cry softly. "Like what?"

"Don't fuss Kathy," Rob said, pulling her close. "I want someone who can be there for the good times and have fun with me, then let me go back to my flying. At first I thought that was what you were looking for too, but now I don't know. You brought up marriage last night - I don't hold that against you - most girls are looking for marriage - but we might not want the same things after all."

"Don't say that," Kathy whispered. She had been coming to much the same conclusion over the past twenty-four hours, but had hoped she wasn't right.

"I'm sorry girl, but I'm not looking for a ball-and-chain," Rob said. "At least not yet. If you are not enough into me, and don't want what I want, I would say it was more sensible to call it off today."

"So sudden?" Kathy gasped. She was truly glad she had not gone into the gymnasium with Rob. How could he ask her to commit to him physically in one sentence, and suggest breaking up in the next?

"That way, I can concentrate on what I need to – my flying; and you can concentrate on what you need to – assignments and exams," Rob said. "It seems the most sensible way to end the semester."

"Maybe," Kathy wasn't convinced. "Couldn't we just wait till the end of semester?" She would have preferred to enjoy his company to the end of term and say goodbye because he was leaving.

"It'll just make it harder," Rob said. "I'll walk you back to the girls' dorm if you want. Or women's assembly area, you might just catch the rest of vespers."

"I couldn't bear vespers," Kathy said. "Just take me back to the dorm."

CHAPTER SEVEN: SECOND GIRL ON BRADLEY'S BIKE

The next morning was Saturday, so Stephanie was still in the room doing her make-up and hair, when Kathy awoke. She blinked sleepily, remembering the events of the night before, when Rob had broken up with her. It would have made sense if she had done the breaking up, but he had gotten in first it seemed.

"Are you coming to breakfast?" Stephanie inquired.

"Yeah, in a few minutes," Kathy said. "When I'm sure Rob has left for the airfield."

"I didn't see you two at vespers last night," Stephanie said. "Are you all right?"

"No," Kathy said with a small catch in her voice. "We broke up."

"I'm sorry," "Stephanie said. "I won't ask you why, but I do know you could do better."

"I know too," Kathy said. "But somehow it doesn't help."

"You have to grieve," Stephanie agreed understandingly.

Kathy sighed and rolled out of bed. Figuring she could shower later, she applied deodorant and dressed casually in jeans and a top. Stephanie was a good friend, but she could be a bit impatient, a bi-product of the tendency to be punctual herself.

Garry was waiting for them at breakfast, and put his arm around Stephanie, as she settled into her seat. He was sitting with Bradley and Andrew, as Dylan was occupied with Annie slightly further down the table.

"How's my girl today?" he asked.

"Fine thanks Garry," Stephanie answered. "How's you guys?"

Garry, Bradley and Andrew all expressed themselves as being in excellent health, and relatively good spirits. The weekend in general served to enhance people's outlook.

Kathy turned to Garry. "How is your mother going?"

"She is waiting for surgery," Garry said. "And doctors are doing all sorts of other tests to make sure they are doing the right thing for her cancer."

"I still pray for her whenever I remember," Kathy said.

Andrew nodded. "Your mother is permanently at the top of my prayer list Garry," he said. "The power of prayer is a wonderful thing."

"No amount of prayer made the tests come back benign," Garry said. "I did hope."

"Sometimes bad thing happen to good people," Stephanie said. "It is unfathomable."

Kathy said took a deep breath. The guys had to know sooner or later. "I've broken up with Rob," she announced.

"Oh I'm sorry," Andrew said. "I hope you are not too upset?"

"I'm feeling a little low," Kathy admitted inclining her head toward Andrew. "But I guess it had been working up. I just couldn't see it."

"We will all be here for you," Garry said, and Stephanie nodded. "Let us know whenever you want someone to hang out."

"It sounds like an occasion for a ride on the bike," Bradley said. "How about it Kathy? I don't have anything else to do today, aside from study, which I can always do when I come back."

"I would love to Bradley," Kathy said, touched by the generosity of the offer.

"Second girl on Bradley's bike - if anyone is counting," Stephanie said.

"I think you're onto a good thing Brad's," Garry said. "Anytime a girl is broken up with, you ask her out for a ride on your bike."

"The strategy certainly has potential," Andrew observed.

Bradley shrugged: "There's only one girl I really need on my bike," he said.

"Well at least wait until I'm off campus, before you move in on Stephanie," Garry joked.

"Oh, of course!" Bradley quipped back.

"While you are at it, you can't have Annie either," called Dylan from further down the table.

"Kathy will be quite enough for me today," Bradley said placidly. "What time do you want me across at the girls' dormitory Kaths?"

"Um we're having breakfast now...what about ten?" Kathy suggested.

"Sure," Bradley said.

After she had finished her breakfast, Kathy hurried back to the room. She showered and washed her hair, drying it with the electric dryer and fluffing up the curls. She knew that she would probably get helmet hair, but she was still excited to be going off campus, and wanted to start the trip looking her best.

Bradley picked her up from the dormitory promptly at ten, and led the way to the student car park where his bike was parked. He handed her a helmet before donning his own headgear, sitting astride the Honda and fiddling with the controls.

The bike was larger than Kathy remembered, but she tried to climb onboard. Bradley was also very tall, whereas Kathy was short. She would be well protected from the wind, she thought as she steadied herself against his back.

"You have bony shoulders Brad," Kathy remarked. The back of Bradley's neck went pink. Was he blushing?

"You have to put your arms around my waist and hold on properly Kathy," Bradley said.

Kathy obediently slid her arms around his lower chest.

"Err, keep still that tickles," he complained.

The temptation was too great. Kathy wriggled her fingers. "Sorry," she said insincerely.

"That would be very dangerous going along," Bradley said. "However, did Rob survive you?"

"We broke up remember?" Kathy said.

"I didn't mean to say," Bradley began.

"You didn't say anything wrong," Kathy interjected.

"Are you settled? Comfy then?" Bradley asked. He cranked the engine. "Now when we are going, lean how I lean."

"Okay," Kathy said.

"Don't lean any more than I do and don't try to fight the bike by leaning the opposite way," Bradley continued. "If I stop suddenly, brace your hands against the front of the bike, if you can reach, so you don't crash into me."

The engine was purring and Bradley began to ease into motion.

"Woa," Kathy said.

"Are you okay?" Brad asked.

"Yes, it just seemed fast," Kathy said.

"That's not fast, you'll know when we go fast," Bradley said.

He steered the bike out of the student carpark and onto University Drive. At the end of University Drive, Bradley turned away from Northcoast, and headed towards the State Forest. As they gained altitude, the road became twisty and the vegetation transitioned toward rainforest. Kathy concentrated on hanging on and moving with the bike.

The sealed road became dirt track, and her ears popped with altitude. Brad seemed to enjoy spinning around the corners. It took the bike about forty minutes to climb up the mountainside, and then he finally pulled to a halt at a look-out.

"You can relax now," Bradley said, and Kathy who had been holding on tight for safety, relaxed her grip.

"That was amazing," she said. "Just like flying."

"Nah," Bradley said. "If we go flying, we are in trouble!"

"You know what I mean," Kathy retorted.

"Yeah," Bradley settled the bike so it would rest on its stand. He was a man of few words.

"Where are we?" Kathy inquired.

"Glasshouse Mountain," Bradley replied. "I like to come up here and look at the view."

"It is beautiful," Kathy said. "I ought to have thought to bring my pastels."

"I have a pencil and paper somewhere here," Bradley said, rummaging in the saddlebags. "Here," he pulled a sheet out of a note-book, while attempting to keep its contents hidden from Kathy.

But the sharp eyed girl had seen. "What's that you are writing – poetry?"

"No," Bradley tried to snatch it away.

"It is," Kathy hooted. She opened a page. "Golden flickers in brown eyes...ooh Bradley...who is this about?"

"That's private let it be," Bradley regained possession of his notebook. "You draw on the paper I gave you."

"Okay, but I need a pencil," Kathy said. "And what are you going to do?"

"Here's a pencil," Brad pulled a stubby pencil out of the saddle bags and stowed his notebook safely inside. "I'm going to chill out. I did all the driving here."

Kathy began to record concept sketches for a painting she could complete later. Brad slouched on the bench and stared into space. After a while, Kathy wondered whether he had fallen asleep. Her sketch completed, Kathy touched his arm. Bradley opened his eyes. How big and bright they were for a boy!

"Do you wanna move on?" he said with his lazy twang.

"Sure," Kathy said. They climbed back on the bike and took off once again. This time Bradley headed towards campus. The stopped at a service station, where Bradley viewed the remaining note in his wallet, and concluded he had better use it for petrol. He then counted his coins and bought a large bottle of cola, which they shared as they had no cups to divide it with. Somehow, after being out on the bike together, it didn't seem weird.

Sunday after sleeping in and enjoying a late breakfast, Kathy attended the Reform Church service. Lunch that day was the first time she passed Rob on campus, and they nodded civilly to each other, but nothing more. Rob was obviously determined to move on with no dramas, and Kathy was beginning to adopt the same attitude. In the afternoon she retreated to her room to work on her History of Christianity essay.

Monday after classes and cleaning, Kathy continued work on her essay. Stephanie usually wrote her first draft well ahead of time, but liked to add the finishing polish just before the essay was due, so she was sitting in the room, proofing her essay.

Kathy paused between points she was writing and looked across the room, "Bradley is quite yummy when you think about it," she said.

"It was nice of him to take you on the bike," Stephanie agreed.

"He is a bit of yum – don't you agree?" Kathy persisted.

Stephanie laughed. "Okay, even though I am going out with Garry, I think I can safely say Bradley is good looking. Are you beginning to like him now?"

"As a friend," Kathy said. She tried to get a glimpse of her room-mate's eyes. They were brown, but did they have any golden flecks? "Did you know he was writing poetry to a brown-eyed girl?"

"Brad is a great admirer of Edgar Allan Poe," Stephanie said. "That's probably one of Poe's raven-haired heroines."

"Oh sure," Kathy murmured. "Why would he act as if it were private then?"

"Bradley is shy about his poetry," Stephanie said. "Even I haven't seen much of it, and we share English class."

Tuesday Kathy was due to perform an observation at the local primary school. The university car picked her up, and dropped her off. She sat at the back of the classroom, taking notes on what was happening. It was a fun class with the children making craft items, from a selection of art materials the teacher had collected in a large box. The noise level was quite high for a middle-primary class, but the teacher appeared relaxed and comfortable with it.

In the evening Kathy attended Aerobics. The class had progressed in the weeks they had been practicing, and the session was now more demanding in terms of intensity and complexity. Some of the dance-like moves were a lot of fun. Annie told the participants that they must be sure to attend the next two sessions, because that was all they had left for the semester. Aerobics would not continue through study vacation and exams, even though the exercise might be good for their brains, because Annie needed the time to study for her own exams. Even though Physical Education sounded like a predominantly practical subject, it had some intensive theory components.

Wednesday Kathy was pleased to find her Victorian bridal set had come safely through the second firing, and the pink glaze she had chosen set it off just perfectly. She spent the afternoon painting her little disks, the majority of which had come through the first firing intact. They would be fired again, and then covered with a clear glaze. Then she would thread some leather through the small hole she had bored near the top of each one, to create a key ring. The following week, all the components of her portfolio were due to go on display around the Art Department. This display would be graded to give her a final mark.

Thursday, Kathy found herself eating lunch with Bradley and Tom. Tom had been Bradley's best friend the previous year. The boys had been almost inseparable, until slightly different timetables this year had parted them in class. They still liked to catch up for a laugh.

"Where's everyone?" Bradley said looking around.

"Cara, Stephanie, Dylan and Garry left lunch early because of some Ecology practical thing; Annie had some fourth year meeting to attend, and David and Debbie are always pre-occupied with each other," Kathy said. "Phoebe's with Hank, and they don't hang with us anymore because of Rob."

"Pooh," Bradley said. "I wanted to remind them to come and watch the Basketball semi-finals. Garry's team is in the B grade of course, and my team is in the A grade."

"I'll come and watch," Kathy offered.

Joelle, who had just slipped into the seat the other side of Kathy, seconded her promise. "I will watch too."

"That would be nice girls," Bradley said. "There was a bit of a fuss last week, because I finally had to suspend Tony Dantean for too many fouls. He's been replaced by Michael."

"I see," Kathy said.

Joelle and Tom exchanged greetings. Tom was an old friend of Joelle's former boyfriend, Milton. Neither heard from Milton much, they presumed he had become deeply engrossed in his family problems. Tom also thought that Milton may have met a new girl, which explained the letters to Joelle ceasing.

"I will see you this evening then," Kathy promised. "I have to finalise and hand in my Psychology essay before then."

"Good luck," Bradley said. "I handed mine in this morning, because of basketball. I don't care if I lose a mark or two from rushing."

"You don't lose many marks Brads," Tom remarked. "You just flow along in that lazy way of yours, clocking up the distinctions."

"So not true," Bradley said. "Why does everybody call me – the captain of the best A grade basketball team - lazy?"

"It's because you never seem disturbed by anything," Joelle remarked.

"Well you can't see inside me," Bradley retorted. "And why should I let you?"

"Goodbye now, have fun with your argument," Kathy said, excusing herself and returning to her room.

The men's basketball semi-finals were not such a big deal as the finals, but they still attracted a fair spectatorship. Kathy and Joelle found themselves a space on the benches alongside Andrew, who they were mildly surprised to see watching basketball. He looked amused when Kathy expressed her astonishment.

"There is sport in the Bible, you know," Andrew said. "Second Timothy 2, verse 5 'And also if anyone competes in athletics, he is not crowned unless he competes according to the rules'. That's only one example."

"So you are here to make sure, they play by the rules," Kathy joked.

"I think that's the referee's job," Andrew returned with mock earnestness.

They settled down to watch the game. Dylan's team lost by a mere margin and was pushed out of the B grade finals. He stopped to chat to Kathy as he left the court.

"It was too close to my Ecology laboratory, I think," Dylan said. "I can't say anything about the rest of the team, but I think I was slightly off my game." He then continued around the benches in search of Stephanie, who was watching from a slightly different vantage point.

The A grade basketball match was bitterly fought. Bradley's team clearly out-ranked their opponents, but the opposing team was determined not to give up without a fight. The scoring was fast, with both teams achieving a record number of goals before half-time. During half-time, Bradley appeared to have entreated his team to increase their defense, as they began to pester the other team, and prevent them from shooting as many goals. The score tipped in favour of Bradley's team, who continued to shoot goals. Soon their lead was comfortable, and by full time, they were the undisputed winners.

Friday lunch time, Kathy ran into Lionel, who she had not talked to much that semester. Lionel and Barbara were still blissfully happy planning their wedding, and Barbara was due to visit the campus that very weekend. She would be staying in one of the third year girl's rooms and attending all the weekend functions at university.

After lunch Kathy had cleaning to do, and then she had promised to accompany Stephanie to Northcoast to farewell Garry, who was going to Wollongong for the weekend. Stephanie explained that it was his last chance for a visit before the exam season began. The university car dropped them at Northcoast station, where Stephanie and Garry kissed and whispered sweet nothings, as if they would never see each other again. Then laden with well wishes, and messages for his mother from both Stephanie and Kathy, Garry boarded the train for Brisbane. From Brisbane he would fly to Sydney, and then catch a train out to Wollongong.

The girls returned to campus in a subdued mood. They ate tea at the cafeteria, and then changed for vespers. Andrew and Cara entered the assembly area separately, and sat with Kathy and Stephanie at vespers to keep them company. A few seats ahead they could see David and Debbie, with Bradley sitting beside Joelle, all seemingly deep in conversation. Tom sidled up to the chatty group, and sat down on the end of the isle next to Joelle.

Kathy had promised her room-mate Stephanie that she would keep her company that week-end with Garry being away. She hoped that didn't mean waking at an unwholesome hour to go to breakfast, she thought as she cranked her sleepy eyes open Saturday morning. However, Stephanie appeared bright and cheerful, and perfectly capable of attending breakfast on her own. Kathy rolled over for another hours' sleep.

Stephanie returned from breakfast talking about having been introduced to Lionel's Barbara, who apparently was as lovely as Lionel had always told them. Stephanie had been invited on a walk with David and Debbie, Larry and Anita, and Andrew Grosvy. She invited Kathy to join them, but Kathy said she had to compile her Infant Maths and Infant Reading resource collections.

It just so happened that three out of her six subjects for the semester required portfolios instead of essays or exams for their mark. It was less stressful to build a portfolio than write an essay or sit an exam, but these collections were lot of work to compile.

Kathy met Barbara at lunch in the cafeteria. She could see why the vivacious brunette held Lionel's interest, despite being off campus most of the time. Not only was she pretty, but she was clever too. Barbara was studying radiology at a major university. This field was not offered at Silver Springs University, which was one reason why she had never been able to join Lionel on campus. However, she was due to graduate at the end of the year, and then would be able to work, making relocating and getting married possible.

In the evening, Kathy would have liked to go to the recreation area, but Stephanie wanted to stay in the dormitory, because Garry was due to call. Kathy persuaded the nervous girl to at least descend to the girl's lounge, and watch *Hey Hey it's Saturday* on television while waiting for the call. At first Stephanie had been afraid she would not hear the public address system, but Kathy had pointed out that the lounge was much nearer reception and she was sure to get to the telephone in time.

They were laughing at the antics of Daryl, Ossie and Plucka, when Stephanie's name was called over the public address system. Stephanie immediately stood up and progressed towards the foyer. A few minutes later she returned and slid back into the seat by Kathy.

"Garry has found out he has been accepted into the University of Wollongong for next semester," Stephanie whispered.

"Well, that's good news isn't it?" Kathy returned.

"Of a sort," Stephanie said. "It makes him leaving Silver Springs seem so much more real, however."

"That's just an illusion," Kathy whispered. "You knew he was staying with his Mum anyway."

"Yeah," Stephanie agreed.

"Be quiet there," one of the other girls muttered. "Some of us are watching the show."

"I can't concentrate on this," Stephanie whispered. "I'm going to read in our room. I'll see you later."

Kathy stayed in the lounge until *Hey, Hey,* had finished and then she joined her room-mate in their bedroom. At least she could get something done on those massive portfolio assignments. Stephanie uncharacteristically had her head stuck in a romance novel, but she supposed her friend could do with the distraction.

Sunday, Kathy made the effort to wake up early and accompany Stephanie to the Inter-denominational praise service. They were joined in the pew by Bradley and Joelle, Cara and Andrew. Tom arrived late, but insisted on climbing past people, until he was settled between Bradley and Joelle.

The service was conducted by Larry, who Kathy had to admit was shaping up into an excellent speaker. Maybe not quite as charismatic as David, or earnest as Andrew, but competent all the same. His voice carried well throughout the assembly area, and his subject matter was well researched.

Later that day, Kathy and Stephanie were combining relaxation and study in their room, by playing the radio as they worked, when Phoebe knocked on the door.

"Hello", Kathy said, surprised to see the other girl. Between the fact that Kathy was currently hanging around a lot with Phoebe's ex-boyfriend, and Phoebe and Hank were hanging around with Kathy's ex-boyfriend, she hadn't seen a lot of Phoebe lately.

"Hi," Phoebe said. "May I come in?"

"I'm sorry we haven't been hanging out lately," Phoebe said. "Campus factions you know."

"I understand," Kathy said.

"I've got some news Kath," Phoebe said. "I'm not sure whether it's good news or bad news."

"Okay go ahead," Kathy said.

"Hank tells me that Rob has been doing what they call doubled-headed days at the airfield all this week," Phoebe said. "He is a post-solo student, so he has been allowed to do so. That is, not counting Sundays, he has clocked up around 5 hours of flight time, per day in the last week and a half."

"He must be near completing his remaining 35 hours then," Kathy said.

"He is," Phoebe confirmed. "He has a few assessments to go, but he will probably be leaving campus before study-vacation commences."

"I'm happy for him then," Kathy said. "I know it is what he wanted."

Phoebe hesitated. "Hank and I thought you might mind," she faltered.

"No, tell Rob 'congratulations' from me," Kathy said.

"Sure I will," Phoebe turned to leave. "I'll be seeing you around."

"Goodbye," Stephanie and Kathy called.

"Wow," Stephanie exclaimed, when Phoebe had left. "Rob sure doesn't let grass grow under his feet!"

"It was always feast or famine with Rob," Kathy said. "That was the problem."

Monday afternoon, Kathy handed her resource files in for Infant Reading and Infant Maths. Dropping the huge boxes off at the Education Department building brought home to her how close the end of the semester had come already.

The evening was also the girls' basketball finals. While the girls' basketball never received the attention on campus, that the boys' basketball did, Kathy and Stephanie attended to support Annie and Cara who were both playing. Dylan, Garry and Bradley joined them to cheer from the benches.

It would have been one thing if Cara and Annie were on the same team, but they were not, they were on opposing teams. Kathy and Stephanie clapped for Cara, because she was their long-term friend, but occasionally they got confused, and cheered for Annie when she did something particularly spectacular, like shoot a goal.

Dylan cheered for Annie all the time, because she was his girl-friend, and was careful never to cheer for Cara because she was an old flame. Garry was stuck in the middle because Cara was an old friend, and Annie the girlfriend of his best mate – so he just cheered a lot! Bradley, being a team captain, was discerning and cheered for all the best moves, no matter which team made them.

Finally Annie's team emerged victorious. Everybody greeted her and congratulated her. Cara was also congratulated upon her team manning a good defense. The players then headed off to the showers and the students to their respective dormitories.

Tuesday morning, Kathy was due to do another observation at the local primary school. Once again, the university car dropped her off, and picked her up after the observation had finished. The children were still working on their art projects. A few finished early, and the teacher sent them to the mat to read quietly from a selection of grade appropriate books stored on the shelf there. Kathy noted this down as an important management strategy for a group of mixed abilities.

That evening was the last Aerobics session for the year. Everyone who had enrolled to earn the credit point made sure that they attended, and were marked off. Phoebe looked thrilled that her project had developed successfully and moved to such a successful conclusion. Annie thanked all the girls for their cooperation with her facilitation, and expressed gratitude for the leadership experience she had been able to enter onto her resume.

Wednesday was Kathy's last formal art session, and she collected everything that had been fired from the kiln. The pots she had stored on the shelf in her room also had to be brought back down to the Art Department, and she had to organize a display of her works. This included her early attempts, a few of which had survived, her matching set, her Victorian bridal bowl and pitcher, and her collection of key-ring disks. Kathy was pleased with her achievement as she laid all the items out.

Thursday evening was the men's basketball finals. The gymnasium was packed with spectators, and extra seating had even been set out around the perimeter. Garry was sitting with Stephanie and Kathy, because his team was out of the B grade competition, having lost their match in the semi-finals.

Bradley and his team strolled onto the court. They were mostly second year students, with the occasional exceptional first year and several third years. The team they were up against was Zach's team, which was composed of primarily senior students, and had sorely challenged them earlier in the year. The only second year student in the opposing team was Arthur Mason and he was very lucky to have made the draw.

The umpire blew the whistle and play commenced. The opposition immediately took possession of the ball, leaving Bradley's team chasing them. The defenders stepped up as they had been instructed, and an attempted goal was headed out of bounds. The opposition tried desperately to regain the ball before it left the field, resulting in one of them being the last to touch it. Bradley's team were awarded the free throw and his supporters heaved a sigh of relief.

However, possession of the ball was lost almost as quickly as it had been gained, and the senior team raced down the field towards the goal once again. This time they managed to score. The ball was returned to the centre of the court and Bradley took possession determinedly. Blocked by the opposition, he passed to a team mate. The team mate was immediately targeted, so he passed the ball back to Bradley.

Bradley caught the ball, prevented himself from stumbling into an illegal 'travel', and pivoted towards the goal. Using his superior height, he heaved the ball towards the goal. It teetered against the edge of the basket and finally fell in through the ring. The score was now two all.

The ball returned to the centre, but all too soon was headed back towards the seniors' goals. The defenders ran interference desperately, but the new score was three to two. Play continued in this fashion until half-time, when the score was in favour of the senior team.

The teams were not even, and although Bradley's team had trained hard all semester, the seniors had an advantage. When play re-commenced, it was evident that Bradley's team had developed a strategy. They could not be better at all things than the opposition, so they concentrated on taking care of the ball. Wherever the ball went, Bradley's team were sure to go, and as likely as not, one of them got their hands upon the ball. Then they returned it to another member of their team. In this way, they kept the seniors running around them, and minimized their scoring.

This tactic alone wouldn't win the game for Bradley's team. They desperately needed to score. As Bradley had been the first to score for his team, the seniors had him under constant surveillance. He fell to gaining the ball in a prominent fashion and drawing attention. At the last moment, he would pass the ball to the vice-captain, who would shoot towards the goal while the seniors were busy blocking Brad. When the opposition got smart to this tactic, Bradley passed to a different member of his team, and the score began to draw even.

Seeing the score only one-down for their team and the last minute on the clock, Bradley abandoned strategy and lobbed the ball high above his guard's head, right at the basket. The whistle blew. The referee indicated 'no goal' and the match was lost, but it was an ending that would be talked about for weeks to come.

Bradley's team gathered around and he smiled tiredly: "I'm sorry guys."

The Vice-Captain clapped him on the shoulder. "You were a great captain Brad, you saved us a hundred times and did not hog the credit for yourself."

"Well, we are the runner's up for the season then," Brad said to his team. "That's not too shoddy." He glanced around the benches and his gaze came to rest on Kathy. "I'll need a date for the Basketball Tea, will you come with me Kathy?"

"Of course Brad," Kathy said, scrambling out of her seat on the bench. Together with his other friends, like Stephanie and Garry, she began to congratulate him on a season well played.

That Friday was the last day of classes for the semester, and any outstanding assignments were due. At five pm that evening, all deadlines closed and study-vacation officially began. Although the students knew that this meant exams were approaching, the general mood was festive.

Saturday morning Brad ate a late breakfast with Kathy, and he offered to take her back up the mountain, to finish her picture. There were a few things he wanted to check at the library in the morning he said, and suggested that they go after lunch.

Kathy heard her name called over the public address system around one-thirty, and hurried down to the foyer. She was dressed practically in jeans and a heavy jacket. This time she was carrying a sketch pad, although it was not a full sized one because nothing over A4 size would be likely to fit into the saddle bags, along with her charcoal and pastels.

Bradley led the way to the student car park and stashed her supplies in the saddlebags. Then he prepared the bike to start, and beckoned Kathy to climb up behind him. "You know the drill," he said with a slow grin.

Kathy climbed onto the back of the bike and slid her arms around his waist. "Ready", she said, finding herself the one to blush this time. Although she knew it was necessary to hang onto Bradley, she could feel his lean torso under her fingers. Going out two weeks in a row, and then to the Basketball Tea, was dangerously close to developing into something regular.

Bradley kicked the bike into action because it had been sitting in the student car park for almost a week. "She sits around too much," he grumbled and Kathy noticed he lovingly referred to the Honda as a female.

The Honda smoothed out and began to cruise as they left University Drive, and headed for the mountains. Somehow amongst the twists and turns in the national park, they ended up at a totally different look-out point.

"I'm sorry," Bradley murmured apologetically. "Will this do?"

"It's perfect," Kathy said, peering over the edge of a small stone wall down into the tree lined gorge. Bradley was standing slightly uphill from her, and she found her fingers itching to draw his outline against the side of the hill and the sky. "Hold still for a minute," she called and he obligingly posed next to his bike.

"You can relax now," Kathy called a few minutes later and Bradley settled the Honda onto the kickstand. He continued to survey the view and his shoulders dropped slightly.

Kathy imagined there was something pensive about his attitude. She crept up beside him. "Brads," she said hesitatingly, "If you aren't romantically interested in me, you don't need to spend all your time on me."

"Ah no," Bradley said. "Don't worry about it, feel free to monopolise me as much as you like."

"But something's wrong, I know it," Kathy said. She ventured to put lay her hand on his arm just above the elbow, which is about where she could reach.

"Well I hate to sound like that soap opera you girls like watching," Bradley said. "That one Channel Seven is talking about cancelling soon...but I have a bit of a *Jesse's Girl* thing happening."

Jesse's Girl was a chart topping hit from a couple of years back, where the guy was hopelessly in love with his best friend's girlfriend. The song was very romantic, but not particularly healthy.

"Well," Kathy said. "Any girl would be mad to ignore you. And if one does - there are plenty of others out there."

"I know," Bradley said. "But I like to be friends for a while first."

"I think that's the best way," Kathy said.

"Thanks for listening Kathy," Brad said. "It's a relief to have told someone."

Kathy settled down to finish her drawing and added colour this time. Bradley explored a little way up and down the path, always promising Kathy he would not be out of earshot, in case an undesirable person came upon her. Then they got back on the bike and travelled back to campus by a circuitous scenic route.

Sunday afternoon Kathy and Stephanie were both in the room studying for their upcoming Education exam. Their pages rustled and papers rattled as they both attempted to study in silence. However, after a while, Stephanie put her book down.

"How did you go yesterday afternoon with Bradley?" she asked curiously.

"Good," Kathy replied. She slid the drawing out of her notebook. "Don't you think that looks like him?"

"Yeah sorta," Stephanie agreed. "You are a very talented artist. So are you two going out now?"

"Just as friends," Kathy said. "Actually Bradley told me he had a *Jesse's Girl* thing happening."

"*Jesse's Girl* by Rick Springsteen?" Stephanie asked.

"Yes," Kathy said. "You wouldn't know anybody he likes, would you?"

"Well," Stephanie said. "They say Tom has been putting the moves on Joelle lately, and she was the first girl on Bradley's bike."

"Hmm," Kathy remained unconvinced. Joelle didn't have brown eyes.

"Brad's too nice a guy to cut a mate's grass, so as to speak," Stephanie said.

"I know," Kathy said. "But sometimes, people can't help how they feel."

"Well, it's none of our business really," Stephanie said dismissively. "And I'm sure Brads wouldn't want it spread around. Now I want to get this revision done, before Garry comes over to collect me for tea. Then I'll be helping him choose his subjects for Wollongong University next semester. They have so many great subjects."

"Do you wish you were going too?" Kathy asked.

"A little," Stephanie admitted. "But I have a lot of good friends here."

Kathy spent Monday circulating between study stations in the room and the library, and the cafeteria for meals. She also spent an hour cleaning the first floor bathrooms, as usual.

The main excitement for the day was the news that Cara had been asked to the Basketball Tea by Kaleb. Kaleb was an African American exchange student studying Theology in Australia. He was tall and confident, and one of the few first years to play A grade basketball. Although Kaleb would not make his preaching debut till his second year, he had taken a few evening worships and was described as an eloquent speaker.

Tuesday was also a study day, with the Basketball Tea the only campus event scheduled. The Basketball Tea would also mark the end of the study-vacation for some students. Because it was a sporting event, the dress code was casual. When Bradley picked Kathy up at the dormitory he was wearing his team T-shirt with his number on it. The basketball shirt had been freshly laundered for the occasion, and the evening was cool, and so he had a bomber jacket over it. Kathy was wearing jeans and a softly woven jumper.

Bradley led the way across to the cafeteria, where Kathy found they had to sit at a table reserved for the grand final teams. Annie and Cara's A grade teams were also placed at the table, which was really a series of trestles which ran the length of the cafeteria. Garry and the rest of the members of the University Basketball League were placed at nearby tables, along with their dates.

Bradley had to leave Kathy part way through the proceedings, and give out the awards. Annie and the rest of the organizing committee assisted him.

Among the girls, Annie herself was awarded 'best and fairest', while Natalie, one of the first year girls who played for B grade, received 'most improved'. Among the boys, Arthur Mason from the winning team received 'best and fairest' and Michael received 'most improved'.

There were whispers that Bradley or the opposing captain ought to have been 'best and fairest', but Brad squashed them with a laugh.

"It would have been like awarding ourselves," he said, and Zach, the opposing captain nodded in agreement.

"Arthur deserves best and fairest, because he was a solid contributing player on a top team," Zach announced.

The only person who did not look happy was Tony Dantean. Michael had been brought up to replace him, and had subsequently been awarded 'most improved'. While Bradley was not the only person who had been involved in the decision to suspend Tony for excessive fouls, the youth mainly frowned in Bradley's direction.

The Basketball Tea usually had lots of fun food. This semester was no exception with party pies, sausage rolls and miniature quiches. Dessert was a hug sponge cake, which the two winning captains cut and distributed in ceremonial fashion. Bradley was relieved to have escaped this duty, and slid back into his seat beside Kathy.

Wednesday Kathy had no exam, but Stephanie had Ecology in the afternoon. Kathy knew this was Stephanie's most challenging subject and understood her companion was very stressed in the morning before the exam. She tiptoed around the room as quietly as possible, until it was time for Stephanie to leave, and then she wished her room-mate good luck.

Thursday morning, Kathy and Stephanie both had Educational Theory. On Friday morning they had Psychology, and Friday afternoon, Stephanie had English. The weekend was more relaxed, because the only remaining exam for either of the room-mates was History of Christianity, which they also shared with the Theology Students.

Kathy was mildly surprised when Andrew Grosvy offered to help her study for History of Christianity on Saturday, but she agreed to meet him in one of the reading rooms off the library anyway. The boy was brilliant when it came to matters theological, and his earnest anecdotes always helped anchor things in her mind.

Monday dawned chilly and bright, and the second year students all hurried down to the hall where the larger exams were invigilated. Three hours later Stephanie and Kathy were free, and the stress of the semester was behind them. Dylan and Garry still had Chemistry to go on Tuesday morning, and Bradley was stressing about Mathematics for Tuesday afternoon.

Kathy, who had no more exams to worry about, spent Tuesday packing her suitcase. The mid-year break was long, because it included two weeks of recreation time and then the students commenced their practical placements of various length. Kathy was due to complete practice-teaching for a fortnight, during which time she would be boarding with a relative in Coffs Harbour.

After lunch in the cafeteria, Andrew offered to walk down to the Art Department with Kathy to help her collect her art work. Her portfolio had been graded, and was now available for retrieval. It took the pair several trips, even with the items all wrapped carefully in newspaper and stacked into cartons.

"Thank you very much," Kathy said when the final trip was complete. "You didn't have to help you know."

"It was my pleasure," Andrew said. "I wanted to see how the pots had all turned out. Bradley Parker wouldn't mind would he?"

"Oh Brad's in a Mathematics exam," Kathy said. "And he and I are just good friends! I don't want to rush into another relationship like I did with Rob."

"Very sensible," Andrew affirmed. "Well, I will see you around next semester then."

"Of course!" Kathy said. "Thanks again for your help with the pots."

On Wednesday afternoon Kathy caught the university bus to Northcoast, and from there she would take the bus to Armidale. Stephanie and Garry accompanied her as far as Northcoast, where they would catch the train to Brisbane.

Stephanie would then board an aeroplane to Adelaide; and Garry would continue via train to Wollongong through Sydney. Garry was burdened with extra cases, because he was not returning to Silver Springs the following semester. He had booked himself all the way on the train, because it offered a larger luggage allowance than the plane.

Kathy wiped a tear out of her eye as she waved goodbye to Stephanie and Garry. Stephanie was clinging desperately to Garry's hand, and their final farewell would be in Brisbane. Kathy could only imagine how her friend felt at the long separation she and Garry faced.

Kathy was almost glad she had no boyfriend from whom to be separated. Owen, waiting down in Armidale, was no longer her concern. Rob was winging his way into the outback for whatever solo adventure caught his fancy, and Bradley was off on his Honda enjoying his first cross-country road trip to Melbourne.

CHAPTER EIGHT: THIRD GIRL ON BRADLEY'S BIKE

It was almost the end of July when Kathy arrived back at Silver Springs University. She had enjoyed her weeks with her parents, and her two weeks practice teaching at Coffs Harbour Primary were quite fun. As a second year student she did not have full responsibility for the classes, but worked in close cooperation with the teacher. Nevertheless, she had been able to try out a few craft ideas with the children, and was exceedingly pleased with their response.

The university car picked Kathy up at Northcoast station on one of its regular circuits.

"Thanks Luke," Kathy exclaimed, always happy to see a friendly face. "How were your holidays?"

"Excellent," Luke said. "Tess and I visited each other's families and we had fun."

"Nice," Kathy said and settled back to enjoy the short ride back to campus. "Has anything changed around here?"

"Define change," Luke said.

"Err, any new buildings?" Kathy suggested.

"Nah," Luke said. "There's talk of a new bus though. Ex-public service."

"Handy," Kathy said.

The short drive over, Luke pulled up close to the girl's dormitory. "Do you want me to help you upstairs with your bags?"

"Thanks," Kathy said.

Luke picked up her suitcase and stepped into reception. He nodded to Annie, who was working on the desk. "Sound the warning," he said. "I'm taking Kathy's bag to her room."

Annie leant over the public address system. "Man in the dorm," she intoned. "Man in the dorm."

Luke carried Kathy's bag up the stairs, and to the door of her room. "I'll see you later," he said.

"Yeah, thanks again," Kathy said.

The room was strangely quiet without Stephanie. Kathy opened her suitcase and unfolded her clothes. She had been shopping with her mother, and acquired several nice new dresses for spring events on campus. She also had a cable knit jumper in a flattering rust colour, and new khaki cargo pants.

The public address system sounded the warning once again, "Man in the dorm," and Kathy heard voices approaching, from further down the corridor. She stuck her head out of the door to see who was coming. It was Phoebe, with Hank carrying her suitcase. He put the case down just outside her room, which was opposite Kathy's, and gave her a kiss on the cheek.

"I will see you tomorrow darling," he said. "Afternoon Kathy."

"Afternoon Hank," Kathy said. "I thought you finished your Pilot's License?"

"I did," Hank said. "Phoebe will fill you in. I have to get out of the dorm while the warning is current."

"Bye then, Hank," Kathy said. She turned to Phoebe. "Phoebe?"

"Come in here," Phoebe said, unlocking her room. "Oh Kathy I'm so happy!"

"Why?" Kathy inquired.

"You know Hank is a mechanic don't you? He applied for work and got a job at the Northcoast Mechanical Workshop. So he is living in Northcoast now. He said he did it to stay around me!"

"That's fantastic!" Kathy exclaimed.

"Hank is also completing his instructor's ticket at the airfield, but that has to be part-time because of his work," Phoebe said. "He will be very busy and some of it will be on weekends, but I can't expect everything."

"I think it's wonderful," Kathy said. "I can't believe how well it has worked out."

"Nor can I," Phoebe exclaimed. "But I am trying."

Stephanie arrived so late that evening, that she must have caught the very last train from Brisbane, and sneaked into the room without waking her room-mate. Kathy, was surprised to wake up and see the bed occupied in the morning. Two suitcases stood locked and unopened, against the opposite wall of the room. Stephanie heard the alarm clock and opened her eyes with extreme difficulty.

"Is it morning?" she asked.

"I'm afraid so," Kathy said. "Whatever happened to you?"

"I booked a flight with a stop-over in Sydney and Garry met me there. We spent a few hours hanging around the airport together and then I caught my connection to Brisbane," Stephanie replied. "I had a special late booking with the university car to pick me up at Northcoast, and it wasn't even Luke driving."

"I hope you enjoyed your time with Garry," Kathy said.

"Yeah, but that's the only time I've seen him since last semester," Stephanie said.

"In a whole six weeks?" Kathy exclaimed. "I thought you might stay with his family again."

"I couldn't possibly impose on the family," Stephanie said. "They are crazy with grief and stress. Garry's Mother's operation is due later this very week."

"That's almost like being broken up, for you two," Kathy mused.

"Please don't say that," Stephanie said. "Garry has already set me free to see other guys."

"What?" Kathy exclaimed.

"He said he wouldn't be in a happy mood the rest of the year, and he knows what campus is like, I would need to go to the events," Stephanie said. "Garry wants to keep in contact of course...and I'm sure he still loves me under it all."

"Yes, but..." Kathy demurred.

"I don't want to see other guys," Stephanie sobbed. "I want to remain faithful to Garry."

The girls got up and went to breakfast in the cafeteria, where they found more of their friends. Then classes commenced. Most of Kathy's classes were similar to her first semester classes. She continued to study Psychology, Infant Mathematics and Infant Reading. Educational Theories continued into second semester but her Art subject had changed; and instead of pottery she was doing basket-making and weaving. Her house requirement was no longer History of Christianity, but Christian Outreach, which was also shared with the second year Theology Students.

Tuesday lunch time, Kathy sat with Stephanie's Advanced Physiology class in the cafeteria. The Biology programme at Silver Spring University was very demanding, which was one reason why the class was small. With Garry gone, it was looking even smaller, except that Annie had transferred into the class.

As a fourth year Physical Education student, Annie had already studied some human physiology, which was counted as a pre-requisite for the second semester subject Advanced Physiology. Another new class member was Herman, an exchange student from Germany. Herman already had a first degree in Science and was completing a one-year coursework Honours in Australia. He therefore also had the pre-requisites for Advanced Physiology. Herman was a great guy and Kathy enjoyed talking to him. She secretly suspected, however, that he was more Stephanie's type than hers. Perhaps he would help her room-mate get through the semester without Garry.

Wednesday Kathy learned that a major component of Christian Outreach involved joining a volunteer programme. Students would keep a journal of their experiences volunteering in the community, and hand it in at the end of the semester. Stephanie appeared to know immediately what she wanted to do, and that was volunteer at Northcoast Nursing Home. Her room-mate explained that Nursing had always been her second choice of career, and she was thrilled by the opportunity to do something related.

Kathy was deep in thought, wondering what to do for her own volunteer involvement, while she walked down to the Art Department. Hence, she was startled when Andrew Grosvy fell into step beside her.

"Hey Kathy, wait up a minute," he said.

"Hello Andrew," Kathy replied. "How were your holidays?"

"My holidays were wonderful, and my practice preaching placement so instructive," Andrew replied. "Thank you for asking."

"You are welcome," Kathy responded, feeling amused.

"I trust you had a pleasant mid-year break too?" Andrew said.

"Yes, thank you Andrew," Kathy said. "I don't mean to be rude, but I'm on my way to Art now."

"Excellent! What are you doing in Art this semester?" Andrew asked. "Still making pots?"

"No, actually basket-making and weaving," Kathy admitted.

"Basket-making is an honourable and traditional art," Andrew pronounced.

"Yeah, I'm sure that is exactly what my Instructor is about to tell me," Kathy exclaimed.

"I removed his shoulder from the burden; his hands were freed from the baskets, Psalm 81:6," Andrew quoted.

"I'm glad you always find my Art so Biblical," Kathy retorted.

"I think I have a text for everything," Andrew admitted.

"No kidding," Kathy affirmed. "Was there anything else you wanted?"

"Well I was wondering if you had decided what to do for your volunteer involvement," Andrew said.

"No," Kathy said. "I must admit I'm open to ideas."

"Have you thought about joining the choir?" Andrew asked eagerly. "That's what I'm doing."

"I don't think I can sing well enough for that," Kathy said.

"Oh no, you don't have to be a great singer, just one voice amongst many," Andrew explained.

"Interesting," Kathy said. "I'll think about it."

"They go on weekend trips too," Andrew said. "Touring around Queensland and North New South Wales to perform at churches."

"It sounds like fun," Kathy said. It also sounded like a welcome break from the campus dating scene. She would be going on outings, but would not require a partner. "I might do it at that!"

"They practice Saturday morning," Andrew said. "But you better sign up by Friday afternoon at the Music Department if you are interested. I'm going to do it."

"Thanks for telling me," Kathy said. "I'll certainly think about it."

Thursday was the first of August. It was also the day of Garry's mother's operation. It was perhaps a good thing that Stephanie had a full day of classes, along with a Biology practical to keep her mind occupied. She asked Kathy to keep an ear open for the public address system calling her name, but expected Garry would not call until evening.

It was an hour after the evening dorm meeting, when the call finally came. Stephanie leapt to her feet and hurried to reception as soon as she heard her name. Kathy waited in the room, her hands clasped in an unconscious gesture of prayer and supplication. 'Please let Garry's Mother be all right.'

It seemed like an age, but was really five minutes before Stephanie returned to the room. "Garry's Mother is not awake yet," she said. "But the Doctor said the operation went well. They performed a lumpectomy, which leaves most of the breast intact. They are hopeful that they got all the cancerous tissue, but apparently the recovery process is slow and painful."

"Oh," Kathy said. "Well some of that sounds good."

"She will have lots of appointments and even require radiotherapy," Stephanie continued. "Garry's father has to go back to work, so Garry is very glad he has taken the time off. He will be able to drive his mother to her appointments between his classes."

"That is good," Kathy said. "At least he feels like he is doing something."

"But I feel so useless," Stephanie cried.

"You let him go to do this for his Mother," Kathy said. "It was the best thing you could do...and you are still here for him to talk to if he needs it."

Friday, after finishing her classes and cleaning the bathrooms, Kathy walked across to the Music Department to sign up for the choir. Joelle was there, practicing the songs for weekend worship with David and Debbie, Anita and Larry and other members of the worship committee. They pointed Kathy towards the choir sign-up list which was pinned onto the cork-board in the corridor.

"You will love the choir," David said.

"I think so too," Kathy said. She crossed to the board and put her name down at the bottom of the list.

Indeed, the more Kathy thought about it, the keener she became on the idea of choir involvement. Music was closely related to Art, and travelling around to perform different places would be fun. In the evening, she tried to sell Stephanie on the idea, but her room-mate demurred.

"I can't sing," Stephanie said. "I've already told Andrew that."

"Andrew said it didn't matter," Kathy replied. "And just think about touring around the countryside with your friends, at no expense to yourself!"

"I can sing a little actually," Stephanie admitted. "I mean I am not in the mood to sing at this point in time. I will be perfectly happy visiting the Nursing Home, and I am serving afternoon tea there two days a week. Just not Thursday because of my Biology lab."

"That's a lot of booking the university car," Kathy observed.

"Brad has offered to give me a lift over there if I have any trouble with the university car," Stephanie said.

"Third girl on Bradley's bike," Kathy murmured. "If anyone is counting..."

"But no one is counting are they?" Stephanie said firmly. "This is entirely different. Bradley has been very supportive toward both Garry and me."

The only drawback with joining the choir was that Kathy had lost her lazy Saturday mornings. Instead she had to wake up with the early-birds, grab a quick breakfast, and front up to practice. Upon arriving at the Music Department, she found herself surrounded by Music students, Theology Students, Theology Student's girlfriends, and generally anyone else who loved a good sing up. Andrew Grosvy saw her arrive and looked particularly pleased.

The Music Master was also the conductor of the choir, so this was a little like taking singing class. They began by performing warm-up exercises and proceeded onto perfecting single notes. Kathy then expected to learn a selection of sedate classical pieces, but was surprised their first piece was the rousing *"Wake me, Shake me,"* which had been adapted as a gospel song, also known as *"Swinging on the Golden Gate"* by White, Smith & Co. in 1984. This was followed by *"I've got Peace Like a River"* arranged by William J. Reynolds. These songs were followed by several classical hymns, more like what Kathy expected.

After choir practice was over, Andrew insisted on walking Kathy over to the cafeteria. He was effusive in his delight that she had joined the choir, and she found herself going pink. Surely it was not such a big deal. Suddenly Andrew grasped her by the arm, and Kathy was about to object, but he spoke urgently.

"Isn't that Jeffrey Mannington over there?" Andrew said pointing. "Wasn't he a bit of a bad boy last year – I seem to remember he gave Stephanie some sort of trouble?"

"Oh, you may be right," Kathy gasped. It did indeed look like Jeffrey Mannington all suited up, and talking to Tony Dantean. His choice of company confirmed it.

"Walk faster," Andrew urged. "They are looking to catch Stephanie alone."

Sure enough, Stephanie emerged from out of the girls' dormitory. She appeared to be crossing to the cafeteria, where she expected to find her friends hanging out, and hoping for an early lunch. Andrew and Kathy increased their pace, but Tony and Jeffrey had the café path under surveillance, and reached Stephanie before them.

The boys greeted Stephanie. "Hey there Stephanie!"

Stephanie hesitated, but she had little option other than to respond to the boys and engage in conversation. However, there was no reason she would desire to speak to either of them.

"Hello, Jeff, hello, Tony," the girl stammered politely.

Andrew and Kathy were close enough to hear the conversation, but not close enough to intervene. However, a black streak crossed campus as Bradley, who had been walking up from the student car park, lengthened his stride. He draped a casual arm over Stephanie's shoulders, and she appeared to relax into his side.

"What are you doing here Mannington?" Bradley drawled casually.

"I'm staying the weekend with my mate Tony," Jeffrey said. He looked Bradley up and down. "Don't I know you? You used to play basketball."

"I play A grade," Bradley said. "In fact I'm a team captain. Now what exactly was it you used to play?"

"B grade," Jeffrey admitted with some reluctance. "And I coached a bit."

"Mm," Bradley drawled. "Play much basketball now?"

Jeff was neatly attired in a suit and although he was not fat, he did not radiate the level of fitness Bradley did.

"No, I'm working," Jeffrey said. "I've got a job in Brisbane."

"I heard something about that," Bradley said. "So what brings you onto campus? Did you hear Garry Merton had left?"

"Yeah, something like that," Jeffrey admitted. "Word gets around you know."

"Tony told you I bet," Bradley said. "Well enjoy your visit. I'll organize some basketball if you want to drop by the gymnasium. However, Stephanie here, she isn't ever going to be available if I can help it."

Andrew and Kathy drew level with Stephanie, and began to edge her away from the boys and into the cafeteria. Stephanie was glad to follow her friends inside.

Bradley stood his ground a moment longer. "So long Mannington," he said. "It's been nice catching up with you!"

Jeff and Tony had little choice but to respond in kind to Bradley's effusive courtesy. Before they knew it, the boys had shaken hands and organized an impromptu basketball match for that afternoon. Jeff and the B grade team Tony now played for, against Bradley's A grade team. It would hardly be a fair match, but the neither Jeff nor Tony had the reputation of being strictly honourable, and some of the younger boys were looking forward to trouncing them.

"Wasn't that sweet of Brad?" Kathy whispered, when they were out of earshot.

Stephanie nodded. "Yeah, but don't read too much into it, he was just being protective."

Andrew merely looked approving. "I know as a Christian I should love everybody," he said. "But unrepentant types like Mannington can stay off campus."

"It's a free country," Stephanie said. "We can't stop him visiting."

"What are you going to do the rest of the day?" Andrew inquired.

"I think Hank was coming over after lunch to take Phoebe for a drive," Kathy said. "She invited us, but I hadn't wanted to intrude on their private time. Under the circumstances, I think we should go Steph."

"Sounds alright," Stephanie said. "And tonight I'll watch television in the girls' dormitory lounge. No guys are allowed in there, and Garry might call."

Sunday Kathy accompanied Stephanie to the Reform Church service, and made sure they were safely seated with a large group of friends at lunch. According to the rumour-mill, Jeffrey Mannington was due to leave campus early that afternoon to return to Brisbane, in good time for work on Monday. Then Stephanie would be free from any apprehension of running into him on campus.

STD (or Subscriber Trunk Dialing) rates remained low all day Sunday and mid-afternoon, Stephanie received the call she had been awaiting. Garry's Mother had begun recovering more comfortably. There was still a sore spot around the incision, and would be for some time because the underarm area was moist, and slow to heal, but the shock of the operation and the negative effects of the general anesthetic had worn off. If all went well, the family would be able to take her home within the week.

The campus social calendar was published on Monday, and was available to pick up around the dorms and in the cafeteria by lunch. Katy was pleased to discover the next scheduled social event was the annual Computer Tea. The Computer Tea was unique in that all students filled out a questionnaire, and then the data was fed through a computer matching programme. The computer was meant to provide students with their "perfect match" like the on the television show.

However, regular couples had been known to outsmart the system by deliberately filling in their sheets with identical answers.

"At least we won't have to worry about getting dates for this one," Kathy laughed and handed Stephanie a spare form.

Stephanie frowned. "Do we really want to be at the mercy of a random dumb machine once again?" she asked.

"I dunno," Kathy said looking through the questionnaire. "It could be fun!"

Stephanie had a point, Kathy reflected as she answered some of the questions, and having no desire to be matched with the only other five foot four student on campus, (who just happened to be an Asian exchange student who intended to return to China at the end of the year), embroidered her height a little.

She put choir down as her favourite activity even though she had only just joined; and selected one of the more charismatic speakers amongst the Theology lecturers as her favourite lecturer, simply because she did not really have a favourite professor.

"Come on Steph," Kathy urged. "Let's drop it into the box before tea."

"I think I'll keep mine just a little longer," Stephanie said folding the questionnaire and putting in her desk drawer. "I don't like to make decisions so rapidly."

"I won't let you miss the tea," Kathy said.

"I promise I won't miss the tea," Stephanie said. "Everyone has to eat that night."

In the ten minute break before Psychology on Tuesday, Bradley slid into the seat beside Kathy and spread out his Computer Tea questionnaire casually. Kathy stared in surprise.

"Let's get this filled out," he drawled lazily.

"Oh no Brad!" Kathy exclaimed. "I've already dropped mine in the box. I forgot, I honestly thought our little agreement didn't last beyond the semester break."

"Oops," Bradley looked mildly frustrated. "My bad for assuming."

"I'm so sorry," Kathy said. "Why don't you ask Stephanie?"

"Stephanie won't let me," Bradley returned, in a raw tight voice.

"Garry told her she could see other guys," Kathy whispered.

"Hmm," Bradley returned his voice still taut. "That appears to mean new guys and complete strangers, but not me. I think I'll go for a ride on my bike that evening."

"You can't do that!" Kathy exclaimed.

"Oh yes I can," Bradley said grimly. "I have my license and the Honda is in good working order, in case you haven't noticed lately."

"Not what I meant," laughed Kathy. "You can't miss a campus event."

"Yes I can if I wish - speaking of campus events, university basketball is back. Will you be coming to watch me play on Thursday?" Brad asked, his voice returning to normal.

"Sometimes," Kathy said. "I don't know how much time I will have with choir now. What are you doing for your community involvement?"

"Well," Brad said, "I'm taking Steph out to the hospital."

"That's not volunteer work," Kathy admonished.

"Really Kathy!" Brad asserted. "I thought I might as well volunteer there too, as sit waiting for her. It's amazing how many patients are waiting for someone to push them around in their wheel chairs, or need a strong arm to lean on as they walk in the corridors. And the old ladies absolutely adore the male tea-lady in the frilly pink apron."

"I'll bet they do!" Kathy was highly amused. This sounded more like the merry, happy-go-lucky Brad she used to know.

Wednesday afternoon in basket making and weaving, Kathy began her first product. Weaving was much easier than pottery to learn, but was frustratingly slow in Kathy's opinion, as she had to construct the actual material as well as fashion the item.

Her first project was only a paper basket such as one might gift an Easter egg in, but by the end of the semester she was expected to have made several large baskets. Kathy could see herself sitting for hours weaving, luckily it appeared she might be able to watch television while her hands were busy.

Thursday tea time, Joelle announced to her friends that she and Tom were now an official couple and of course were rigging the Computer Tea so they could go together.

"Tom got to know me last year when I was going out with Milton," she said. "We were just friends then of course – and just friends all last semester too."

Tom took over the story: "But we corresponded through the mid-year holidays, and decided we did really like each other."

"Ah that's sweet," Kathy exclaimed.

"I'm glad it has worked out for you both," added Stephanie.

"Who would have thought it would work out like this last year?" Annie exclaimed from her seat beside Dylan. "Me and Dylan, you and Tom."

Herman had not known any of them last year, so he could not comment. "Congratulations," he said anyway. "I hope you two will be very happy."

"I'm sure we will," Joelle said. "It has been a long slow road getting to this point."

"I'm interested in something you said earlier," Herman said. "Das arrangiert den Computer Tee, how do you do?"

"Do you mean rigging?" Tom asked. "I'll show you mate." He pulled out his questionnaire. "You see this paper full of questions? You and the lady of your choice sit down, and if you write exactly the same thing in each space, the computer ought to put you together."

"Einfache daten matching routine?" Herman asked. He turned to Stephanie. "Will you do this rigging with me?" he asked.

"Ah, Of course," Stephanie said. Her questionnaire form somehow mysteriously materialized out of the back of her Physiology folder. "Just as friends, getting to know someone new, eh?"

"I arrive in Australia three weeks ago," Herman said. "Every girl I would like to get to know is new to me!"

"I understand perfectly," Stephanie said. "It should be a lovely evening, and I would enjoy your company."

Kathy did not want to be a snitch, but when she went to watch Bradley play basketball that evening, she felt obliged to warn him that Stephanie had organized a date with Herman. Of course she waited until his match was over for the evening, and he came across to her to chat.

"That new bloke in her Biology class," Bradley said. "She somehow sees Garry in him."

"I think it's just that he's new, and it can't possibly be a serious date." Kathy suggested.

"Let's hope so," Bradley said, with an uncharacteristically fierce glint in his eye. "I was willing to step aside for Garry because he was a mate, but I'm determined not to let a new guy have her."

"What are you going to do?" Kathy asked curiously.

"What can I do?" Bradley said. "Just be good old Brads. Funny, happy, lazy, part-of-the-furniture, always a good friend, Bradley."

"You stood up to Jeffrey Mannington," Kathy said.

"That was different," Bradley said. "That was defending Stephanie from a guy she didn't want to have around her. I can't go against Stephanie's own wishes."

"Maybe you should kiss her or something," Kathy suggested.

"Not until the time is right," Bradley was adamant.

"Well I expect this new guy will get the idea soon enough," Kathy said. "You and Stephanie are the hottest non-couple on campus since Dylan and Cara."

"Bad example," Bradley said. "Look what has happened to them. Try you and Andrew Grosvy."

"Me and Andrew?' Kathy exclaimed. "We are just good friends."

"Tell that to Andrew since you joined the choir to be with him," Bradley observed. "Well as you were the only girl nice enough to watch me play basketball this evening, I had better walk you back to the dormitory."

Friday at lunch, the Biology class was sitting at a table, with the insularity it usually developed before or after a lecture. Cara was sitting with Kaleb, whom she had continued to see after the Basketball Tea. They were comfortably moving through the 'just-good-friends' stage towards being something regular. Dylan and Annie were still a couple, and Stephanie had been partnering with Herman in laboratory sessions.

Kathy prodded Bradley towards their table: "Come on, say hello," she said. "I'm not taking no for an answer. You can't let this thing get blown out of proportion. Break the ice and it won't seem half so bad."

"I'm sure I don't know what you mean Kathy," Bradley objected, but he followed her anyway.

Kathy walked up to the table and sat down beside Herman. "How are you today?" she inquired politely. Herman looked flattered Kathy was talking to him.

"Sehr gut danke frauline," he said. "I am very well. You are Stephanie's room-mate aren't you?"

Bradley pulled out the chair on the opposite side of the table next to Stephanie, and as he did so, his hand unconsciously rested for a moment behind Stephanie's shoulder. It was a small gesture that Stephanie, who was used to Bradley's presence, barely noticed him make, but it was picked up by Dylan and Herman both. Herman looked slightly confused.

"This is my friend Bradley," Stephanie said. "I'm sure you guys have met?"

"Ah freund," Herman said, only looking slightly more informed.

"We volunteer at the Nursing Home together," Stephanie added. "Brad is kind enough to provide me with transport every week."

"Sehr gut," Herman said. "Very good."

Bradley looked more assured now that Stephanie had granted him a role in her social hierarchy. He leaned back in his seat and eyed Herman casually. "Did you play any sport back in Germany?" he asked.

"Basketball spielen," Herman replied. "I played basketball and some football..."

"Rugby?" Dylan asked with interest.

"Nein," Herman said. "You would call it soccer."

"Well you're in luck," Bradley said. "If you come into the gymnasium tomorrow morning, I'll see if I can find you a team for basketball. We'll have you spieling in no time."

"Keine Zeit zum Spielen?" Herman looked slightly alarmed. "No time to play?"

"He meant schnell spieling," Annie said, looking mildly amused.

"Playing quickly, Herman. Watch the colloquialisms please Bradley."

"Danke Annie," Herman said. "I would be honoured to play basketball with you tomorrow, Bradley freund."

"Ah sport, it is the universal language of the male," Kathy sighed.

"And some of us girls too," Annie observed. "Bradley, Dylan and I will be spieling in the gym with you tomorrow too."

"Me and Kaleb as well," Cara said, "I like a bit of spieling - I think."

"Well while you are all spieling, I will have choir practice," Kathy said. "But I hope you all have fun."

The next morning at choir practice, they rehearsed the songs Kathy had begun to learn the previous week, and the Music Master introduced one or two songs by Handel. He had an ambitious performance scheduled for the end of year festivities, he announced, but the choir would learn all the pieces gradually to make it easier to prepare.

Lunch time the friends who had met for impromptu basketball in the gymnasium all entered the cafeteria together, and sat down beside Kathy. She was surprised to see Stephanie was not with them.

"Where's Steph?" she asked.

Cara shrugged. "Studying," she said. "You know our Stephie, as soon as new assignments are announced, she goes right into panic mode and completes them all."

Apparently Herman and Bradley had got along well, and now Bradley was debating whether to slot Herman into an A grade team, where he would most likely spend most of his time waiting in reserve, or a B grade team, where he would become a star player. Herman was dealing with his own dilemma in understanding Bradley's role in Stephanie's life.

Annie had broken out her schoolgirl German to try to explain "freund nicht lieb", but Herman appeared convinced that "lieb" had something to do with it. Annie tried explaining there was a friend called Garry who had been Stephanie's boyfriend, but Herman pointed out that Garry was no longer around and Bradley was, with perfect German logic.

Herman was of half a mind to offer Bradley his seat at the Computer Tea, when their dilemma was solved by a most unexpected source. Damaris had been wary of the second year students, ever since Andrew had set her in her place so thoroughly, but she approached the group and said she could not help over-hearing.

"As a hospitality student, I have direct access to the seating plan," Damaris said. "If Bradley really wants to sit with his friends, I can arrange it."

"Wouldn't that make the seating uneven?" Kathy inquired.

"Not if I put him on the end of the table," Damaris said, "There are sure to be a few lone people attending."

"Not so keen," Bradley drawled. "I don't want to be obviously alone."

"Or," Damaris blushed and hesitated, "I could put him down as my date. I won't get to sit all evening, I'm responsible for one of the courses, but it would keep the numbers even."

Kathy half-expected Bradley to explode at this. It was nearly as bad as being allocated an unknown date, who might turn out to be someone perfectly nice, but you never knew. However he seemed to be considering the idea.

"She's a pretty little thing after all," Dylan whispered in Bradley's ear, "I don't mind red-heads."

Annie kicked Dylan under the table, and so did Cara. The girls barely missed kicking each other, which was lucky. So far there had been no major conflicts between Dylan's girlfriend and his former flame in class, but it was only the beginning of the semester.

"Forget I mentioned it," Damaris looked embarrassed as Bradley hesitated. She turned to leave.

"Come back Damaris," Bradley called. "Should I pick you up at girl's dormitory before?"

"No I'll be cooking," Damaris said. "I'll meet you down there." The hospitality student hurried towards the dishwasher area, looking slightly pink.

"Someone has a little crush," Annie remarked.

"I'll deal with that," Bradley said. "It is flattering – I've gone from third wheel to desired property."

"I don't understand how you could be a wheel Bradley," Herman said.

"It's an Australian saying," Annie explained. "Most bikes only have two wheels...they don't need three."

"Ah is she getting on your motor bike Bradley?" Herman asked.

"I don't know if it will get that far," Bradley said. "We'll see."

Stephanie arrived just then. "What's new?" she asked.

"Bradley has a date for the Computer Tea," Kathy informed her room-mate.

Stephanie did not miss a beat. "Very nice," she said and sat down with her tray. She did not even bother to ask who it was.

"How did your assignment go?" Bradley asked.

"Great," Stephanie said. "How did your basketball go?"

"Very good," Bradley said. "Herman is an excellent player."

CHAPTER NINE: A PERFECT MATCH

After the morning church services and lunch, the male and female population of campus segregated, as the girls spent the afternoon on hair and make-up for the Computer Tea. Kathy felt a frisson of excitement at the thought of meeting her mystery date. There was nobody on campus that she consciously wanted to date, but she had a wild idea that the computer might find someone whom she saw every day, and had somehow overlooked.

At six o'clock Stephanie's name was called over the public address system, which was the agreed signal for both girls to descend the stairs. As Kathy was unaware of the identity of her date, he would be unable to pick her up at the dorm. When the girls arrived at reception, they saw that both Herman and Bradley had come across to meet them.

Herman greeted Stephanie with formality, and handed her a wild-flower picked from along one of the bush walks. Kathy fell into step alongside Bradley.

"It's going to be an interesting night," she whispered. "Just remember Stephanie is Herman's date."

"However could I forget?" Bradley drawled. "Anyway, I have my own date tonight remember."

"I'm almost sorry for poor Damaris," Kathy said.

"Why, am I that bad a date?" Bradley was mock offended.

"No, you are just a very naughty boy," Kathy said.

"You know me Kathy, I'm always nice," Bradley assured her firmly. "I will show little Damaris the utmost respect."

The little party arrived at the cafeteria, and stopped at the podium by the entrance to find their seating allocations. Herman and Stephanie were seated side-by-side, so their matching questionnaires had outsmarted the system successfully. Bradley was seated opposite the couple, as had been promised by Damaris.

Kathy collected her ticket and set off to look for her mystery date. She was surprised to see Andrew Grosvy seated in the chair corresponding to her own ticket.

"Hello," she said. "How did this happen?"

"I don't know," Andrew said. He spread his open palms above the table. "I'm truly innocent of any trickery."

"You would be," Kathy said, grimly taking her seat. "What did you put down as your favourite activity?"

"Choir of course," replied Andrew.

"So did I!" Kathy exclaimed. "Favourite lecturer?"

"The Theology lecturer of course," Andrew said.

"Mine too, because there wasn't a lot of choice. I don't do Science or Math and there were no Art lecturers listed," Kathy admitted.

"Height?" Andrew inquired.

"I told a little lie and put down five-foot-eight," Kathy blushed.

"Well I told a little truth and put down five-foot-eight too," Andrew said. "So whose fault is it we are seated together?"

"Mine it seems," Kathy admitted.

"Admit it, you secretly wanted to come here with me," Andrew said.

"I could do worse, I guess," Kathy said. "In fact I have dated worse, and that by my own choice.

Phoebe and Hank were seated close-by, and expressed themselves highly amused by this little interchange. Phoebe explained they had to purchase a ticket for Hank to attend, because he was living off-campus.

The food was excellent, although it represented a blend of cultures. The first course was traditional Greek salad, accompanied by souvlaki on skewers. The second course however, was butter chicken or its vegetarian equivalent. It was served on fragrant steamed rice. The final course was orange self-saucing pudding with home-made ice-cream.

After the Computer Tea finished, Andrew walked Kathy back to the dormitory. He gave her a quick peck on the cheek which struck just the right note of courtesy and friendship.

"I'll see you in class," Kathy said.

"And in choir," Andrew said.

"Ah yeah," Kathy agreed. "I can't wait until our first trip away, can you?"

"It will happen as soon as we know enough songs," Andrew said. "Good night now Kathy. Sleep tight."

When Kathy returned to the room, Stephanie was already there preparing for bed. "Hi, Kathy," she said, "Did you have a good evening?"

"Yes, it was very interesting," Kathy said.

"Who were you with - we were a little too far away to see?" Stephanie asked.

"Andrew Grosvy would you believe," Kathy exclaimed. "I described him exactly when I filled out my questionnaire it seems."

Stephanie laughed: "Perhaps he is just what you need!"

"I don't know whether he is even interested - you know how Theols are very hard to read," Kathy admitted. "How was your evening?"

"Very nice," Stephanie said.

"Who walked you back to the dorm - Brad or Herman?" Kathy inquired curiously.

"Herman of course, he was my date," Stephanie said. "Bradley stayed to help Damaris pack the dishwasher, apparently she couldn't leave until that was done. Did you know the orange pudding was her dish? Getting the sauce to pour just right is a real challenge. And it is a lot of work to make home-made ice-cream thicken."

"So Damaris was a hit?" Kathy inquired.

"Yeah, Bradley has asked her to go and watch his basketball game on Thursday night," Stephanie said.

"Hmm, Stephanie, what sort of game are you and Bradley playing?" Kathy could no longer restrain herself from asking.

"No game," Stephanie's voice was firm. "I cannot use Bradley by going out with him. He would take it seriously, and then what if Garry should return?"

"Then you would have too gorgeous guys competing for your attention," Kathy said. "I sorta fail to see the problem."

"I couldn't possibly hurt Bradley," Stephanie said.

"The way I see it, you have been hurting Bradley every day, since I don't know how long ago," Kathy declared.

"Did Bradley tell you this?" Stephanie demanded.

"Not exactly, but you could ask him," Kathy suggested.

Monday was a busy day full of classes, and the mild gossip which always followed a campus social event. In the evening, Kathy walked over to the gymnasium to watch Cara and Annie play basketball, as their teams were once again opposing each other. Dylan and Herman were both there watching the girls play. After a while, Bradley wandered into the gym, and sat down between Kathy and the boys.

"Hello Brads," Kathy said.

"How did things go with you and the fire-cracker after the Computer Tea?" Dylan asked.

"We had a nice little chat," Bradley said. "And she is an amazing cook."

"You might need to be careful," Dylan said. "I believe she got a bit clingy with Andrew G a while back there."

"I know," Bradley said. "But it's all under control."

"Why then did you invite her to watch your basketball match?" Kathy asked curiously.

"She really does have a hard time making friends because of the extended hours of her course," Bradley said. "And the gym will be full of hot sweaty males all playing basketball. I can introduce her to anyone she fancies."

"Bradley als schlange wie schlau du bist," Herman said. "As cunning as a snake."

"Thanks, I think Herman," Bradley said. "Damaris did me a favour, so I'm doing her one." He subsided quietly, giving his attention to the remainder of the women's basketball game.

When the game finished, Annie and Cara bounced up to them.

"Hello everybody," Cara cried. "What did you think?"

"Hello Dylan, Bradley and Kathy," Annie cried. "Willkommen Herman!"

"Hey Annie," Dylan said frowning slightly. "I'm not sure I like the sound of that. Herman are you stealing all our women?"

Herman looked alarmed. "Nein – nicht, is not my intention!"

"Don't listen to these guys," Kathy said. "They have always been great jokers."

Tuesday evening Kathy attended Aerobics. She was only casually enrolled for this semester, as she had earned the available credit point the previous semester, and had a new activity that took her time. However, she still found exercising to the rhythmic music a lot of fun. Annie was progressing as a facilitator too, introducing more fun movements, and smoothing out her instructions.

In Art on Wednesday, Kathy had now graduated from weaving paper Easter baskets to macramé plant hangers. The same technique could be used to make string tote bags, purses, wall hangings and even mats. A lot depended on the yarn used, the complexity of the weave and the beads included.

Thursday evening Damaris attended Bradley's basketball match. Apparently she brought the product of her afternoon cooking class, which was a variety of savory scones, and Bradley reported that most of the single members of the basketball teams were already half in love with her.

"She won't have any trouble getting a date for the next campus function," Bradley chuckled.

"It doesn't hurt to be sponsored by one of the A grade captains," Kathy said. "You had better not drop her cold, Brads."

Bradley pretended to look hurt. "I wouldn't do that would I?"

Kathy turned to Andrew, who was sitting between her and Stephanie: "I haven't seen much of you this week," she said.

"Ah no, sorry," Andrew said. "I was studying for a Greek test."

"Hmm," Kathy said. She wasn't sure what to think. Andrew had told her before that Greek was very challenging, but he also might have been playing it cool around her, since their pseudo-date at the Computer Tea.

Guys did that sometimes when they were not really interested.

"What are you making now in Art?" Andrew asked.

"Macramé," Kathy said. "Weaving with ropes," she explained when Andrew looked blank.

"Ah nets," Andrew said.

"A whole fishing net would be a years' worth of work surely," Kathy exclaimed.

"Mathew four, verses 19-20: "Then He said to them, 'Follow Me, and I will make you fishers of men.' They immediately left their nets and followed Him," Andrew quoted. "The fishermen sat by the fire and made nets in the off-season, I think."

"I don't really get an off-season," Kathy remarked.

"Nor do I unfortunately," Andrew said. "Greek calls. Kathy dear, I will see you at vespers tonight."

"See you then Andrew," Kathy said. She turned to Stephanie. "Is 'see you at vespers tonight' a date do you think?"

Stephanie considered: "I shouldn't think so, not unless he intends to come and call for you at the dorm. It sounds more like a 'please save me a seat' than anything else."

"I'll call for you at the dorm if you like," Bradley said impudently.

"That won't be necessary," Kathy laughed. "What are you two doing today?"

"After lunch we are going to the Nursing Home for the afternoon," Stephanie said. "We will be back by vespers if you want company, however."

Kathy took extra care with her hair and make-up, before vespers that evening. She listened for her name to be called over the public address system and it never came, so she descended the steps when Stephanie was called downstairs by Bradley. Kathy doubted that Stephanie was allowing Bradley to call their outings together 'dates', but he was never shy about coming across to girls' dorm to collect her anyway. The trio entered women's assembly area, and selected a pew with ample space for their friends to join them.

Andrew appeared to arrive minutes later and slid into the pew beside Kathy.

"Did Greek go well?" Kathy asked.

"Ah yes, that is out of the way until next test," Andrew said. "I must say you are looking nice tonight, Kathy."

Kathy was pleased by the compliment, but Andrew had always been polite and observant. It wasn't proof of anything special. Cara and Kaleb chose to join them just then, followed by Annie, Dylan and Herman.

The vespers program was very pleasant, led by Larry. Despite being a Theology student, Larry kept up to date with developments in society. He spoke about the recent spate of werewolf, zombie and other horror movies released into the cinema, and how a Christian could be confident in their future, and read the Bible to find out what would happen to them after death. With a few slight Theological variations, most denominations on campus believed the future was safely in God's hands.

After vespers, Andrew turned to Kathy and said he would see her in choir practice the next day. He wished her goodnight, and left the women's assembly area. Several other friends stayed behind to chat, and one even observed that Andrew had looked very tired that evening.

Saturday morning in choir, everyone was excited by the announcement that the next weekend would involve a trip. It was only a short trip to Gympie Baptist Church, where they would perform several of the songs they had been practicing during the service time. After the service, the congregation would be hosting a shared lunch, and members of the Silver Springs Choir would be guests of honour.

During choir practice, Andrew invited Kathy to join a small group who were planning to 'workshop' their journal writing. They would be meeting in the café lounge after finishing their mid-day meal; then discussing and recording the things they had learned from involvement in the choir. He suggested Kathy bring her journal and pencil.

"This way, we can help each other with ideas, and do our major assignment for Christian Outreach," Andrew suggested. "It's not cheating as we don't write each other's journals."

"Thanks," Kathy said. "I have made a few notes, but I'm not used to writing that self-reflective, religious experience oriented, sort of thing."

"That's why I thought it might be helpful," Andrew said with more of his usual earnestness, than he had displayed all week.

Kathy obediently brought her journal to lunch, dropping it into one of the lockers at the cafeteria entrance. After eating her meal with a selection of friends, she packed her tray away in the dishwasher slot, and proceeded to the lounge. David and Debbie, and Larry and Anita were already there. They greeted Kathy effusively. After a few minutes, Andrew arrived with Luke and Tess.

"Let's get started," David said, assuming his natural role as leader. Everyone agreed that as it was a Bible subject, it would be helpful to say a prayer, and Larry was nominated to pray for the group. After the prayer, David turned to Kathy. "I'm sorry to put you on the spot, but as our newest member, would you like to tell us how you are going with your journal?"

"Um – I have the dates of practice and names of the songs we sung," Kathy said.

"That's a good start," David said. "But what about feelings?"

"Um – at first it was all strange and new…" Kathy ventured.

"That's a good start," David said. "You need to be open to admitting that in words…"

"What exactly are you learning?" Larry asked.

"Um – new songs," Kathy said.

"New songs is okay," Debbie said. "But what the lecturers really like to hear is new skills."

"I've got teamwork, voice and performance," Luke added. "I also had to upgrade my driver's license slightly, because we are using the new university bus, which seats fifty persons."

"The driver's license aspect is unique to Luke," Debbie said. "And I would leave the performance skills to later if I were you, so I had something to talk about other than scenery on our trips."

"Making friends," Kathy suggested.

"We sort of knew each other already," Anita said. "What about getting to know each other on a different level? Sometimes as friends, other times as fellow singers."

"What are the aims of the subject?" David said. "If we want maximum marks, we should target our discussion towards them."

"Community involvement," Kathy said.

"Have we done any of that yet?" Tess asked.

"I think we have," Debbie said. "But so far – it has been internal to the university. When we go out next Sunday it will be external outreach."

"Feeding the flock and growing the flock," Andrew said. "Are two different areas of ministry."

"This is all very helpful," Kathy said. "Thank you for inviting me to join the group."

That evening in their room Kathy relayed some of the hints she had gained to Stephanie. Stephanie was interested to hear the other student's opinion, as to what the lecturer's required in the journal, and said she would pass the ideas onto Bradley. However, she said the parallels between the Nursing Home work and Christ's healing ministry were fairly clear, and she was not having much problem making appropriate theological reflections.

Kathy invited her room-mate to the recreation area to play pool, or otherwise hang for the evening, but Stephanie said she would be happy watching television in the girl's lounge and waiting for Garry to call.

"He doesn't call as often now, unfortunately," Stephanie confided with a wry expression. "He has commenced at Wollongong University, so he has his studies and he is very much involved in his Mother's recovery."

"Are you sure you need to keep waiting on him like this?" Kathy asked. "Surely an evening in the rec area would not hurt?"

"Maybe not, but it's my choice," Stephanie declared stubbornly. "The television in the girl's lounge is as good as the one in the recreation room, and if you are honest, the seats are better."

"True," Kathy observed. "But the company is more limited."

"If I miss Garry's call he may not call again for a week," Stephanie said obstinately.

"If you are living with those sort of fears, you may need to let go," Kathy said. "I think our prayers have been answered that the doctors were able to get the cancer. What happens next is up to the Lord once again."

"Now you sound like our mutual friend, Andrew," Stephanie laughed. "Why don't you phone boy's dorm and ask him to hang in the rec room?"

"I couldn't do that," Kathy said. "I'm not sure he likes me that way. He hasn't been himself since the Computer Tea."

"Maybe he worries about whether you like him," Stephanie said with a yawn. "You made such an issue about preferring guys like Rob earlier this year. Try to sort it out before the two of you go to Gympie next weekend, or it could be quite awkward."

Sunday remained Kathy's only day to catch a sleep-in, so she lazed through the morning, only arriving in time for the Reform Church service to commence. Scanning the seats for her friends, she noticed something peculiar. Herman and Annie were sitting on one row, while Cara, Kaleb, Andrew and Dylan were sitting in another row some distance away. Dylan's face was like thunder.

"What's wrong?" Kathy whispered as she slid into the seat beside Dylan.

"Annie is not sure about our relationship anymore," Dylan whispered in return. "Apparently she enjoys practicing her German with Herman so much, that she would like to spend more time with him."

"After asking you not to waste HER time and all," Kathy muttered.

"Exactly," Dylan said. "Then she went and wasted – how many of MY weeks?"

"Maybe the novelty of talking to Herman will wear off," Kathy suggested.

"With those blonde good looks, and being higher on the basketball chart than me?" Dylan scowled. "I don't think so."

"Well you still have your other friends," Kathy whispered.

"Fancy a walk this afternoon? I really need to get off campus and blow off some steam," Dylan said.

"Ask Andrew too," Kathy whispered.

"Oh like that is it?" Dylan whispered. "Sorry for sitting between you."

"That's okay," Kathy whispered. "Nothing is happening."

"Hey Andrew," Dylan murmured. "Nature walk this afternoon? See some of God's wonderful creation?"

"Sure," Andrew said. "If you two will stop whispering in church."

"I think God understands," Dylan said. "They say Jesus suffered every temptation that we do. Although I can't find some of them listed in the gospels."

"I may be able to help you with that inquiry later," Andrew returned with perfect seriousness.

Dylan chuckled. "Let's see him find a text for wanting to strangle your ex-girlfriend," he whispered to Kathy.

Andrew silently handed Dylan a Bible. It was open to Judges Chapter Two. Dylan quietened down, and began reading. Kathy took a peek across his arm. In this chapter God complains about being betrayed by an entire nation that he lavished his blessings on. You can't get much worse than that!

That afternoon Dylan, Kathy, Andrew, Cara and Kaleb set off for an ambitious walk around the perimeter of campus, and along some back roads. Stephanie and Bradley also decided to forsake the motor bike for an afternoon, and take to foot to enjoy their friends company. Everyone in the group, with the possible exception of Kaleb, who had not known Dylan for as long, could understand his frustration at being dumped. The general consensus was that, while Annie had the right to do as she wished, her behaviour had been in mildly bad form.

Monday it was back to lectures once again. Classes had been going for about three weeks now, and it was around the fourth week that a lot of lecturers liked to schedule a test. Just to see how students were understanding the units it seemed.

The Educational Theories and Psychology lecturers followed this pattern and Kathy found herself with some revision to do. She was sitting in the room around mid-afternoon, resolutely reading the less than fascinating textbook, when Stephanie appeared. Her room-mate was loaded with library books for some paper, or practical session write-up.

Stephanie fumbled with the door trying to close it with one hand, while clutching all the books with the other, and her shoulder bag fell to the ground. Pens, pencils and other writing implements fell out. A small square box with a hinged side and rounded lid, also rolled across the floor. It came to rest in front of Kathy and she picked it up.

"What's this?" Kathy cried. "It looks like jewellery."

Blushing, Stephanie retrieved the gift box and cracked open the lid. It contained a flat golden ring featuring two hearts side-by-side. A tiny diamond chip was embedded into one of the hearts.

"Who gave you that - Garry or Bradley?" Kathy demanded.

"Bradley," Stephanie admitted.

"But you are not wearing it?" Kathy observed.

"Not yet," Stephanie said. "I told Bradley I would have to think about it."

"Don't think too long," Kathy advised. "Or Bradley may tire of waiting."

"I think Bradley knows exactly where I am coming from," Stephanie said. "Don't judge him by your own experiences Kathy."

"Well I did seem to run into two men who were exceptionally low on patience," Kathy retorted slightly huffily.

"I'm sorry, I didn't mean anything by it," Stephanie said. "I'm sure you have found a patient one now in Andrew."

"Maybe too patient," Kathy complained. "He's not knocking our door down, or showering me with invites."

"Does he make you worry that he might have an interest in anyone else?" Stephanie asked.

"No, he just seems happy to be good friends," Kathy observed.

"Maybe that is what he thinks you want," Stephanie suggested. "Now please, don't tell a soul Bradley gave me the ring. I have to at least explain to Garry first, even if I decide to go out with Bradley."

"My lips are sealed," Kathy promised.

Tuesday once again the highlight of the day was the aerobics session in the evening. Annie had now incorporated some of the latest hits into the class. These included: "*Like a Virgin*" by Madonna, which was a catchy tune, but quite ironic, as Kathy reflected the majority of the girls were still virgins, and "*Sussudio*" by Phil Collins. Nobody knew what "*Sussudio*" meant, but it was rhythmic and fun for exercising.

Wednesday in Art, Kathy commenced a more ambitious weaving project, which was an owl wall hanging. The pattern had a stick at the top, which was mostly hidden by the owl's wide head and large eyes. The eyes were woven round circles, with tufted fringes extending some distance from the weave. A large wooden bead was knotted into the centre of each eye. The body was a basket-like weave, and the two feet were composed of the wool being gathered together, and wrapped around a prominent stick, upon which the owl appeared to be perching. Its tail was composed of one large knot, and then a long tassel of wool ends.

Thursday evening Kathy wandered down to the gymnasium to watch the men's basketball. Damaris was there, basking in the glory of being Bradley's main cheering-squad. Kathy sat down beside the younger girl.

Stephanie wandered in a little later, because she had a Biology practical all afternoon, which also frequently made her tardy for tea.

"How did it go?" Kathy asked Stephanie curiously, knowing the small class would be rife with additional tension, now that Dylan and Annie had broken up.

Stephanie shrugged. "Herman is now partnering with Annie, and I am working with Dylan and Cara," she reported. "Annie seems happy enough, although Herman seems confused. Not much is said between the two groups except for the occasional – pass me the scalpel please."

"The scalpel?" Kathy exclaimed. "That bad eh?"

"Coincidence," Stephanie retorted. "We were dissecting mice."

"Disgusting," Kathy exclaimed.

"Don't worry, I have washed my hands," Stephanie laughed.

Andrew wandered by the gym on the way back from the library, and seeing Stephanie and Kathy sitting there, he sat down. "Hello Kathy," he said. "Hello Stephanie."

"Hello Andrew," Stephanie said. "What's new down your end of campus?"

Andrew wrinkled his nose. "Nothing much, everything around boys' dorm is now looking smelly and old. Kathy did you hear we actually have two bookings in Gympie on Sunday? In the afternoon we visit the Christian Community Church. They are non-denominational, and have only been going around two years."

"Oh wow!" Kathy exclaimed.

"Extra-long practice on Saturday morning," Andrew said. "Did you hear?" He suddenly seemed too shy to look Kathy in the eye.

Bradley's team won their match easily, which would put them one space higher on the campus chart for the semester. Bradley got himself a drink, and then crossed to the spectators' benches.

Damaris cracked open the lid of a Tupperware container; it contained mini-pikelets this week. Damaris gave one to Andrew, to show there were no sore feelings from earlier in the year, and Andrew ate it obediently.

"She loves the position of number one fan," Stephanie observed.

"That she does," Bradley drawled. He took Stephanie's hands in his and observed them closely. "And until further notice, she really is my number one."

Stephanie blushed. "I still have to speak to Garry," she said.

"I wonder," Bradley said, "Whether you could call him for once, instead of just waiting for him to call you?"

"I don't know when he is free with all he has going on," Stephanie hedged.

"Try it, just for me," Bradley urged.

Friday was generally a busy day for Kathy, but she was vaguely aware of Stephanie's tension, as her room-mate had been unable to get Garry on the telephone the previous evening. Bradley had suggested they miss vespers that evening to call him together, and failing that, was threatening to ride down to Wollongong on his bike.

In the evening, Kathy descended to vespers with Cara and Phoebe, who were called over the public address system by their respective boyfriends, Kaleb and Hank. She carefully left a little space beside her on the pew, and Andrew joined them, looking very shy.

"Don't forget extra practice tomorrow Kathy," he whispered.

"Of course I won't," Kathy scoffed gently. "Although," some imp entered into her and made her say, "It might help if you came and called for me at the dormitory in the morning, just in case I sleep in."

Andrew went pink, but his face was solemn. "If that is what you require Kathy," he replied.

After vespers, Kathy returned to the room and Stephanie was there reading a novel.

"How did it go with Garry?" Kathy asked. "Did you get through?"

"Oh yes," Stephanie said.

"Did you tell him?" Kathy pursued.

"Yeah. He said his mother was due to begin radiotherapy in the next week or so, and side effects of chest treatment could include nausea and difficulty breathing and swallowing," Stephanie said. "He also said Bradley looking after me was the best news he had received since his mother fell ill. He told us to be happy."

"I see you are not wearing the ring," Kathy observed.

"It's my decision, I'm waiting till the moment is right," Stephanie said. "I just sorta got dumped again, you know."

"Garry had told you not to wait for him," Kathy reminded her roommate patiently.

"Yeah, but I did, I really loved him," Stephanie said.

"What about Brads then?" Kathy asked.

"I love him too," Stephanie admitted. "They are both different."

"Marry one, be a friend to the other," Kathy suggested.

"Yeah," Stephanie said. "That's the plan."

"I ordered Andrew to pick me up at the dorm tomorrow morning," Kathy said. "I don't know why I did it. Something got into me."

"Did he say he would?" Stephanie inquired.

"Yes," Kathy said. "But he didn't look happy."

"Poor boy, he's clearly terrified of asking you out," Stephanie said.

"Don't romanticize," Kathy said. "I'm not sure he likes me that way.

He seems to have a one date, then 'good friends' policy. It worked that way with Damaris, then Cara."

"You are not Damaris or Cara," Stephanie observed.

"Too right I'm not," Kathy exclaimed. "Andrew's going to have to learn that."

Saturday morning Andrew picked Kathy up from reception in girls' dorm looking prim and proper in his weekend casual attire.

"Would you really have slept in and missed practice, if I hadn't picked you up Kathy?" he enquired as they walked across to the Music Department.

"It's a distinct possibility," Kathy said. "I used to enjoy my sleepy Saturday mornings last semester."

"So early practice is like – a cross to bear?" Andrew deduced.

Kathy laughed. "I'd better put that in my journal," she said, feeling more relaxed than she had all week. "No really Andrew, I've been lonely this semester."

"Since Rob left," Andrew said. "You never told me why you two broke up. Was it just the distance?"

"No, we broke up before he left," Kathy said. "He wasn't the man for me."

Anyone else would have asked Kathy whether she had any idea who was the man for her, but not Andrew. Instead he went pink and kept on walking. "What exactly was the problem?" he finally ventured.

"I thought he was a lot of fun at first, but in the end I found him frivolous I think," Kathy observed.

They reached the Music Department and walked through to the main practice room. There the Music Master led the choir through the songs they would be singing in the morning at the Baptist Church, and on the afternoon visit to the Community Congregation. Anything he felt was not quite perfect, he drilled again and again, until the crew were quite exhausted. Then he finally released his victims with instructions to assemble for the bus bright and early in the morning.

"It's a forty minute drive to Gympie," The Music Director announced. "But I've allowed us an hour just in case."

Andrew and Kathy walked straight from the Music Department to the cafeteria, which was already serving lunch. They collected their trays and selected a table beside the window with Cara and Kaleb.

"Oh look," Cara said, glancing outside and down into the gardens. "Bradley and Stephanie together at last."

"I don't think they know we can see them," Kathy observed as Bradley bent his head to give Stephanie a kiss. Stephanie looped her arms around his neck, and raised her face to receive the caress.

A few minutes later, Bradley and Stephanie entered the cafeteria hand-in-hand. There was a slight glint of gold on Stephanie's right ring finger and Bradley was walking extra tall for his usual six-foot-three.

CHAPTER TEN: THE COURTSHIP OF A PRIEST

Andrew called for Kathy at the girls' dormitory around seven-thirty the next morning. He looked a little self-conscious, because he had not been invited this time, but explained he had thought she might want help with her bag. There were no plans to make the Gympie trip an overnight stay, but between their regulation issue choir gowns, and a change of casual clothes, the students all had bit of luggage.

"I see you have lost your sleepy Sunday too," Andrew observed sympathetically as Kathy yawned, and settled into the seat in the bus. With the exception of a few single Theology Students and Music students, the choir was mostly composed of couples, and it made sense for Andrew and Kathy to sit together. There were no other unattached members of their group going along.

As the bus approached Gympie, it passed the Woondum National Park, replete with subtropical rainforest and spectacular rocky rock pools. The town of Gympie was situated on the Mary River, which was prone to flooding. Major floods had been reported in 1893, 1955, 1968, and 1974; yet the town remained where it was, loyal to its roots in the history of goldmining in Australia.

The Silver Springs students arrived at the Gympie Baptist Church around eight-thirty, give or take a few minutes, and were shown in to a large hall, where they could change into their choir robes. The congregation had thoughtfully provided screens between the men's and women's areas, but these were hardly necessary, as the loose robes were pulled on over their church clothes.

The service commenced around nine o'clock. Kathy had experienced a number of service styles from Silver Springs, but still missed the liturgy, whenever she attended a reform style service. The choir were called upon to sing three times during the service, in order to punctuate segments of the proceedings. The songs they sung were *"Peace like a River"*, *"Amazing Grace"* and *"The Old Rugged Cross"*. With the exception of *"Peace like a River"* these pieces were traditional hymns.

After the service, the congregation accompanied the students to the Memorial park, where the food had been set up in the rotunda. The rotunda was surrounded by plants that bloomed in spring, and Kathy could see the beginnings of the display already, as it was late August with September rapidly approaching.

Kathy had always considered herself an outgoing type of girl, but now she discovered one of the most demanding aspects of being an ambassador for her organization, which was mingling with strangers. Kathy made a note to herself not to enter this into her official journal, but she was very glad of Andrew by her side.

The congregation naturally looked to him, before they looked at her; and in the context of a parish, Andrew was transformed. Instead of the shy boy she knew on campus, he was a young man who had something gracious to say to everyone. His habitual courtesy, which seemed stilted and excessive when the other students were all casually joking on campus, suddenly appeared highly appropriate at church.

After lunch they bid goodbye to the congregation and piled into the university bus for a short drive away from the Mary Valley towards the lakes. Instead of meeting in a traditional building in the centre of Gympie, the Christian Community Church actually met on a farm in Lagoon Pocket. There were negotiations underway to move the congregation to James Nash High School, but at this stage they were still in their temporary accommodation.

The special afternoon meeting commenced around two-thirty. What this congregation lacked in elegant surroundings, they made up for in sincerity and enthusiasm. *"Peace like a River"* was now one of the more sedate of the choir's offerings, along with Handel's *"Halleluiah Chorus"*, and *"Jehovah Jireh"*, which was a Jewish style, modern Christian song written in the 1970s.

It was almost tea time when the meeting closed, and once again this congregation offered them a picnic style meal. After the eating and compulsory socializing, Kathy was tired, and welcomed the chance to climb back into the university bus. As they drove back through the falling dusk, her head nodded, and she found herself leaning against Andrew's shoulder. He was too polite to push her off of course, but regarded her with indulgent amusement.

After the excitement of the trip Sunday, Monday seemed very dull, and Kathy was mildly lonely. Stephanie was barely ever in their room, now choosing to study in the library with Bradley, or hang in the gymnasium of an evening, once again with Bradley.

In contrast to her absentee room-mate, Andrew seemed to be close whenever Kathy wanted something. He was her companion in the classes they shared, and offered to take her tray to the dishwasher after each meal. However, he largely avoided personal subjects, and had not officially asked her out again.

Come to think of it, the computer had put them together at the Computer Tea, so he had NEVER really asked her out. Moreover, Kathy had seen him hang around with both Damaris and Cara after their dates, and yet no relationship had developed with either girl.

Tuesday Kathy had a Psychology test, and Wednesday she had an Educational Theories test, so she spent Monday and Tuesday afternoons studying in her room. As far as she could tell she passed both comfortably. A few boring hours with the text book had paid off.

Wednesday at lunch time Kathy was early at the cafeteria, waiting for the lunch rush to begin, when Andrew arrived from the direction of the Music department looking excited.

"Guess what Kathy?" He exclaimed.

"I cannot imagine Andrew," Kathy responded sedately. She had learned long ago that minor things could be of great excitement to Andrew. His enthusiasm was a quality she envied.

"I have just found out that we are going to have a HUGE practice this Saturday because the choir is going on a trip again next week," Andrew cried.

"Where is it this time?" Kathy was now interested.

"Toowoomba," Andrew exclaimed. "Because that is over three hours' drive, we will be camping out in the church hall Saturday night, and returning Sunday evening."

"Oh wow, and seeing something of the town too, I hope," Kathy exclaimed.

"Toowoomba in the first week of spring, when the flowers are out and the festival season is about to begin!" Andrew exclaimed.

"It sounds romantic," Kathy ventured.

"It does too," Andrew looked slightly stricken. "But it doesn't have to be."

"I beg your pardon?" Kathy asked.

"I promise solemnly to behave myself," Andrew said. "You can trust me Kathy. I will always be your friend."

"When have you ever misbehaved?" Kathy inquired.

Andrew blushed. "Earlier this year, I thought I might like you," he admitted. "But you told several of our friends that you would never marry a minister."

"Oh!" Kathy murmured. It was her turn to blush. "You weren't supposed to hear about that."

"Please don't blame anyone," Andrew requested earnestly.

"I think I should clarify," Kathy said. "I would never marry an occupation. Only a person - a person I had gotten to know well."

"Irrespective of their choice of the ministry?" Andrew enquired earnestly.

"I'm not sure," Kathy said. "You see earlier this year, I was also recovering from the break-up of a long term relationship. I didn't want to think about getting serious with anybody."

"Don't you worry then Kathy," Andrew said. "I won't be embarrassing you by expressing my feelings, or putting the hard word on you. I will be the epitome of patience and restraint."

"Er, thanks," Kathy muttered. Their friends were filing into the cafeteria and beginning to fill the rest of the table, so the subject was dropped.

Thursday morning Kathy combed her naturally wavy hair as flat as possible and added a scarf at her neck in case her collar appeared too low. She was puzzling between her favourite court shoes, and some canvas flats when Stephanie returned from breakfast.

Her room-mate stared in surprise: "Whatever are you up to?" Stephanie exclaimed. "Trying to hide a love-bite?"

"I'm trying to look more like a girl who would marry a minister," Kathy said. "Someone told Andrew I said that I wouldn't, and he has promised not to bother me with his feelings on our choir trip to Toowoomba."

Stephanie laughed. "I would take that scarf off at once," she said. "You know what everyone around here assumes about them… Andrew has always liked you just the way you are too, so you better fix that hair too."

"You don't think it's too eighties?" Kathy asked.

"I'll let you in on a secret," Stephanie said. "This is the nineteen-eighties!"

"Very funny," Kathy said. "Who do you think told Andrew I wouldn't marry a minister?"

"Not me," Stephanie assured her. "But you did say it a few times around the group. Maybe Dylan, he has the biggest mouth. It shouldn't matter really, just tell Andrew your feelings have changed."

"They haven't exactly," Kathy said. "I have no desire to marry most of the ministerial students here. I just like Andrew."

"You have given me relationship advice a hundred times or more," Stephanie said. "I can't see why you would find it difficult to bother Andrew with your feelings, if he really won't bother you anymore with his!"

"You know I like assertive guys," Kathy objected.

"Well, he has at least told you what the problem is," Stephanie said. "I would expect you to be free to have fun with it from here on. The old Kathy would."

After much thought, Kathy requested Andrew meet her after lunch on Friday, to help her fill out her journal. Secretly, however, she filled in an entry especially for him to read, and slid it between the sheets of her journal proper. The genuine entries all dealt with her skills development during performance, and growing sense of evangelistic mission during the trip. Andrew read these through and nodded with approval.

"Your journaling is coming along nicely," he observed.

"What about this?" Kathy said.

Andrew picked up the page with the false entry and began to read it through.

"This seems a little personal," he observed. "I don't think the lecturer needs to know who you sat with on the bus."

"I'll make a note of that," Kathy murmured as gravely as possible. Andrew read further down the page. "And this part – I'm glad you feel I have just the right thing to say to everybody in the congregation – indeed I'm truly flattered, but you may want to phrase it as a skill you would like to learn yourself."

"Good idea," Kathy murmured. "Any other suggestions Andrew?"

"I think this is a little wrong...I don't remember...now Kathy you are having a joke with me!" Andrew exclaimed. He tugged the page gently and the loose leaf fell free of the journal. "Now why would you do that?"

"I don't know," Kathy murmured demurely. "I just thought..." She cast her eyes down and fluttered her eyelashes.

"Are you trying to tell me that you have had a change of heart since the beginning of the year?" Andrew said.

"Yeah," Kathy whispered. "I have."

Andrew grasped both her hands in his. "While I would love to believe that, Kathy dear," he said, "I feel I have to protect us both against your having another change of heart."

"I won't," Kathy shook her head.

"Think about it," Andrew said. "Your first boyfriend was impatient to get serious, and you two broke up. Your second boyfriend was very exciting but wasn't serious enough. Now you think you want me. I am patient and I take things slow – I am not exciting – but I am serious. Do you see a pattern here at all?"

"It's called learning what I want," Kathy said.

"Is it?" Andrew asked. "In six months' time, maybe you will want someone fun and exciting again."

"No, no," Kathy protested. "I will want you. You are good and kind, caring and true. I know you are clever, and you have a refined sense of humour. You also love God and that is important to me."

"I'm sorry Kathy," Andrew said. "I think we should stay just friends, unless you can convince me I am truly what you want."

Kathy pouted and preened, but was unable to persuade Andrew from his cautious stance.

Stephanie did not sound very concerned when Kathy told her Andrew's response. "It sounds as though you have Andrew very near where you want him, even though he insists as classing it as 'just friends'," her room-mate said. "Give it a week or two..."

A week or two sounded like eternity to the vivacious Kathy, and she felt a flash of resentment. Since Stephanie had admitted she loved Bradley, things had become very intense between the young couple. Stephanie could barely concentrate on study, which was most unlike her. She was also writing random bits of poetry, such as odes to Bradley's leather jacket and bony shoulders. The couple were planning to celebrate their 'one week' anniversary on Saturday, with a trip somewhere on Bradley's bike.

"I want something better," Kathy muttered. "What would convince someone I truly care for them?"

"Time," Stephanie said. "Time and attention. Isn't that what you wished your previous boyfriends gave you?"

Saturday's practice was pretty intense, as the choir continued to learn *Handel's Messiah*, and also practice for the upcoming performances at

Toowoomba. After practice, Debbie and David, Anita and Larry, Cara and Kaleb all declared their intention of going straight to the cafeteria for an early lunch.

The group met Dylan in the cafeteria, and Kathy invited him to sit with them. Dylan was still bitter about his break-up with Annie; and according to Stephanie, this had put an end to the easy comradery the Biology class had enjoyed for almost two years.

Kathy could empathise with Dylan's disillusionment, and went out of her way to include him in the conversation, asking him how his studies were going, and what he was doing as his community involvement. Dylan explained that he had become involved with a local animal rescue group. Members of the group collected sick and injured native animals, and cared for them, until the animals were well enough to be released into the wild once again.

Kathy was pleased to hear Dylan had found something which might take his mind off Annie. Her caring attitude bought an approving smile from Andrew, who also concentrated on making conversation with Dylan.

Sunday was the first day of spring, and one of the few remaining days before the rains commenced. After the morning services and lunch were over, Kathy persuaded Andrew and a few other friends, to go for a leisurely afternoon walk. She took her sketch book along, and drew small botanical sketches of the wild-flowers that were blooming.

Monday, classes launched again, and as there were only three more weeks in this half of the semester, Kathy had to put her personal concerns aside and hit the text books. She had two essays to do one for Psychology and one for Educational theories, in addition to teaching aids to create and demonstrate for Practice Teaching.

Tuesday, Kathy had the university car booked to take her to the local Primary School, where she would hear the children read for an hour. This was part of her Infant Reading subject. She had elected to stay another hour and observe a Maths lesson for her Infant Mathematics subject as well.

Wednesday afternoon in Art, Kathy graduated to weaving baskets with cane. The students began by choosing a pattern and a flat wooden base for their basket. Then they cut a number of pieces of cane into matching lengths and scraped them ready for use. A number of small holes were drilled around the perimeter of the basket, and upright canes were threaded through these holes.

After that, the weaver began circling the circumference of the basket, and weaving in and out of the upright canes, to make the edge. Every second row followed an alternate pattern to the first row. Some more ambitious baskets had stronger support canes, which were threaded around the sides half way up, to hold the shape. Towards the top, the weaving had to turn back upon itself to create a finished edge.

Kathy was surprised to find her basket had an uneven, variegated colour when she was finished. She was told that a perfect looking basket might be sprayed with a neutral cane coloured spray, or even clear coat, to make it appear even in finish. She elected to use a clear coat, because she thought it would give the most natural looking finish.

At tea that evening, Kathy was happy to be able to tell Andrew that she had finally completed something he would consider a 'real traditional' basket. Andrew laughed, and said he always enjoyed hearing about her Art.

Thursday evening, Kathy accompanied Stephanie to the gymnasium to watch Bradley play basketball. Stephanie believed matches were more exciting now that she and Bradley were going out, but Kathy did not agree. Bradley was still the star for his team. Most times they won easily, but occasionally they battled desperately against their opponents.

Tonight they were up against one of the tougher teams. When this happened, Brad's team was inclined to rely on him, and he had to encourage the other members to stay on the ball. Through much catching and passing, and guarding opposition players, Bradley's team managed to draw ahead; with the score being one to their advantage by half time. The opposition fought back, scoring several goals in the second half, but Bradley's team also scored, so they emerged victorious.

After he had a drink, Bradley crossed to the benches, where both Stephanie and Damaris billed and cooed over him. Damaris was still bringing snacks, and tonight she had some little cheesy puffs. Both teams crowded around the little cook as she passed the bite sized appetizers around.

Stephanie regarded the group with amusement. "Do you think Damaris has developed a favourite yet?" she whispered to Bradley.

"You mean outside of me?" Bradley returned provocatively. "I am of course the king for introducing her to this little gig."

"You are my king," Stephanie said. "Of course outside of you – wasn't that the whole point?"

"I think she inclines a bit towards Michael," Bradley said. "In fact, I heard a rumour that he had asked her to the up-coming Chinese Night."

Kathy and Stephanie exchanged glances.

"Um, those particular guys can be a bit juvenile," Kathy ventured. "Should we warn Damaris?"

"I don't think so," Stephanie said. "If he truly likes her, he might shape up."

"Michael and Arthur were only on the very edge of the snobby crowd last year," Bradley said. "And it's been a whole year since. I wouldn't hold it against them anymore. Come on, let me walk you two ladies across to the dormitory. No Andrew tonight Kathy?"

Kathy blushed. "I didn't tell him I was coming over here."

After completing her classes, her cleaning and most essential study, Kathy spent Friday afternoon packing for the trip to Toowoomba. During the performance she would be covered by the choir robe, but she needed Sunday best to go under the robe, some pajamas or a track suit to sleep in, and casual clothes for any hiking or picnicking the choir might do. The Music Master had promised the trip would not be limited to performance oriented activities.

Friday evening at vespers, Kathy could hardly contain her excitement and listen to the message, which was a pity because David had made an effort in his sermon preparation. Andrew gazed at her fidgeting with indulgent amusement, where once he might have been mildly disapproving.

Saturday morning, Andrew collected Kathy at the girl's dormitory, and helped her carry her case and sleeping bag, across to the Music Department, where all the choir had piled their luggage. The Music Master insisted they have one more proper practice before they left, so it was almost lunch before they were all packed into the bus and under way.

The route the Music Master had chosen took them through Kilcoy instead of Brisbane. Kilcoy's main claim to fame was that the half-man, fur-covered beast known as the Yowie, had been sighted around there in the late 1970s. While the creature apparently had its roots in Aboriginal mythology, several theology students remarked cynically they were not surprised the most frequent sightings were during the hippie era, when many men had long hair and beards.

The bus stopped at the Fred Greensill Lake, where they ate a picnic lunch from eskis packed by the cafeteria staff. Kathy's favourite sandwich was the curried egg, but the beef lettuce and tomato were also very delicious, as was some mysterious vegetarian spread, that you would swear was chicken paste. They washed this down with juice from the large flagons.

After lunch the Music Master allowed a half-hour break in which to 'stretch their legs'. Some of the wilder students elected to go for a 'Yowie' hunt, returning with sightings of Willie Nelson, John Lennon and Jon English as well as a few 'mystery Yowies'. David borrowed Debbie's mohair beanie and pranced around the picnic area announcing himself as the "Silver Springs' Yowie".

"I've never seen acting them so crazy," Kathy whispered to Andrew.

"That's because you don't often see the Theology students when they are alone," Andrew whispered back. "Everyone has to have a bit of good clean fun you know."

After the lunch break, the members of the choir clambered back on the bus, and travelled for about an hour, before taking a brief toilet break at Esk. After Esk, they passed through the Deongwar State Forest, before finally arriving at Toowoomba. Toowoomba was around the sixth largest city in Queensland, and was also a centre of education, business and government services.

The choir were booked to stay that night at Toowoomba Anglican College and Preparatory School. The school had a twelve acre campus, ovals and a beautiful chapel. It was a boarding facility and in many ways reminiscent of Silver Spring University for a younger clientele.

The choir would be given temporary accommodation in the sporting facilities, where they could lay down mattresses, and use their sleeping bags. The showers and toilets normally used for changing after sport, would serve the visitors.

The bus arrived around four pm, and members of the choir had almost an hour to set up their make-shift bedding, shower and change if they desired, before attending the school cafeteria for a meal. After tea, they donned their robes and attended vespers in the stunning Saint Aidan's Chapel.

The school had its own noteworthy choir, and the Music Master and Conductor of the School Choir had been exchanging excited emails for some time, regarding things the two choirs could learn from each other. The school vespers program was a relatively sedate enough affair where both choirs assembled and sang several special items each. This was followed by a Bible reading.

After the vespers program had finished however, the two Music Masters indicated that school and university choir members alike were to remain, while the other attendees filed away to their respective dormitories. Then they pulled their music books out and began an impromptu 'sing-off'.

It was hard to say which choir was better. The members of the school choir were younger, but their choir was a permanent choir, and enjoyed regular music lessons. The Silver Springs choir was a mixed choir, and despite their professional presentation, they were a part-time musical group with single weekly practices. In any case, a good time was had by all participants.

The next morning, the students scrambled to pack up their make-shift beds, and return most of the luggage to the bus. Then they attended a service at St. Stephens Uniting Church, where they sang beautiful pieces from their growing Handel repertoire into the soaring arched ceiling of this incredible building. Established in 1863, the building of this church represented an amazing act of faith, because the local congregation were relying upon visiting Presbyterian pastors and the future growth of the parish. The structure was now one-hundred-and-twenty-two years old and as beautiful as ever.

The congregation of the Uniting Church provided them with lunch, and once again, the Silver Springs students were challenged to socialize with a group of strangers. After lunch, they climbed into the bus, and commenced the journey back to Silver Springs. This time the bus took the road through Brisbane, where they met briefly with one of the city churches more directly affiliated with Silver Springs University, who provided them with an evening meal in exchange for a song at their twilight prayer session.

It was dark by the time the choir climbed into the bus for the last leg of the journey. They were also quite exhausted. Three performances in three different organisations, and a little sight-seeing on the side made for a hectic weekend. Kathy fell asleep with her head against Andrew's shoulder. Sometime on the way back she seemed to hear him asking her whether she had a good time.

"Mm, yeah," she murmured.

"I have to talk to you when we get back to campus," Andrew whispered. "But not tonight, we are both too tired."

"That's all right," Kathy muttered, half asleep and very comfortable against his shoulder. "No hurry."

"The Chinese Night might be a good time," Andrew said. "You are coming with me aren't you?"

"Anytime," Kathy murmured. "You know there is no one else."

"Damaris says, The Chinese Night is basically an excuse to ensure the Hospitality students practice their Asian cooking skills," Andrew said, "But it sounds like fun and there is no trip scheduled next weekend."

"Yeah," Kathy murmured.

When the bus drew into the car park on campus, Kathy was surprised to see Stephanie waiting to greet her despite the late hour.

"There is a surprise for you," Stephanie said. "It arrived this afternoon."

"Oh?" Kathy exclaimed. She couldn't imagine what it could be.

"We didn't know what to do with him, and he would not go away when we explained you were on a trip, so we put him in Bradley's room," Stephanie whispered.

"Who?" Kathy cried. "What are you talking about?"

"Owen of course," Stephanie exclaimed. "I remember him a little from last year – he wandered in here - bold as bold, and asked for you."

"We've barely spoken since July," Kathy said. "Indeed, we barely spoke even when I was home in July. I wonder what he could want."

Kathy turned to look for Andrew, who had been faithfully by her side all weekend, to find he was shaking his head. "You have to work this one out yourself," he declared.

Andrew helped carry her baggage to the foyer and then melted into the shadows. He was incredibly principled and discrete.

"Oh no," Kathy exclaimed. "Just when things were finally working out with Andrew!"

"You have to talk to me," Owen was saying intensely, Monday at breakfast. Bradley had managed to restrain her ex-boyfriend overnight, but he had found Kathy as soon as it was morning. "We were together for a couple of years – I even thought we were serious enough to propose."

"I know," Kathy said, desperately looking around for Andrew out of the corner of her eye. He was around somewhere, but was keeping himself surrounded by his Theology student friends. "But in the end, you did not respect what was important to me – my course here! And you were not prepared to wait even another year for me."

"I know my mistake now," Owen said seriously. "I've wasted almost a year, during which we could have been keeping in contact. You graduate at the end of next year even. It seems so close now."

"I appreciate your being able to see things that way, now," Kathy said. "I really do. However, I have changed since we were going out."

"I heard a rumour you were seeing some guy first semester," Owen said. He held up his hand for Kathy's silence. "I know you did not tell me, but I had my sources. Your Mother, for one, could not help letting it slip."

"That is over now," Kathy said.

"I heard that too," Owen said. "And according to your parents, you are not with anyone new this semester."

"Not really," Kathy said. If she had ever described Andrew to her parents, it would have been as Stephanie's good friend, and all round nice-guy, not specifically a boyfriend candidate.

"So please, please let us get back together," Owen cried.

Kathy considered for a moment. This little visit was blowing things with Andrew wide apart, and Owen had been a good boyfriend - at least the first year of their relationship. There would have been a time when she would have thrilled to hear his current protestations.

However, she had moved on too far since then. Even if she had to re-build her friendship with Andrew from nothing, she would prefer his sunny equivocal disposition to that of any other male on the planet.

"No thank you Owen," she said. "Please go home to Armidale."

"You can't mean that Kathy," Owen cried.

"I do indeed," Kathy said. "I admit, last year when you gave me an ultimatum, I was shattered."

"I'm sorry about that," Owen muttered.

"Then I had to pick myself up again and get on with life," Kathy continued. "I had to watch you getting close to Isabella and I had to navigate the dating scene once again myself. As a consequence, I am stronger, and I understand myself much better. I would not go backwards for a million dollars."

"I'm not asking you to go backwards, Kathy," Owen said. "I'm asking you to forgive me and move onwards with me."

"I forgive you Owen," Kathy said. "However, I must move forwards alone."

"Do you truly mean that?" Owen asked.

"I truly do," Kathy said. "I am not angry anymore, I am not hurt, and I am no longer trying to replace you. I have found peace. I am sorry that you have made a trip down here for nothing."

"It was not for nothing," Owen said. "I had to face you and talk to you. I knew a letter or phone call would not get me an absolute answer."

"You have your answer," Kathy said. "I hope you somehow find peace too. Please let me go now, I have classes to get to."

"Would it be alright if I hang around a little longer?" Owen asked. "Bradley said I could chill in his room."

Kathy shrugged. "Who am I to throw you off campus after the journey up here? Consider yourself Brad's guest not mine."

Tuesday night, Andrew slid into the seat beside Kathy in combined assembly. The mild Theology student had been giving Kathy space for over a day now, and she had almost begun to despair his ever making a move back in her direction.

"I take it you've had a talk to your ex?" Andrew asked.

"Yeah," Kathy murmured.

"Was your conversation a healing one?" Andrew inquired.

"I'm not sure," Kathy said. "I forgave him. But we are not getting back together."

"I could see that, as he has been hanging with Bradley," Andrew observed. "Not with you."

"Owen asked if he could stay a while," Kathy said. "I'm not clear why. I don't own campus, so I had to say he could."

"Curiosity I suppose," Andrew said. "The campus lifestyle is unique."

"Brads seems okay with it," Kathy said. "You know how easy-going he can be."

Bradley is easy-going about everything except Stephanie," Andrew said.

"Yeah," Kathy laughed.

"Are you still coming to the Chinese Night with me?" Andrew asked tentatively. "Or is this not a good time?"

"It is an excellent time," Kathy said. "I feared I had imagined you asking."

CHAPTER ELEVEN: HOME FOR THE HOLIDAYS

Wednesday afternoon the Art students were challenged to make baskets from raw materials. The class walked out into the campus bushland area, and selected light plants that might be of use for weaving. After harvesting a reasonable amount of material, while taking care to leave the bush or tree with the ability to grow again, they took their gleaning back to the Art Department.

The twigs were partially dried, and then prepared as fibre for the baskets. The natural materials had to be woven, while they were still green and flexible. Kathy enjoyed the truly natural process of creating something from the environment, and while her selected plant was difficult to work with, she promised herself to experiment with other plant fibres.

Thursday afternoon, Kathy went shopping in Northcoast with Phoebe, Joelle and Debbie. The university car, driven by Luke, dropped them off in Northcoast, but the plan was for Hank to meet them after his work finished, and drive them back to campus. None of the girls could afford a new dress at this point in the year, but each hoped to get just the right element to transform something from her existing wardrobe into a new outfit.

The girls entered the teen shop first, as the prices here were usually lower, and there was often something on sale. Phoebe was lucky because she immediately found a scarlet top in a jersey knit. It had a boat neckline and frill which hung from the neckline, and even extended across the sleeves. It was not a peasant style, but tended more towards the highly fashionable eighties' bat-wing silhouette.

"I will wear this over my black skirt," Phoebe announced.

"That should look very nice," Joelle pronounced. Living in such close proximity, the girls were familiar with each other's wardrobes.

"This is nice," Joelle said next, picking up a chiffon blouse with cap sleeves, in a fabric that featured large black spots on a white background. "But didn't someone have something like this last time?"

"Does it really matter?" Debbie asked. "To a certain extent, being in fashion involves being similar."

"Maybe," Phoebe murmured. "It's really up to you."

"I think I'll look a little further," Joelle said. She picked up a top which was denim in colour, but lightweight in fabric, more like cotton. It was singlet style, except it had been cut just over the chest-line and a ruffle had been inserted. The ruffle continued all the way around, even crossing the sleeve. "Different," she remarked.

"Actually I love that," Kathy exclaimed. "Playful but not too sexy, hand it over if you do not want it."

"What will you wear with it?" Phoebe inquired.

"I don't know," Kathy said. "Maybe my white skirt."

"I don't think I'm going to find anything in here," Joelle announced, looking around. "Let's go to the import shop."

The girls' continued up the hill to the store which had tie-dyed and other imported clothing. Joelle chose a long yellow wrap skirt with a black leaf print. She planned to wear this over a plain black skivvy.

"Does Stephanie want anything?" Phoebe asked. Last time they had gone shopping, Kathy had been commissioned to purchase material for her room-mate.

"No," Kathy said. "Stephanie is busy unpicking the hem of a tartan bolero, that she made during the holidays, and combing the ragged edge into a fringe. She has also sewn sequins at intervals on the pattern."

"Creative," Phoebe commented.

"Outré," Joelle remarked. "Stephanie's sense of fashion always mixes eras. I used to tease her about wanting to see her wearing the latest trends, but she always preferred her own designs."

"Given that Brads will probably wear his leather jacket, Steph's doubtless got it right," Kathy observed.

Their shopping completed, the girls walked towards the Northcoast motor repair workshop. Although it was late night shopping for the retail stores, the workshop would close at five-thirty, and Hank would be free to join them.

They girls arrived a few minutes early, and had to wait around for Hank to finish. While they were sitting out the front, on a bench conveniently placed on the main street, Joelle noticed Bradley's bike pull up at the train station. When they saw his passenger remove their helmet, Kathy recognized Owen.

"Excuse me a minute," Kathy said to the other girls and crossed the road. Although it was a train station, the bus to Armidale left from there as well. "Hey there guys!"

Owen looked pleased to see her. "Hello Kathy," he said. "I tried to call you at the dormitory, but there was no answer."

"Are you leaving?" Kathy asked.

"Yeah," Owen said. "Bradley has been good enough to look after me most of the week, but I do feel I'm in the way. With our relationship over, I don't really have any reason to hang around."

"I'm glad you enjoyed your stay," Kathy said.

"I've seen you occasionally sitting with a particularly clean-cut young gentleman," Owen said. "Something tells me that is the way the wind is blowing in the future. Am I right?"

"That is Andrew," Kathy said. "I probably mentioned him as a friend last year, but I hope he will be much more one day."

"Well with this Chinese Night coming up, it would have been weird if I'd still been around and you had a date," Owen said.

"One day, I hope it won't be weird," Kathy said. "You can attend with Bella or whoever you have found, and I will attend with my partner."

"If we even live anywhere near each other by then," Owen said soberly. "Where is this Andrew from Kathy?"

"Canberra," Kathy replied. "But as a minister, he could really be transferred anywhere."

"Exactly!" Owen exclaimed. "Well I hope it works out for you this time Kathy. I had my doubts about the other one, your parents liked him, but they had never met him."

"That was over as soon as it began really," Kathy said. "I must admit, I was really only filling in time."

"It is interesting you should suggest I get back with Isabelle," Owen said. "I sometimes get the feeling she wants to try again."

"You two seemed really suited," Kathy pronounced generously. "While I was hurt, I was almost surprised it had not happened earlier – when we were long distance. And I think it was rough on her that you were so quick to break it off."

"Time will tell," Owen said. "At least I've seen what is really going on here with you."

Bradley was gesturing frantically that the bus to Armidale was approaching. Owen kissed Kathy on the cheek and picked up his luggage. "So long Kathy."

Kathy turned back to the girls who had been waiting at a discrete distance. They were trying not to appear nosy. None of them knew Owen very well, and they figured it was not their business.

"Hank is ready now," Phoebe announced. "Do you girls mind if we drop by his house so he can grab a quick shower? He is covered in grease. You will be perfectly safe – he is boarding with a middle-aged lady."

During lunch on Friday Kaleb asked Andrew about the small prayer group, that Andrew had run for a while the previous semester. Cara had attended once or twice, and apparently it had been instrumental in their romance.

"The prayer group was also good for me because I don't preach yet like you second years," Kaleb explained. "I was wondering if you are not planning on running it this quarter, whether you would mind if I did?"

"I'm certainly happy for you to lead the group," Andrew said. "Between preaching and choir, I am very busy. If you choose the right afternoon, I could still attend however."

"What about you Kathy?" Kaleb inquired.

Kathy nodded. "I would be happy to attend," she said. Andrew looked pleased and after much discussion a time was selected. The prayer meeting would be held on a non-trip, non-event Saturday night. Many of the Theology students had little interest in the evening television, and would be happy to have another group to attend.

Andrew escorted Kathy back to the girls' dormitory after vespers that evening. He stopped in a pool of shadow, just a few paces before the lighted door, and with uncharacteristic boldness, gave her a peck on the lips.

"You taste sweet," Kathy cried, throwing her arms around his neck and returning the kiss. His mouth did taste sweet, considerably sweeter than Owen ever had and far sweeter than Rob. With kisses like that, Kathy speculated, she would never have a weight problem, because she would never crave chocolate or cake.

"Really?" Andrew said looking slightly embarrassed when Kathy allowed him to come up for air. "I hope I am doing it right."

"Whatever you are doing - it is perfect," Kathy sighed.

"I had better let you go inside now," Andrew whispered.

"The door doesn't lock until ten-thirty," Kathy murmured.

"But people can see," Andrew said. "I will collect you tomorrow early for choir practice."

"You said you wanted to ask me something," Kathy said. "Or has this anticipated it?"

"I still want to ask you something," Andrew said. "And tomorrow night at the Chinese Banquet would be perfect. Let's not get the cart before the horse."

"Alright then, see you in the morning," Kathy said. She was tired after all, and choir made an early start.

During choir practice the next morning, the Music Master concentrated on the pieces from *Handel's Messiah* he hoped the Choir would perform just before graduation. It was an ambitious learn for a small choir, but they would have the support of a professional music department, with music majors stepping in to sing the solo passages. The music was a little high-brow for Kathy's taste generally, but she found she felt shivers of anticipation along her spine at the thought of being in the gala performance.

After lunch, the girls got to the serious business of making themselves irresistible for the Chinese Night. There had been no indication that it was a costume evening, but the theme had caught the girl's imaginations. Kathy and Phoebe both decided to forego skirts for dress pants, just in case they arrived at the cafeteria, and found everyone was kneeling on cushions instead of sitting on chairs. There was much straightening and crimping of hair, instead of the usual curling, and artificial lotus flowers proved to be a popular hair ornament.

Andrew picked Kathy up at the girl's dormitory around six o'clock. He admired her new ruffled top, and then helped her drape a loose white cardigan across her shoulders, in case of a slight chill as they walked across to the cafeteria. Once inside the cafeteria, the air was warm and scented with Asian spices, and Kathy was able to remove her wrap.

The café was a blaze of colour, with table cloths of red, white and gold plastic, sourced from a party supplier. Hundreds of red paper lanterns also hung from the ceiling. Nineteen-eighty-five was the Year of the Ox in the traditional Chinese calendar, so bright yellow oxen had been cut out of paper and hung around the walls at selected intervals.

Instead of each attendee receiving their own plate, huge bowls of Chinese food had been placed on the table, and the students served themselves using flat Chinese spoons provided for the purpose. The first course was composed of finger foods such as spring rolls, won-tons and dim-sims. Chop sticks were provided, however students were not expected to be able to manage them.

Kathy and Andrew were sitting alongside Stephanie and Bradley, and opposite Michael and Damaris. Despite having to leave her seat at intervals, to help carry bowls of food out, or clear tables for the next course, Damaris was entertaining company, telling them about the ingredients in the dishes and the traditions associated with Chinese feasts.

Michael was from Brisbane and his family had money, so the previous year he had gravitated towards one of the more snobby groups on campus, and even at one stage, made fun of Andrew for his taste in ties. However,

Bradley had ridden Michael strictly in the university basketball league, showing him that a place in the A grade could only be earned by skill and sportsmanship, so he was much better company this year, than he had been the previous.

The second course consisted of large bowls of Mongolian beef, honey chicken, sweet and sour fish, and a delicate ginger chicken. The great thing was that no one had to choose between dishes, but could serve themselves a generous combination of everything. The sweet-meats were accompanied by a vegetarian 'special fried rice' suitable for all.

After they had eaten their main course, Andrew leaned forward and took Kathy's left hand in his right hand. "Kathy dear," he began.

Yes Andrew," Kathy breathed, all tingling and expectant.

"Have you booked your travel for the mid-semester break yet?" Andrew asked.

"No Andrew," Kathy answered in puzzlement. The question was not what she had expected at all. "I can ring the bus company, or go to Northcoast anytime. I was thinking of doing it Monday actually. There are several busses to Armidale a day."

"I was thinking," Andrew said seriously. "That instead of flying from Brisbane to Canberra, I could catch the bus with you through Armidale. It is time I met your parents, and asked their permission to court their daughter."

"You would do that for me?" Kathy's eyes were wide.

"If I was welcome," Andrew said. "I know your parents might not be expecting me..."

"My parents won't mind," Kathy said. "What about staying the first weekend? We would arrive late Friday, socialize with the family Saturday, and attend the local Evangelical Church on Sunday. Then you could continue on to Canberra via Sydney."

"Unless you would prefer me to go straight to Canberra and come back on the last weekend to pick you up?" Andrew suggested. "Then you have more time to prepare your parents."

"I think I would rather tell my parents sooner," Kathy said. "Oh I'm so excited."

"Me too," Andrew said. "I wasn't sure you would say 'yes' quite yet."

"I can't wait until Monday," Kathy cried.

"Let's book over the phone tomorrow then," Andrew said. "Then we just have to go to Northcoast and pay on Monday. We can call your parents and tell them too."

Desert was a novelty combination of pineapple fritters, banana fritters and fried ice-cream. Unlike the mains, these were served in individual servings. Platters of moon-cakes were also laid out on the table, in acknowledgement that the closest of the Chinese festivals was the Autumn Festival, although it was currently spring in Australia.

After the social ended, Andrew walked Kathy back to the girls' dormitory, and kissed her once again on the lips with more confidence. Now that they were going to tell her parents, it seemed he did not mind who saw them kiss. Each kiss was as sweet as the last, and Kathy sincerely hoped that sensation was there to stay.

Sunday morning, Kathy slept in and Andrew thoughtfully waited until time for the Reform Church service to call for her at the dormitory. After lunch, Kathy placed a call to her parents. Andrew had wanted to make the call with her, but she asked him to wait outside the telephone area, in reception. Her parents were intrigued when Kathy requested permission to bring a 'special friend' home. She did not refer to Andrew as her boyfriend, because she was not sure when Andrew wanted to declare them officially a couple. After he had met her parents it seemed.

"Of course you are welcome to bring someone," her father said. "Kathy is bringing a 'special friend'." He relayed to her mother off-line.

Kathy could hear her mother talking in the background. "It's not that Rob is it?"

"Tell Mum it's not Rob," Kathy said, and her father obligingly repeated. "It's not Rob."

"Good!" Her mother exclaimed. "Is it Andrew who was just-a-friend?"

"It is Andrew," Kathy said. "My special friend."

"It is Andrew," her father repeated.

Kathy heard a muttered, "I told you so," in the background as her mother re-counted how many times the name had come up in her letters.

"We haven't booked the tickets yet," Kathy said. "I will ring you back after I have called the bus company. Love you Dad."

"Love you Kathy," Father said. "Call back soon."

Monday afternoon, Andrew and Kathy went to Northcoast to pay for their tickets. The university bus dropped them off at Northcoast station, and they trekked into the small local travel agent. The agent advised them to book their returns at the same time, because the weekend they would be returning would be Labour Day in New South Wales. It was not a public holiday in Queensland, but could be busy nonetheless.

Kathy turned to Stephanie when they both returned to their room that night. "Did you over-hear our conversation during the Chinese Night?" she asked. "Andrew is coming to Armidale to meet my parents. We have just paid for our tickets."

"It sounds wonderful," Stephanie said. "I am not going back to South Australia these holidays either. Bradley is taking me to Melbourne to meet his parents."

"Oh wow," Kathy exclaimed. "Are you going on the bike?"

"We have had a couple of arguments about that," Stephanie said. "It's twenty hours on the bike, and I'm scared."

"Brad will be careful," Kathy said. "I'm sure."

"I wanted to fly," Stephanie admitted, "But Brad said he had the bike, and we ought to use it."

"You will need to take a break or two," Kathy suggested thoughtfully.

We have booked motel rooms at several towns along the way," Stephanie said. "And please don't tell anyone, but the rooms are doubles. Two singles would be a waste of money."

"It sounds romantic," Kathy sighed. "And you will have a lot of fun."

"Half of the holidays will be taken up travelling there and back," Stephanie observed. "We will have less than a week with Brad's parents. And I won't be able to pack many clothes!"

"But think of the wonderful memories you will have," Kathy said. "Memories to treasure for a lifetime. And Bradley will probably like you better without clothes."

"It's not like that!" Stephanie objected. "We will be in Melbourne for our one month anniversary though. I wonder what we will do to celebrate?"

"I'm teasing," Kathy said. "Visit me in Armidale on the way back. You can stay over one night."

"That would mean taking the New England Highway, not the Newell," Stephanie said. "I'll talk to Brad."

Tuesday was the last Aerobics session for the half-semester. Kathy and Stephanie both made the effort to attend, although they both had reading reports to finalise before the break, and time was flying fast. However, the exercise seemed to clear their heads and function as an excellent study break.

Wednesday in Art, the students were still experimenting with natural materials. Kathy had picked some lighter plants this time, more like sturdy grasses, and she found they were highly malleable if not strong. The basket she produced resembled a bird's nest, and she joked about putting it outside in a tree.

"You are doing remarkably well Kathy," the Instructor said. "I have been meaning to talk to you about something."

"What?" Kathy asked, mildly apprehensive.

"I wondered whether you would consider making an entry into the Noosa Shire Art Competition, which is coming up soon."

"Well," Kathy said, considering. "I am flattered you suggested the idea. But then wouldn't we be facing the old art versus craft divide? If a product requires skill and is reproducible, it is downgraded to craft by people who judge that sort of thing."

"I am suggesting the idea to all my best students," the Art Instructor said. "I know you are multi-talented. Perhaps you could work with several media, and throw in something different."

Kathy hesitated.

"I know it is extra work on top of your studies," the Instructor said.

"I would like to," Kathy admitted. "Let me work on a few ideas over the holidays."

Thursday was the last day of classes, and all their readings had to be handed in for the first half of the semester. There was no match scheduled for the men's basketball, as the guys wanted to pack, and a few had left campus already. Kaleb called an impromptu meeting of the prayer group even though it was not a Saturday night.

Cara and Kaleb, Kathy and Andrew, and a few close friends who were not leaving campus until the morning, assembled in the cafeteria lounge after their respective dormitory formalities were finalized. Stephanie had declined to join them as she was tired from her Biology laboratory, and Bradley intended they leave on the bike early in the morning.

Cara volunteered Dylan's mental health as a subject for group prayer, as he continued to be cynical, and lacked his normal comic sparkle since his break-up with Annie. Kathy volunteered Garry's mother's health for group prayer. Although Garry had left campus, many students remembered him. Kaleb added a prayer for protection for all the students travelling that night, the following morning, and any time throughout the mid-semester break.

"What are you doing during the break?" Kathy asked the African American student.

"I am staying here in the dormitory," Kaleb said. "One of the weeks I have to practice preach at Northcoast Uniting Church."

"Ah yes," Andrew said. "First year students practice preach in September. Second years have a longer placement on July."

"It will be quiet around here," Kaleb said. "But I am looking forward to the experience."

"You are not going to Geelong to visit Cara's parents then?" Kathy asked.

"No, Kaleb said. "Perhaps another time. It was not wholly Cara and my decision."

"Oh?" Even Andrew was puzzled.

"The Theology Lecturers want to be able to supervise my first practicum themselves," Kaleb explained. "They felt that in some areas, the novelty could detract from my practical experience."

"What novelty?" Kathy exclaimed. "Your American accent?"

"That too," Kaleb said. He extended his arms in front of them. With the exception of Cara, who had heard this before, his friends stared at him in confusion.

"Because you are dark?" Andrew exclaimed. "But that is racist!"

"Black," Kaleb said. "Say it! I am Black and proud of it."

"We never notice," Kathy stammered.

"You are young and educated," Kaleb said. "In my own country, it would be different, some congregations are predominantly Black. I would serve those congregations."

"I thought segregation was abolished in 1964," Andrew murmured.

"It is voluntary," Kaleb said. "People enjoy fellowshipping with people who they feel are like themselves. I wanted the overseas experience. In Australia, your society is mixed, and yet many cultural groups feel like they are in a minority."

"I still don't understand their proscribing your experience," Andrew said.

"It was not a proscription," Kaleb said. "They just want to see me get my confidence. I want that too."

"Surely Geelong is not such a backwater," Kathy said. "Why it is just west of Melbourne!"

"You would be surprised," Cara said. "There are a few prejudiced people around! It doesn't mean Kaleb can never come home with me - just when the time is right. We want to have a happy visit. Not Christmas unfortunately, because his scholarship supports a trip home for Christmas."

"Another time," Kaleb flashed his brilliant smile. "I don't want to miss seeing my family at Christmas."

Friday morning dawned dull and drizzly. Stephanie hugged Kathy and said, "Goodbye", before the regular six-thirty alarm went off even. It was important to set off before the morning traffic got underway, as Bradley and Stephanie hoped to cover many miles that day, and would have to travel carefully given the weather.

An hour later, Kathy was dressed herself, because Andrew and she intended to catch the mid-morning bus from Northcoast to Armidale. There, he would finally meet her parents, which was an exciting thought. The only other boy she had ever taken home, had been Owen and her parents had already known him.

CHAPTER TWELVE: THE ART COMPETITION

Kathy's mid-semester holidays were a roaring success. Instead of experiencing the usual schism between university life and home, she had visitors from Silver Springs either side of the holidays. Andrew accompanied her to Armidale, with intention to stay the first weekend. He was a huge success with her parents, and soon after meeting them, sat down for a serious conversation with her father.

Mr. Shipton was not the sort of father who loomed threateningly over his daughter's boyfriends, but he was pleased to hear how seriously Andrew had thought things through, and how sincerely he promised to always take care of Kathy. The ministry was important to Andrew, and he was determined to make sure his partner understood what it might demand, but he also considered a relationship a sacred trust, and would endeavor to be attentive to a wife and children.

These things were music to Kathy's parent's ears, as they suspected Kathy had been treated unfairly two times in a row by previous boyfriends. Owen they had known for a long time and partially excused, upon grounds of his extreme youth when commencing dating Kathy, but Rob sounded like the sort of good-time boy, that no parent wanted their daughter dating.

Andrew had attended the local church with Kathy on Sunday and allowed himself to be introduced around as her 'boyfriend'. Monday morning he had reluctantly continued his journey to Canberra for the rest of the holidays. He had called several times in the evenings during the subsequent weeks.

Kathy's other visitors were Stephanie and Bradley, who roared in on the Honda around lunch time, the Saturday before the holidays concluded.

Kathy was proud to introduce her room-mate to her parents as well. Kathy's parents appeared to like the steady Stephanie and her even-tempered boy-friend.

Mrs. Shipton was a little inclined to advise Stephanie to persuade Bradley to trade the Honda in for a car, which she considered "so much safer". Stephanie agreed with Kathy's mother, that a car might be more convenient at least, and she hoped Bradley's interest would eventually turn in that direction. However, Stephanie had too accommodating a nature, to actively persuade Bradley against the motor-bike.

Stephanie and Bradley spent a happy afternoon and evening with the Shipton family. They then stayed the night, leaving just after breakfast to commence the last leg of the journey back to Silver Springs. Kathy herself boarded a bus for Silver Springs on Sunday around noon, arriving at Northcoast around eight o'clock in the evening.

Andrew had commandeered the university car, and was waiting with Luke to meet Kathy at Northcoast station when the bus arrived. The bus driver unloaded her cases, and the boys stowed them in the boot of the car.

"Welcome back," Luke said.

"It is good to see you, Kathy dear," Andrew said, and gave her a big kiss.

They climbed into the car and drove back to campus, where Andrew helped unload her bags, and carry them to the room on the first floor. Then knowing university regulations would not allow him to linger in the girl's dormitory rooms, Andrew promised to see her in the morning and left.

Kathy was surprised to find she had beaten Stephanie back to campus. When Stephanie arrived nearly an hour later, she explained that it had been safer to stop and take a rest every two hours than aim to arrive back at campus in day-light.

"I'm swimming in soft drink and junk food," Stephanie said. "But that won't matter as we won't get much during the semester."

Monday afternoon, with classes and other chores completed, the couples were sitting on the lawn outside the cafeteria, enjoying some sunshine. Bradley was sprawled out on the grass with Stephanie seated between his long legs, and was playing with her long dark hair, which reached nearly to her waist. Stephanie hated knots in her hair, so she had taught Bradley to braid. One long twist completed, Bradley rested his chin on the top of Stephanie's head.

"I'm so happy," Bradley said. "If I died tonight, I would go straight to heaven."

"That's very poor Theology," Andrew remarked.

"It's bad Psychology too, Bradley," Stephanie said. "I wouldn't want to lose you."

"If human love is this good," Andrew remarked from a similar position, where he was relaxing with Kathy, "Imagine how powerful God's love must be."

"Who let the Theology police in here?" Kathy inquired, and Andrew nuzzled the tip of her nose.

"You know you love me like this," Andrew said.

"Yeah I do," Kathy agreed happily.

"Oh Stephanie," Bradley complained, "Do put that book down."

"I've got assignments Brad, and I can never rush them last minute like the rest of you," Stephanie objected.

"Do you know what this one did?" Bradley exclaimed. "We couldn't take her books on the bike, so she joined the public library in Melbourne."

"Imagine that," Andrew said. "Luckily the main book I need is a Bible and it can go most places with me."

Tuesday evening Kathy and Stephanie were getting ready for bed, after completing their Aerobics session which, had been a satisfying work out. Kathy turned to Stephanie thoughtfully.

"Please don't mind me asking," Kathy said. "You don't have to answer if you don't want – but did you and Bradley go 'all the way' when you stayed in the motel rooms?"

"No, we didn't," Stephanie said. "We were far too happy kissing and cuddling."

"You have two more years of your course before you can get married," Kathy said. "Are you really going to wait that long?"

"I don't know," Stephanie frowned. "I would like to wait until at least a significant anniversary, like one year. I also dislike the idea of sneaking around campus trying to pretend we don't do it together."

"That would be a downer," Kathy agreed.

"While we are on the topic, did you and Owen ever go all the way?" Stephanie asked.

"No we were too young," Kathy replied.

"Said who?" Stephanie asked.

"Said me!" Kathy answered. "We were high school kids and just wanted to have fun. Then I came here and we were long distance."

"Rob?" Stephanie asked.

"I didn't want to," Kathy said. "Scared, lack of attraction I guess. You and Garry?"

"Not together long enough," Stephanie said. "Two holiday breaks where we corresponded, and one semester really."

Wednesday in Art, the students returned to weaving with cane and they were also introduced to rush, which had to be moistened before use, and Chinese sea grass. The work was tedious, but Kathy persisted because she knew that only practice could bring proficiency and neatness.

During the lesson the Art Instructor approached Kathy. "Have you thought any more about the Noosa Shire Art Competition?" the Instructor asked.

"Yeah," Kathy said. She pulled one of the sketches of Bradley looking out over the valley she had done earlier that year out of her folder. "I thought, not just a portrait, but I might build the mountain up in three-D below him."

"Hmm, who is the boy?" the Instructor asked.

"Bradley Parker, my room-mate's boyfriend," Kathy replied.

"You might need permission from him, but otherwise it sounds great," the Art Instructor said. "Let me know if you need more access to the room and materials."

There were only six weeks left in the men's basketball competition, and Stephanie begged Kathy to watch all the matches with her. Her room-mate explained that it could be dull sitting alone, or with only Damaris for company, depending on how many other girl-friends and spectators attended.

"Bradley's team is almost at the top of the chart again," Stephanie cried. "I'm sure they will make it to the finals."

Kathy agreed, although as she was a little behind her room-mate in completing her assignments, she took that week's Education reading down to the gymnasium. Hence she missed much of the game, which Stephanie assured her was very exciting.

"I'm sure Brad is wonderful," Kathy said, her eyes glued to the page. "I'd be happy to look if only the Education Lecturer had not made any reading due this week."

Stephanie relaxed her efforts to talk to Kathy, and began to talk to Damaris. Apparently the Hospitality student and Michael were still dating; and Michael had likened her cooking to the menus of some exclusive restaurants in Sydney and Brisbane.

"He says he will take me someday," Damaris said. "As I'm from Newcastle and he is from Sydney, we really aren't too far apart."

"Dylan is from Newcastle," Stephanie said. "Did you two ever meet before Silver Springs?"

"We know a few of the same people," Damaris said. "But no, he is a couple of years older than me and we didn't go to the same school."

"What is Newcastle like?" Stephanie asked curiously.

"It's cool," Damaris said. "The main central business district is on a steep hill, and I've heard there were competitions between the churches regarding which one could build on the highest point."

"It sounds interesting," Stephanie said.

"There are several newer shopping complexes just opened in the suburbs," Damaris said. "That has made it a lot more fun to live there."

"Yeah," Stephanie said. "I love shopping, but I never have the money."

"I will be working after the end of this year," Damaris said. "But of course, a girl never has enough money for shopping."

"Where would you like to work?" Stephanie inquired.

"Depends," Damaris said thoughtfully. "I've sent my resume to a few places already. Restaurants in Newcastle, a hospital that needed a chef in Brisbane, Sydney so I would be near Michael's family, even here."

"The cafeteria here?" Stephanie asked.

"Yeah," Damaris said. "That would be handy."

"It certainly would," Stephanie said.

Bradley shot the final goal for his team and the match ended. One more step up the ladder, and now his team would have to defend its position, until the end of the season. Kathy packed her reading away, and prepared to offer her congratulations to the winning team.

Kathy had not really been keeping up with viewing *Neighbours*, nevertheless she was shocked when she dropped by the recreation area, to be told that Channel Seven was axing the show. Students who were keen fans, were avidly tuning in to the final month of episodes, and following the intense media speculation that another station might pick up production of the show. It was rumoured Channel Ten was interested, but no one knew for sure.

Saturday morning choir practice commenced again. Andrew collected Kathy at the reception of girls' dorm and the couple walked across to the Music Department together. The choir was a little rusty after the break, and the Music Master put them through all the preliminary drills and voice exercises again. Then he reviewed their known repertoire, reminding them of all their parts and how to harmonise as a group, before introducing one or two more Handel pieces.

Although they had not been learning *Handel's Messiah* in order, the choir now knew most of *Part I*: including the "*Sinfony*", "*Comfort ye*", "*For unto us a child is born*", and "*Glory to God*". There was much excitement when the Music Master announced that the following week would bring another performance. They would be going to Maryborough, which was only one-and-a-half to two hours away. The trip would only be a day trip.

As the present weekend contained neither a major social event, nor a choir trip, Kaleb called a meeting of the prayer group. David and Debbie,

Larry and Anita, Andrew and Kathy all attended, as of course Kaleb's steady girl-friend Cara.

One of the first things the group prayed about was giving thanks to God, for his protection over the holiday period. As far as was known all Silver Springs University students and their families had travelled safely on the roads, both to and from campus.

Kaleb had also prepared some current events for the students to pray about. Issues of concern included Israel's conflict with the PLO, President Gorbachev's diplomatic missions, and the safe landing of the space shuttle missions Atlantis and Challenger.

After Kaleb had presented his substantial prayers on current events, Kathy felt a little silly putting forward her concerns, which were assignments due in the next few weeks. However, as it turned out, that was a personal concern for most students, and was accepted as a fit subject for prayer.

After the prayer meeting closed, the couples lingered in the cafeteria lounge talking. As the café lounge was one of the few venues open to both males and females in the evening, it was as good a place as any to spend a Saturday night. Finally Andrew walked Kathy back to the dormitory and kissed her good night.

Sunday morning, Kathy slept in as long as she could, which was to a little after nine o'clock, because she knew Andrew would be picking her up for the Reform Church service. When he arrived, she was surprised to see he was carrying a bouquet of flowers.

"What is the occasion?" Kathy exclaimed.

"Tomorrow will be exactly one month since I asked you to take me home to meet your parents," Andrew said.

"At the Chinese Night - I remember," Kathy said.

"And you said 'yes'," Andrew said. "I don't know about you, but I consider that our anniversary."

"These are beautiful," Kathy said, burying her nose in the flowers. "Where did you get them?"

"The service station at the end of University Drive I'm afraid," Andrew said. "There is nowhere else around here on a Sunday."

"It is very romantic of you," Kathy said. "Thank you."

"I would like us to go out to Northcoast tomorrow afternoon to celebrate," Andrew said. "Not just hang around campus. Your assignments permitting of course."

"I do need to work on assignments, but I'll see if I can spare an hour," Kathy said coyly. "What about your Greek?"

"I seem to have got the hang of that at last," Andrew said with a grin. "I'll wait here if you need to go back to your room, and put those flowers in water."

"It could make us late to the Reform Church service," Kathy warned.

"Let's forget the Reform Church service for once," Andrew said. "Neither of us belongs to that denomination, and we had worship last night basically. I would like to go for a walk with you instead."

"Andrew, that is living dangerously," Kathy exclaimed. "I never thought I would hear you wanting to miss a church service!"

Kathy ran back to the room and collected one of her hand-made vases. Then a quick trip to the bathroom to get some water, and the flowers made a proud display on her desk. As a quick afterthought, she kicked off her high heels, and donned a pair of flat shoes. Then she ran back down to the foyer.

Andrew was waiting, and the couple linked hands and headed towards one of the campus walking trails. They had about two hours to spare before lunch, so they wandered along at a leisurely pace. Eventually they came to a style, which Andrew gallantly helped Kathy over. Beyond the style was a rough road, and in the distance, they could see the small mountain after which their town was named. Mount Silver Springs was situated on private property, but permission could be sought to climb the small peak.

Andrew and Kathy did not want to go too far and miss lunch, so they turned back and made their way gently towards campus. While they were deep in the tree covered area, Andrew pulled Kathy off the path and into a small clearing sheltered by bushes.

"Do you trust me?" He asked.

Kathy nodded, and Andrew bent his head to give her a kiss. Kathy slid her arms around his chest and pulled herself closer, please to feel Andrew's arms closing around shoulders. Any fears she may have harboured that a young man aspiring to be a minister would not be an affectionate partner were soon laid to rest.

Stephanie was impressed by the flowers and remarked that Andrew had good taste. "Of course he has to because he is going out with you!" her room-mate joked.

During class, Kathy agonised about what to get Andrew as a present. Nothing seemed too little, and most things seemed too much. In the end she visited the campus gift shop between classes. She knew that Stephanie and Bradley had exchanged cards on their early anniversaries, because Stephanie had a few in her bedside drawer. It was hard to find a card with the right words, but she eventually found a blank card with a suitable picture.

Kathy knew Andrew would love one of the bookmarks imprinted with a Bible text, so she bought one and slipped inside the card. The bookmark had John 15:12 printed on it: "This is My commandment, that you love one another as I have loved you," which Kathy found highly appropriate. The quote was from the New King James Version, which combined a nice amount of poeticism and readability.

After eating lunch in the cafeteria with Andrew and her friends, Kathy returned to her room to lightly touch up her make-up, and prepare for their anniversary date. Andrew arrived to collect her about half an hour later. They linked hands and strolled toward the university car pick-up area.

"I found out that the university car could be booked to take us a few places other than Northcoast," Andrew said. "So I have taken the liberty of booking a trip to Eumundi. It is close and while it is apparently quite small, I have never been there."

"Nor have I," Kathy exclaimed. "You are very clever Andrew. Eumundi sounds much more romantic than Northcoast."

"There is no market today," Andrew warned her. "The market runs on the weekend."

"That's okay," Kathy murmured. "There is sure to be something."

They boarded the university car and traversed the short distance to Eumundi, which was turned out to have a romantic Morton bay fig lined main-street. The couple strolled down the avenue hand-in-hand, and looked at the few stores in town. These included several fashion stores, a bookstore and timber furniture workshop. Then they stopped at an old bakery, and celebrated their anniversary with fresh orange juice, together with slices of delicious black forest cake.

The couple sat on a bench in the park for a while talking, and then the university car drew up to take them back to campus. Andrew half apologized he had not organized a longer anniversary date, but Kathy pronounced the timing to be just right, given they both had assignments waiting back on campus.

Andrew was dropping her off at the girl's dormitory, when she remembered the card she had tucked into her purse.

"This is for you," Kathy said with a blush.

"Thank you," Andrew said, going slightly pink. "I have something for you too. I was waiting for the right moment."

He produced a small package which was slightly lumpy, and an envelope that probably contained a card. Kathy unwrapped her package and found an ornamental hairbrush. During the 1980s, where hairstyles were bouffant, hairbrushes were very prized possessions, designed to give the right amount of body and lift to their curls. Andrew's selection wasn't too bad, it was a little fancier than the one she usually used, but at least it was not too fine.

"It is lovely," she exclaimed.

"Look it has your name on it," Andrew said, pointing to the handle.

"So it does," Kathy observed. "Now I won't lose it!"

"I didn't know what girl's liked," Andrew said. "That wasn't to imply your hair was messy or anything!"

"No it's perfect," Kathy exclaimed. "Just personal enough to be romantic. Please open your card."

Andrew was pleased with the personal message she had written in the card and thrilled with the gift of a Bible book-mark. "Thank you," he said, giving her a kiss.

Tuesday afternoon, Kathy took the Art Instructor's offer of extra time in the studio literally, and spent the afternoon working on her entry for the Noosa Shire Art Competition. Bradley had willingly given permission for her to use the sketch she had made of him. Kathy had checked with Stephanie too, making sure her room-mate would not be offended by Kathy painting a portrait of the other girl's boyfriend.

Kathy had decided to work in layers, with the mountain and background scene being the first layer. That afternoon she concentrated on painting a beautiful background, as the landscape would form the majority two thirds of the picture.

Wednesday in Art, Kathy began to weave a fan. This relatively easy item was designed to give her practice weaving. The fan was shaped like a popsicle, and woven around a central piece of dowel, which would form the handle. The desired finish was smooth, as this would demonstrate the most progress in her technique. She also thought she could paint a fancy design on the fan with enamel paints. The idea was drawn from a number of cultures. Kathy hoped that an attractively painted fan or two could be added to her entries in the Noosa Shire Art Competition.

Thursday evening Kathy accompanied Stephanie to the gymnasium, to watch Bradley's basketball match. Michael was playing as well, and Damaris was sitting on the bench watching. Upon seeing the other girls, she moved her bag to allow them to sit next to her.

"Thank you Damaris," Stephanie said.

"Hello Stephanie, Hello Kathy," Damaris said.

"Hello Damaris," Kathy said. "How are you?"

"I'm good," Damaris said. "You two?"

"We are very well thank you," Stephanie replied.

"How is the game going?" Kathy Inquired.

"Good, I think," Damaris answered. "It's hard to tell who will win tonight."

"Ah good, I like those matches," Kathy murmured.

"Umm," Damaris appeared to assess the other girls and make the decision to confide something. "Michael likes to show off a bit doesn't he?"

she ventured.

"Most guys do," Stephanie said. "Even Bradley on occasion."

"Last weekend, because there was nothing much happening on campus, Michael took me to Brisbane," Damaris said. "We caught the train at Northcoast like normal students, but once we got there, his family, who were visiting his married sister in Brisbane, had organized their own transport. I wanted to check out the new Sizzler in Annerley, so we went there for lunch on Saturday."

"So far it all sounds lovely," Kathy remarked.

"It was," Damaris said. "It's - hard to explain – Michael wasn't quite himself. He wore a suit, even though Sizzler's is a family restaurant and neat casual was acceptable. And he seemed a bit aloof – like mixing with the other families was below him."

"I'm not sure what to say," Kathy remarked. "To tell the truth, Michael was not part of our group last year."

"I know, Bradley told me," Damaris said.

"Did you get the feeling Michael's attitude was directed at you or the environment in general?" Stephanie inquired.

"It was a general thing, like when he is on campus he is grounded, and knows where he fits in the scheme of things. Off-campus he is no longer sure," Damaris said.

"Did you meet his parents?" Kathy asked.

"Briefly," Damaris said. "They were in a hurry to get back to Sydney. Other than that, they seemed lovely. Although they appear quite well-off, and I couldn't tell what his mother really thought."

"I'm not sure how to put this," Stephanie said. "But Michael has matured a lot since coming to university. There was a time when he might have hung with Tony Dantean and his crowd – but now he hangs with Brad."

"Tony certainly wouldn't have Michael hang with him now that Michael has replaced Tony in the A grade," Damaris observed. "Michael says Tony that still holds a grudge against Bradley over the matter."

"It was Tony's own fault for rough play on court," Stephanie remarked.

"Of course," Damaris agreed. "Bradley just did what an administrator ought. I think Bradley is wonderful. He is really the glue that holds you all together isn't he?"

"I think Bradley is wonderful too," Stephanie laughed. "Please remember that Damaris."

Damaris shrugged. "I've always known Bradley was crazy about you Stephanie! We only did each other a couple of favours."

"If the mature Michael continues to develop, I think you two will be very happy anyway," Stephanie murmured.

"That is about the shape of things," Kathy said. "It might be better if you don't tell Michael we said anything however."

"Of course not," Damaris said. "This is just between us girls."

Friday morning, Kathy handed in her reading reports for both Educational Theory and Psychology. After lunch she completed her cleaning duties, before writing in her journal for Community Outreach and spending some time weaving her baskets. In the evening Andrew collected her for the Uniting Church vesper's programme which they both enjoyed.

Saturday morning's choir practice combined preparation for the Maryborough performances with learning melodies from *Part II* of *Handel's Messiah*. This included "*Behold the Lamb of God*" which was a chorus, and "*Lift up your heads*", which had a delightful echoing effect when sung in parts.

The choir had already learned the *"Hallelujah"*, and Kathy was happy they did not have to learn the solo sections, which would be sung by full-time Music students.

Sunday morning, Kathy had set her alarm to wake her before Stephanie usually stirred. It was an hour-and-a-half to two hour drive to Maryborough, so the Music Master had requested that the students be waiting by the bus, ready to depart by 7 o'clock. Although Kathy did not normally relish waking early, it was almost fun creeping around the dormitory before most of the girls were awake.

Andrew was waiting for Kathy in the foyer around-ten-to-seven, but he did not have her called over the public address system due to the early hour. He picked up her bag for the day, and they walked around to the bus area. After a quick head count and roll call, everyone climbed onto the vehicle, and they were on their way along the Bruce Highway. They passed through Gympie, Curra, Bauple and Tiara before approaching the outskirts of Maryborough.

Their destination was a large town that had prospered from links to mining, farming and industry. The Music Master explained that in the past, Walkers Limited had built both trains and ships, but now as part of Downer Rail, the Maryborough workshops were limited to locomotive construction. There were also some remaining sugar mills, and fishing as a channel connected Maryborough to the Coral Sea. As they passed through the centre of the town, the students noted that many of the heritage buildings had been preserved.

The bus's purpose was the Marybourough Church of the Nazarene. Although many of the students were not familiar with the Church of the Nazarene, during their visit they learned that the church had developed out of the Wesleyan Methodist movement, and despite their association with the Pentecostal movement, retained many connections to the Methodist Church. The Church of the Nazarene also shared many traditional beliefs, including the Trinity and Infant Baptism.

The choir had been booked to participate in the Sunday morning service, which was scheduled for around ten o'clock. They arrived early and were shown into a side room, where they could don their robes. The clouds, which had been grey up to this time, began to drop rain, and the students were forced to huddle in-doors. Finally it was time to take their places near the front of the church. They sung a combination of gospel songs and their Handel repertoire. Kathy thought the Handel pieces sounded especially fine in the large church building.

After the Sunday service concluded, the congregation offered the visiting students a light luncheon in their hall. The food was predominantly healthy salads and fruit, and the drinks were water and juice, because the Nazarenes believed in avoiding drugs of any sort.

Their definition of 'drugs' also included alcohol, tea and coffee. It would be easy to assume this was a typical 'temperance' or 'abstinence' stance, but their reasons ran much deeper. The Nazarenes considered these stimulants, and other societal evils such as gambling, fundamental causes of poverty, and it was one of their denominational undertakings to help the poor. They ministered by example and also by running charitable campaigns.

Around two o'clock, the choir were forced to leave the Church of the Nazarene because they were due at St. Paul's Anglican Church. This ecclesiastical building was an architectural beauty, constructed around 1879 to replace a wooden building which had stood on the site previously.

Surprisingly, in the early days, Maryborough parish was considered part of the Diocese of Newcastle, some 1,000 kilometers (or over 620 miles) away! Kathy reflected this was a day's travel on a bus with two drivers, so she could only guess how long it would have taken bishops to travel by horse and cart.

The beautiful church was somewhat overshadowed by the impressive hall and tower, that had been built on a few years later. The interior of the church was different than Kathy expected, as it had many internal posts supporting the high arched ceilings. The effect of the posts was rather Baroque, whereas Kathy was used to Gothic church architecture. The worship area was also designed to form a rough cross shape.

The choir were situated to one side of the pulpit where they could partially see the congregation, and from there, their upraised voices blended with the quality tones of the organ. The Anglican community was favoured with a selection of Handel pieces from *Part I* and *Part II* of the *Messiah*.

After the programme, which had lasted around an hour-and-a-half, many people lined up to greet the choir, before ushering them into the hall for a light meal and fellowship. The Music Master apologized that they could not linger more than half-an-hour or so, because of the two hour journey back home.

Around four-thirty the bus commenced the return journey to Silver Springs' campus via Cooloola Road. This route was a little longer, but the Music Master had promised they could drive through the beautiful Tuan State forest. The sun began to set around five-thirty, and the light dwindled till just after six o'clock. Luke switched the bus lights on and the party completed the rest of the trip in the dark.

After the excitement of the trip to Maryborough, Kathy found it hard to concentrate on essays and assignments, which seemed exceedingly dull in comparison. Observing this, Monday lunch-time Andrew suggested that she bring her notes to the library, so they could work side-by-side and support each other, even though they were working on different subjects.

Tuesday afternoon Kathy continued work on her entry for the Art competition. One of the wood-work students had obligingly cut out the outline of a slim male figure, that Kathy had traced onto light ply. She was paining this to look vaguely like Bradley, and had the brilliant idea of weaving the figure a jacket from wicker materials.

The outer jacket would be woven around the figure, but she had to wait for the cut-out to dry, after painting on the features and basic clothing. Kathy had also begun molding the mountainside from clay, and fired it once. When it was ready, it would be built up from the lower edge of the frame and secured into place with glue.

Wednesday was Kathy's regular Art class. She worked diligently weaving fans for her assignment. The Art Instructor also allowed her to borrow a few minutes of class time to work on her art competition entry. This involved painting the clay mountain base, and setting it in the kiln for its second firing. Kathy also completed weaving the jacket on the boyish figure and painted it black. She set it aside to dry, as the whole masterpiece would need to be assembled and glued on Thursday afternoon, in order to be ready to meet the submission deadline on Friday.

Thursday afternoon, Kathy was extremely busy completing woven fans and adding painted patterns. She planned for each fan to be unique and different. As some fans would be submitted for her assignment, she had worked hard to make more fans than required, and submit a selection into the Noosa Shire Art Competition.

The Art Instructor unlocked the studio for her especially, and Kathy was relieved to find her mountain base had survived the second firing, and heaved a sigh of relief, because she would not need to use her crude back-up attempt. Kathy struggled to glue the mountain securely to the base, finally accepting Andrew's suggestion, that she screw a small slat of wood along the lower edge of the frame, to form a shelf and support the clay mountain.

With its own little shelf to sit upon, the mountain accepted the gluing process with much more grace, and began to look like it would be secure once the glue had dried. The male figure stood on a flattened ledge Kathy had created near the summit of the clay mountain, and was easily secured using glue.

The Art Instructor had offered to drive Kathy into the Nooosa Shire Council Chambers, to submit her entry into the Art Competition on Friday afternoon. Noosaville was about twenty minutes' drive from Silver Springs, and the university car would have taken Kathy, but the Art Instructor wanted to make sure the entry arrived safely, by helping deliver it in person.

They arrived at the council chamber complex and were directed towards the library, where one of the librarians was taking care of registering entries. The friendly librarian appeared to know the art instructor, and addressed her by name:

"Hello Louise, how are you?" the Librarian queried.

"I am well, how are you?" Instructor Louise answered.

"I am fine," the Librarian responded. "Do you have an entry for us this year Louise?"

"These are from one of my talented students," Ms. Louise said, gesturing for Kathy to bring her painting and fans forward.

"Ah, I see," the Librarian said. "Very creative indeed! We will be proud to display them in the gallery. We are also very lucky this year because Lyn McCrea has agreed to be one of our judges."

"That is wonderful," Ms. Louise said. "I really haven't heard much from her since she moved to Brisbane. How is she?"

"She is enjoying consulting with the corporate sector and doing marketing, but she has not forgotten her love of the community, and wants to encourage young artists such as your friend here," the Librarian explained. "As I said, we are very lucky to have her."

Ms. Louise and the Librarian exchange some more gossip which meant very little to Kathy, who was busy trying to catch a glimpse of any competing works of Art, that had been already delivered to the competition. A shiver of apprehension ran down her spine. What if her entries were not good enough, and she was making a fool of herself by entering?

"I am ready to go now, if you are," Ms. Louise said, and Kathy returned to the real world with a start.

"Yes thank you, Ms. Louise," Kathy said.

"I thought we might grab a celebratory piece of cake at a bakery somewhere," Ms. Louise said.

"I like the sound of that," Kathy said.

"Well come along dear," Ms. Louise said. "Your entry has to stand by itself now. Nothing we can do until the judging is over."

"What if it doesn't win anything?" Kathy asked anxiously.

"It might win, it might not," Ms. Louise said. "The Art world is full of trends, I must admit. The important thing is to have entered."

"Do you really think so?" Kathy cried.

"Oh yes dear," Ms. Louise said. "What is the good of making beautiful things if no one gets to see them?"

Ms. Louise led the way into a bake-house which had a selection of buns and pastries. "What would you like dear? My treat."

Kathy pointed to a wholesome looking piece of apricot pie. "That looks nice."

Ms. Louise bought two pieces of the apricot pie, and ordered two drinks, a coffee for herself and a flavoured milk for Kathy. Ms. Louise began to tell Kathy how she had become interested in the Arts and studied at a university in Brisbane.

The only problem with being out with a lecturer Kathy found, was that she felt obliged to agree with most of what Ms. Louise said. This was probably her own hang-up, Kathy reflected, but it seemed imprudent to contradict someone who had not finalized her mark yet.

Saturday Bradley and Stephanie celebrated their two month anniversary, as they were about one month ahead of Kathy and Andrew. Kathy could not help notice there was much billing and cooing between the couple at breakfast and lunch. According to the calendar, their anniversary would more correctly have been Thursday, but due to Stephanie having a Biology practical in the afternoon, and Bradley playing basketball in the evening, the couple had decided to do something special on the weekend.

After lunch Stephanie showed Kathy the gift Bradley gave her. It was a stuffed rabbit with soft body and long floppy ears. The toy rabbit was crouching loosely on all fours, and had big brown-gold eyes Bradley had assured Stephanie reminded him of her eyes. The plush fur was an orangey-brown with a slight pile, which made it look absolutely adorable.

"Bradley said it was something to cuddle whenever I missed him," Stephanie said. "Not that we are apart much at university – but I guess there are the long holidays."

"I think it is sweet," Kathy said. She was rather wondering how she could drop a hint to Andrew that she might like something similar, their next gift giving occasion.

Stephanie settled the rabbit down on her bed-side shelf just as her name sounded over the public address system. "That will be Brad now. We are going for a ride to the beach."

"Have fun," Kathy said. "If you pass the Art Exhibition in Noosaville, be sure to drop in and view my entry in the contest."

"I'm not sure whether we are going that way," Stephanie said. "But I will ask Bradley if we can. It's so exciting you are in a competition."

"Well, I'll see you later then," Kathy said.

"Bye," Stephanie said. "I may be late – although not past curfew late!"

CHAPTER THIRTEEN: BONFIRE NIGHT

That weekend, Andrew who enjoyed all the religious services, attended the Inter-denominational praise service, before collecting Kathy from the girl's dormitory for the Reform Church service. They arrived at the campus meeting hall and climbed the stairs. Once in the main area they located a seat beside Debbie and David, Cara and Kaleb. The speaker for the day was Larry, and Anita was helping with the song service. Joelle was busy playing the organ.

"Thanks for letting me sleep-in this morning," Kathy whispered.

"I thought it was only fair," Andrew murmured in return. "However, I think it's only fair to let you know, I think you missed the better service."

"I can believe you," Kathy said. "They should swap the services around."

"I don't think the different groups would be willing to let go their time-slots," David who had overheard, remarked.

"Just a thought!" Kathy said. "Maybe in the future there will be more progress."

"Maybe," Debbie laughed. "Times do change, even in the Christian community. Have you thought about what we are going to do this afternoon?"

"I thought we would hang with the others, maybe go for a walk," Kathy said. "Stephanie and I were talking, and we observed it has been a while since we all hung out. Now that we have boyfriends we all tend to go in different directions."

"I think that's partly the fault of the vehicles," David said. "Stephanie and Bradley are often off campus on his motorbike, and Hank is always taking Phoebe back to Northcoast."

"What's on the university social calendar?" Andrew inquired. "For us poor Theology students, who cannot afford vehicles to ferry our ladies around."

"Quiz night this evening if we want to go," Kathy replied.

"I would like a vehicle," David said. "What would you have if money were no problem Andrew?"

"New Sigma I think," Andrew said. "Economical and practical."

"If we are not considering money or practicality," Tom said. "I would like a Honda Accord."

"I would not purchase an Australian car," Kaleb observed. "But I would love to own a Cadillac Eldorado Biarritz back in the US."

"Earth to the boys," Debbie said, tapping the table to regain their attention. "Back here on campus, where we are all poor students - do we want to attend the quiz night?"

"I don't know," Joelle said. "It is not really a recreational activity for us. We have tests and exams all the time."

"This is different!" Kathy said. "We book a table with our friends, eat a meal and compete against the other tables."

"How many to a table?" David asked.

"Eight I think," Kathy replied.

"Well, if Joelle and Tom don't want to – we have six. Debbie and David, Cara and Kaleb, you and me," Andrew observed. "Where will we get our other couple?"

"If Stephanie and Bradley join us, between them they have about a quarter of the brains on campus," Debbie observed.

"I will go and register us then," David suggested. He walked across to the proprietor's desk and penciled his name in as leading a team.

That evening the friends gathered in the cafeteria to participate in the quiz night. A number of tables had been set aside for participants, while students who were not competing could sit on the other tables and spectate. David's team was assigned to table one.

Lionel, Annie and several others from the graduating class, were responsible for asking the questions. Lionel stood up holding a microphone so everyone could hear him clearly.

"We thought we would start with a few easy questions," He said. "Number one – who is the president of the United States?"

Cara's hand shot into the air. "Oh wow," Lionel exclaimed. "Someone beat Kaleb to the draw." Titters ran around the room because Cara's boyfriend, Kaleb, was well known as the only American exchange student on campus. "Cara?"

"Ronald Reagan," Cara replied.

"Correct!" Lionel said. "Question number two – what is a Dell?"

The teams all consulted with one another, puzzled. Stephanie muttered that she thought it was a shaded clearing, but felt that was too obscure for the quiz.

Bradley finally put up his hand. "I think it might be a new brand of computer," he said.

"Correct!" Lionel said. "Question number three – who is the premier of Queensland?"

There was much laughter as many students knew this answer. Someone beat David in raising their hand. "Joh Bjelke-Petersen," they said.

"Correct!" Lionel agreed and assigned a point to the opposing team on table two. "Question number four – who are Michelangelo, Leonardo, Raphael and Donatello?"

Stephanie raised her hand. "Four Renaissance Artists?"

Lionel laughed. "That is one answer I suppose. If I admit it is a trick question – can someone give me another answer? Ah, table three."

"The teenage mutant ninja turtles," someone from table three answered.

"Correct in this context," Lionel said. "Sorry table one. Question number five – who won Wimbledon last year?"

"John McEnroe," answered someone on table three.

"Correct! And for bonus points who won the woman's section?" Lionel continued.

"Martina Navratilova", answered Kaleb.

"Another point for table one," Lionel said.

The questions continued hard and fast, with a battle being pitched between tables one and three. Finally table one drew ahead, and table three had to concede defeat. The prize was meal coupons for the cafeteria. David looked very pleased as his parents were due to visit the next weekend, and he would be able to bring them into the cafeteria to eat.

The others said they would be happy for David to use the prize, although Kathy asked for one ticket to give to Phoebe, so the girl could bring Hank along to the next special event.

Monday night was the semi-final of the women's basketball season. Kathy and Stephanie were going to support Cara and Annie, who were playing against each other that evening, as they were on opposing teams. Although Dylan was still very touchy on the Annie subject, he had been persuaded to attend to support Cara. In fact, Kathy thought he secretly hoped Cara would win, to avenge his hurt feelings. Andrew, Bradley and Kaleb did not normally watch the women's basketball, but as two friends were involved, they also attended.

Cara's team won the toss, and began the game well by taking possession of the ball. Annie's team expertly tackled, and the forward on Cara's team lost possession, without having shot a goal. The forward from Annie's team then went upon the attack, scoring a goal. The back and forth interaction was fierce throughout the game, and the scoring was very even. It seemed almost a coincidence that the referee blew the whistle for fulltime, when Annie's team was one goal ahead. Annie and Cara stepped forward and shook each other's hand.

"Great game," Annie cried.

"Good luck in the finals," Cara said.

Dylan looked disgusted. He turned to leave, but Stephanie caught his arm. "Stay for a minute and speak to Cara," She said.

"It was nice of you to come down Dyls," Cara said crossing to the bench to greet her friends. "I know it's been tough for you."

"Thanks," Dylan said. He avoided looking across the gymnasium to where Herman was congratulating Annie.

"Good game babe," Kaleb said. "A pity Annie's team beat you."

"Thanks," Cara said. She gave Kaleb a quick hug. "I had better go back to the dorm and shower. I will see you at breakfast Kaleb."

"Night babe," Kaleb said. "You want me to walk you to the dorm?"

"Oh sure," Cara laughed.

Kaleb turned to Dylan, "You are welcome to come with us man."

"I think we'll be walking back too," Stephanie said, taking Bradley by the hand. Kathy and Andrew followed more slowly, as the evening was pleasant, and the stars were beginning to come out. It was also a nice night for kissing just around the corner from the dormitory door.

Tuesday Kathy had a full morning of classes, and after eating lunch in the cafeteria with her friends, she cleaned the first floor bathrooms. As she had devoted a lot of time to her Art competition entries the week before, Kathy needed to catch up with reading reports for Educational Theories and Psychology. She also had to produce learning aids for Infant Reading and Infant Maths.

After tea, Kathy felt like she needed a study break, so she had a shower and did her hair nicely for combined assembly that evening. When Andrew called for her at girls' dormitory, he exclaimed that she looked very nice.

Wednesday afternoon in Art, Ms. Louise told Kathy that she had phoned the organisers of the Noosa Shire Art Competition, and been given the news that Kathy's entry had scored an "honourable mention". The exhibition would soon be finished, and Kathy would be able to collect her Art works by Friday.

Thursday evening was one of the men's basketball semi-finals. The team Bradley was facing was Zach's team, which had won the final last semester. That meant this match was very intense because if Bradley's team did not win, they would not make it to the finals at all this semester.

At first it appeared everything was against them. The opposing team won the toss, took possession of the ball, and scored several goals in quick succession. Bradley felt his team almost break under the pressure, and began to do most of the work himself, always a risky strategy for a captain. However, with his superior height, he was able to intercept several balls and score baskets from improbable distances.

The effect this had on the opposite team was to make them all cluster around Brad, who seeing that his vice-captain was now in the open, made an unexpected pass, hoping his team-mate would pick up the action. The vice-captain caught the ball and dribbled before shooting another basket for their team. Half time, the scores were even, but Bradley was absolutely exhausted.

The team met in a huddle, and Stephanie and Kathy on the spectator's bench imagined Bradley was exhorting his team mates to, "Up their game," and support him. When play recommenced, the pep-talk appeared to have worked. While the opposing team nervously circled Bradley, his supporters in the forward positions shot several goals. By the time the senior team worked out the strategy, Bradley's team was safely in the lead. It appeared that Zach's team were not used to falling behind, and their catch-up strategies were wild and desperate.

After Bradley's match concluded, he went outside to get a drink, before joining his friends on the bench to watch the B and C grade matches. Kathy had no close friends in the B grade, and Dylan's C grade team had not made the finals, so she and Andrew left the gymnasium to walk leisurely back to the girl's dormitory. Stephanie remained at the side of her conquering hero and joined Kathy in the room much later.

Friday afternoon Kathy had the university car booked to take her to Noosaville to collect her entries into the Art Competition. Andrew accompanied her to keep her company, and help with the carrying. As she did not expect to be long in the gallery, Kathy asked Luke to keep the car waiting while she collected her materials. He agreed, on the condition that she would be ready, by the time he was due to make his next pick-up in Northcoast.

Kathy found her painting was still on display in the gallery. As it had some extra weight, it had been placed on a supportive stand instead of being hung on the wall. Her certificate of merit was lightly attached to the frame, and her fans were spread out on a low table nearby.

The librarian who had helped Kathy register her entry recognized her and gave approval for her to remove her art works. "They were really good quality for a beginner," the Librarian said. "I'm not surprised you got a certificate."

Kathy and Andrew returned to the university car, Andrew was carrying the painting, which he stowed carefully in the boot; and Kathy was clutching her precious certificate.

"I wonder," she said reflectively to Andrew, "Do you think it is vain of me to exhibit my works?"

"I don't see why," Andrew commented. "God does it all the time - Psalm 19 verse 1: 'The heavens declare the glory of God; and the firmament shows His handiwork'."

"That's sweet," Kathy said.

"I think your creativity is a gift from God and you ought to use it," Andrew pronounced.

"What about 'no graven images'?" Kathy quoted loosely from the commandments.

"Well, we are not going to worship your pots or your paintings," Andrew said. "So they don't transgress the law as far as I see it."

The university car stopped at Northcoast station just then, and Joelle and Tom got in. "Hi guys!"

Saturday the choir continued to practice *Part II* of *Handel's Messiah*, and also learned some movements from *Part III*. The main choruses were "*I know that my Redeemer liveth*" and "*Since by man came death*", with much of the third part being sung by soloists.

The Music Master caused great excitement, when he announced that a last minute trip had been organized, to perform at Caloundra the next day. Caloundra was about fifty minutes south-east, and was the last major town on the lower edge of the Sunshine Coast. The trip would only be a day trip, with one performance scheduled, but it would be fun and the students would get to see the surrounding country-side.

That afternoon, Kathy met David's parents. They were a nice middle-aged couple, both very much like David himself. They were also very proud that their son was training for the ministry. It made Kathy think about the special moment she expected would come very soon, probably sometime around Christmas or the New Year, when she would get to meet Andrew's parents.

The next morning, members of the choir climbed on the bus around eight o'clock. They were due in Caloundra around ten o'clock, but the Music Master was cautiously early as usual. They climbed onto the bus and drove for around an hour, travelling down the Bruce Highway until they passed the Big Pineapple. The Big Pineapple was a sixteen metre tall statue of a pineapple. It housed cafes and souvenir shops.

The Music Master would not allow the bus to stop in the morning because they were on their way to divine worship, but promised they might stop on the return journey. The bus turned east after the Big Pineapple, and passed though the beautiful tourist area of the Sunshine Coast, finally arriving at Caloundra.

The town of Caloundra had been established around 1875 from the development of land purchased by Robert Bullock. It became a popular tourist attraction because of its beaches and was also a key site for defense installations during World War II.

The choir were booked to perform at the Baptist Church in Caloundra. The regional Baptist community was known for its efforts in providing for the needs of disabled persons around the Sunshine Coast area.

The Caloundra Baptist congregation was also remarkable for undergoing a revival in recent years due to their acceptance of some charismatic principles. In recognition of this circumstance, the Music Master had designed a program which included some of their more rousing choruses, some classic Handel and a traditional hymn or two. After the service, the students mixed with the congregation, who all proved to be lovely community minded people. They ate a shared lunch in the church hall, and visited the nearby botanic gardens.

On the return journey, the Music Master was true to his word and allowed the bus to stop at the Big Pineapple. The students were all glad of the free time to browse through souvenirs, and stroll around the grounds. Kathy bought a pencil case as a reminder of the trip, and it was almost time for tea when the bus arrived back at Silver Springs.

Monday evening was the women's basketball grand final and a number of girls from the Aerobics class went along to support Annie. Kathy, Cara and Stephanie were amongst the group of spectators, much to Dylan's disgust. Kathy reflected that it really was awkward finding themselves in a tug-of-war between friends.

Kathy had always thought of Dylan as a fun guy, and he had always taken his rebuff from Cara so docilely, that no one had expected to find this bitter side to him. She could only imagine what it was like in Stephanie's Biology class – although Stephanie assured her that everyone concentrated hard upon their subject tasks.

Annie's team won and Herman escorted the older girl back to the girl's dormitory in triumph. Their relationship appeared to be settled onto solid grounds, despite its rocky foundation in the jilting of Dylan. Kathy wished them all the best, although she wondered whether Herman would go back to Germany at the end of the year.

Tuesday was Guy Fawkes Day, which commemorated a failed attempt to blow up the British Parliament in the year 1605. In honour of this holiday, the campus social committee had planned a bon-fire evening, for the coming weekend, to be held on the beach where it would be safe to light a fire and let off fire-works.

The other notable thing about Tuesday, was that while Kathy and Andrew, Bradley and Stephanie were lingering in the women's assembly area after combined assembly that evening, Stephanie heard her name called over the public address system. Hastening to the foyer, she accepted a call from Garry.

Calls from Garry were less frequent now the couple were no longer dating, but they still kept in touch. Garry said that his mother was feeling somewhat poorly from the radiation therapy. She was experiencing some difficulty breathing a swallowing and the doctors were monitoring her heart. This was due to localized treatment of the chest area.

However, on the whole, it appeared the treatment was successful, and there was no sign of cancer regrowth or any cancer cells outside the area. Kathy was happy to hear the news, as she still had the prayer group praying for Garry's mother on the occasions they met.

Wednesday was Kathy's last full length Art workshop, before her portfolio fell due the next week. She spent the time industriously weaving and painting. As her competition entries had been returned in good time, she added the extra fans to her portfolio. The picture of Bradley on the mountain did not fit the weaving assignment, but Ms. Louise had asked to be allowed to display it in the foyer of the Art Department anyway.

Kathy's certificate of merit from the Noosa Shire Council Art Competition was pinned to the notice-board alongside her winning entry. She felt very proud, and grateful to Ms. Louise for suggesting that she enter.

Thursday was the men's basketball finals, and as Bradley was playing, Kathy and Stephanie attended as his personal cheer squad. There was much laughter and friendly rivalry between the two teams, as they lined up before the match. Both teams were thrilled to be playing in the grand final; and even Zach's team, who had been defeated the week before, turned out to watch the game.

Bradley also found himself playing against Michael in the grand final, which was mildly amusing for anyone who remembered, that it was Bradley who had sponsored Michael's transfer into the A grade, to replace Tony Dantean, who had been delivering an excess of fouls. Michael had since been seconded from Zach's team to replace an injured player in the current opposing team.

The match started well, with both teams actively scoring. The watchers cheered loudly, as a high scoring match was always popular with spectators. After the ball went out of bounds, it was returned to play and Michael captured it. He began to dribble, but was intercepted by a player from Bradley's team and was forced to pass. The pass was successful, and another goal was scored for the opposition.

This time when the ball was returned to play, Bradley captured it and dribbled to within shooting distance. At the last minute he passed to his vice-captain, who actually scored the goal. Scoring passed back and forth between the teams, and the spectators were thrilled. At half time it was anybody's game.

During the second half, Bradley's team pushed to score, and were active in defense, slowing the scoring rate of Michael's team. They began to pull ahead, and looked likely to win. Michael, who had often practiced with Bradley, began to guard him in an attempt to hamper his team. However, the team was too well trained, and continued to score, even though Bradley was frequently blocked.

When the final whistle blew, Bradley's team had clearly won. However, everybody agreed Michael's team had played very well. Michael accepted everyone's congratulations, and retreated to a place beside Damaris on the spectator's bench. Bradley came to sit with Stephanie and Kathy. As it was the Grand Final, they all stayed to see the outcome of the B and C grade matches.

Friday evening the last *Neighbours* episode screened on Channel Seven. Some students sneaked away from vespers to watch the programme. It was rumoured that *Neighbours* would return to television on Channel Ten the next year, however, no one knew whether the show would be the same once it was produced by a different station.

Kathy had to content herself with accounts from students who had watched the concluding episode, because Andrew wished to attend the Uniting Church vesper's programme. As she had not watched *Neighbours* consistently throughout the year this counted as only a minor sacrifice, and one of the acceptable changes she had made to become the girlfriend of a Theology student.

Saturday the choir settled down to serious practice of all three movements of *Handel's Messiah*. The Music Master told them he would not be accepting any more bookings for performances that semester, and they would now focus upon the graduation concert. The Music students had all been learning their parts separately, and it would soon be time to put the performance together into a proper rehearsal.

Sunday after the Reform Church service had concluded and lunch had been eaten, Kathy went to have an hour's lie down. Around mid-afternoon Andrew called at the dorms to collect her, and they climbed on the university bus to be transported to the beach for the bonfire night.

Kathy was excited because while she had heard of Guy Fawkes Day, she had never attended a proper bon-fire and fireworks display. The social committee had applied for all the right permits, so they would not be breaking the law lighting a fire on the beach and setting off fire-works.

Some Reform Church authorities disapproved, saying that burning an effigy was not a Christian activity, whatever had happened during the sixteenth century. Other members of the faculty argued that the historical re-enactment was a good lesson, and everybody knew the figure was just a scarecrow made from some old clothing stuffed with straw.

The bus arrived at the beach and the hospitality students helped the café proprietor to unpack the picnic hampers. These were set up on some folding tables ready, however they would not be opened until the right time for the evening meal. In the mean-time, the students were free to walk along the beach as they wished.

"We are lucky it is not raining this afternoon," Andrew observed, looking at the sky, which was relatively cloudless.

"We are lucky it rained most of last week, however," Cara replied. "If the weather had not been wet, the Adventure Club might have lost its permit to light a fire this evening. Then we would have had to make do with a mere picnic on the beach."

"That would have been a bit disappointing," Stephanie said. "I do love a good bon-fire."

"I also like fireworks," Bradley said. He had experienced fire-works before, because consumer fireworks had been legal in Victoria. (New restrictions had been introduced that year, but even under the *Dangerous*

Goods Act 1985, Chinese firecrackers and sparklers were still legal, so long as they were handled by license holders who were over 21 years of age.)

"Come along," Kaleb said. "I will race you to the far sand dune, Bradley."

Bradley and Kaleb sped away both loping along on their long thin legs, while Andrew followed more sedately with the girls.

"The boys are officially mad!" Kathy exclaimed, as Kaleb and Bradley paused alongside the rocky cliff face, and the slightly sturdier Bradley hoisted the extremely thin and athletic Kaleb, onto his shoulders in an attempt to reach a ledge that was visible.

"Bradley is just happy he won the basketball season," Stephanie said.

"And Kaleb?" Kathy inquired.

"Enjoying his visit to Australia – can't you tell?" Cara laughed.

"Obviously!" Stephanie agreed. "But do you ever worry about what would happen if Kaleb decided not to stay in Australia?"

"I honestly try not to think about it," Cara said. "He is here now, and I would have missed so much happiness if I had not gotten to know him."

"You are right not to worry." Andrew said. "Mathew 6 verse 25 and following, roughly paraphrased: 'Therefore I say to you, do not worry about your life...Look at the birds of the air, for they neither sow nor reap... yet your heavenly Father feeds them. Consider the lilies of the field, how they grow...Now if God so clothes the grass of the field...will He not much more clothe you, O you of little faith?'"

"Thank you Andrew," Cara said. "Yeah, Kaleb and I are leaving the future up to God. We don't even know how long his scholarship will last."

"You don't know what will happen, even with Australian guys," Stephanie's face was clouded as she thought briefly about Garry, but then she brightened. "I am so lucky to have Bradley."

"I like to think I have a future with Andrew," Kathy murmured.

"Of course you do sweetie," Andrew said. "Mathew 28 verse 20: 'and lo, I am with you always, even to the end of the age.' That is a promise from God and from me."

"Do you have one for me?" Stephanie asked curiously. "You had a text for Cara and for Kathy."

"Um, it's not a party trick, but you seem like a Psalm 23 sort of girl," Andrew said. "The Lord is my shepherd; I shall not want. He makes me to lie down in green pastures; He leads me beside the still waters; ...Yea, though I walk through the valley of the shadow of death, I will fear no evil; for You are with me; Your rod and Your staff, they comfort me."

"Part of that's awful Andrew," Kathy objected, but Stephanie said it was all right.

"I've had my moments," Stephanie said. "I lost my Grandma, last year Jeff was not the ideal choice of boyfriend, Garry's mum got sick...and God has helped me through those things. I like to think he will be there for me in the future too."

"I love my text," Cara said. "Andrew you should go into the greeting card business!"

They caught up to Bradley and Kaleb, and the merry group divided into courting couples once again. While they were all good friends, and loosely hanging out together, each couple kept their eyes open for rocky outcrops to shelter behind for a kiss or two. Finally Bradley announced that he was hungry. Despite his lean profile, Bradley burnt through his food at an amazing rate, and was always eager to get to the cafeteria for a meal.

On arriving back at the picnic area, they approached the folding tables and began to collect their food. The cafe proprietor had set up a large portable barbecue and hot sausages were sizzling. The organisers catered for all needs, making certain both the vegetarian and traditional sausages were available. There was also a selection of salads, cheese and bread.

The group decided to send the boyfriends to brave the queue beside the hot-plate, while the girl's selected their salads. Bradley collected a couple of hamburger patties and buns, and came racing back to Stephanie, who had filled a plate with her favourite potato, curried egg and Waldorf salads.

"This is bliss," Bradley said, his mouth full.

"Thanks Andrew," Kathy said, accepting the plate he proffered to her. It contained her favourite Kabana sausage and caramelized onion, with a slice of bread and butter.

Cara frowned at the jumble of food Kaleb had on his plate. "He's been here six months and still doesn't know what to do at a barbecue."

"I see food and eat it," Kaleb returned good-naturedly. "You worry about putting it between bread."

"Yeah I do," Cara said, selecting a sausage and piece of bread and butter from the plate. "It's much nicer that way."

"But to a man, it's all food," Kaleb insisted. He demonstrated by consuming great gulps of sausage and onion. Bradley and Andrew laughed as they agreed it was all about the taste, and not about the appearance of the food.

The sun set and the day began to cool off. The leader of the Adventure Club lit the huge pile of wood set up for the bonfire, and it began to burn, at first slowly, but then as the larger logs caught, with a steady glow. The fireworks were safely stored some distance from the fire, and Annie, who was one of the licensed seniors, began to set them off one by one.

Kathy and Andrew settled down in the sand, some distance away from the others, to watch in comfort. As the darkness fell, they could barely see the couples around them, even Bradley and Stephanie, who were the closest.

Andrew bent his head and began to kiss Kathy. He had never undressed her in any way, but his hands still managed to find some of her sensitive areas. Usually Kathy gently pushed him away, but tonight she did not. She lay back in the sand, her head pillowed on a folded jacket and allowed the sensations to flow. She was flooded with warmth, and began to shiver feverishly. Her breathing quickened and Andrew noticed.

"Is something wrong?" he whispered.

"You had better stop," Kathy whispered back. "I think I am getting turned on."

"I'm sorry," Andrew whispered.

"Don't be," Kathy replied. "I'm just a little embarrassed, as we are not alone."

"I know what you mean, but it is a gift from God really," Andrew whispered.

"It's not a gift I feel comfortable thanking him for during prayer meeting," Kathy whispered.

"Agreed - it's a little personal," Andrew said. "So not now, not tonight."

"When do you think?" Kathy whispered.

"I don't know," Andrew said. "When the time and place are right."

"Just kiss me normally," Kathy whispered.

The fireworks continued to go off around them, but Kathy and Andrew were oblivious for the next few minutes. After a while the crackling of the rockets ceased, and Andrew sat up.

"I think they are going to put the dummy on the fire now," he whispered. "Do you want to go closer and see?"

"Sure," Kathy whispered.

Lionel and some of the senior boys dragged the dummy towards the fire. They stopped, braced themselves, and heaved the figure onto the fire. It was an eerie feeling watching the dummy catch alight. Kathy had to remind herself several times that it had never been alive – and had never been human. She could see why some people did not like this part of the celebration.

"I wonder whether the real Guy Fawkes was burned as his punishment?" asked Stephanie who had come up behind them. "I must look it up when I get back to campus."

"No, he was actually hung," Bradley said.

Stephanie looked surprised. "How did you know that?"

"I knew you would get curious, so I looked it up before we came across here," Bradley said. "Now you will be able to sleep easy tonight even though the library is not open."

"I do love you," Stephanie said.

"I love you the most," Bradley returned.

"I love you more," Stephanie retorted.

"I love you the morest," Bradley returned.

"No such word," Stephanie crowed. "I love you the utmost."

"That might be a word," Bradley said. "But it sounds silly. I love you constantly."

"And I love you endlessly," Stephanie responded.

The couple continued having the cutest competition to say they each loved each other the most extravagantly, until Bradley stopped Stephanie's pert little mouth with a kiss. The fire burned low, the café proprietor and his student assistants re-packed the bus, and the students eventually climbed on-board to be conveyed back to campus. Everyone agreed it had been an exciting evening.

CHAPTER FOURTEEN: FOREVER YOUNG

Monday afternoon, Kathy heard that the students could visit the student services office, and have their portraits taken by a professional photographer, who was currently in residence. This service was primarily designed for the graduands, who were costumed in cap and gown, ready for graduation in their portraits, however many couples were attending to have their relationships documented.

As it would be Andrew and her two month anniversary on Thursday, Kathy persuaded him to attend and they had their portrait taken together. When Kathy mentioned the idea to Stephanie, her room-mate ran off to persuade Bradley to participate, and have their portrait taken as well. By the time the picture had been processed, Stephanie and Bradley would be due to celebrate their three month anniversary, and Stephanie thought it was a brilliant idea.

Tuesday night was the girls' last Aerobics session for the year. Kathy and Stephanie had both been attending casually, but they made sure they attended the last evening, and celebrated the first (and as it turned out only), year of the all-girl Aerobics activity on campus. Phoebe, who had been instrumental in organizing the activity, and continued to administer the roll, presented Annie with a bunch of flowers, and thanked her for facilitating the classes.

"We are conscious of all the work you have put in selecting songs, choreographing exercises and leading the classes for us," Phoebe said.

"It has been my pleasure," Annie said. "I have developed a lot of confidence in myself as an exercise leader while running this class, so I have to thank you in turn for the opportunity." Several people clapped and then they all fell upon the orange juice provided by the café for their finale. Aerobics could be a thirsty activity!

Wednesday Kathy had to cart all her weaving down to the Art Department and arrange a display, so that her final mark could be assigned. Andrew helped her carry the items down, and she selected one of the more prominent cupboards to set-up as a showcase for her work. The studio was open for any last minute dabs of paint or twists of twine, but the projects were expected to be essentially complete by this stage.

Thursday was Andrew and Kathy's two month anniversary. It also just so happened to be the Basketball Tea, so they had a double celebration. During the afternoon, they took a walk along one of the bush walks, briefly sheltering under a tree during a shower. The raindrops were barely noticeable under the dense rainforest canopy, and the privacy was just great for kissing!

In the evening, Stephanie was wildly excited, because Bradley would be receiving the A grade season trophy, on behalf of his team. She rushed back to their room as soon as her Biology practical was finished, and began doing her hair and make-up. Kathy, who was adding the final touches to a poster for Infant Reading, laughed to see her normally levelheaded room-mate so enthusiastic.

Bradley and Andrew called for them over the public address system, and the girls descended to the foyer. Andrew was wearing smart casual – which for him was jeans and a nice cotton shirt. Bradley was wearing his team shirt and his best jeans.

The friends crossed to the cafeteria, where they had to part; as Stephanie and Bradley were assigned to one of the team tables, while Kathy and Andrew were seated with all the non-competitors. The first course was savoury bruschetta topped with sun-dried tomato, olives and cheese, followed by a choice of interesting lamb or vegetarian wrap. Dessert was raspberry coconut bites, which were a macaroon-like square topped with genuine fresh raspberries. Vanilla ice-cream was available on its own for anyone with berry allergies.

The presentations began after the savoury was eaten and thought to be sufficiently relished. First Annie stood up, and presented the trophies for the girl's B and C grade winning teams, and out-standing players. Then, as it would have seemed weird for Annie to present the trophy to herself, Bradley took over and presented the women's A grade trophies.

While Bradley was on the podium, he continued to award the men's B and C grade trophies. Then Annie stood again, and awarded Bradley with the men's A grade team trophy. Bradley accepted the trophy and made a speech thanking all his team.

"I have loved being the team captain, but the captain does not make the team alone," he announced. "Every player is important, and every player contributes to each game. I would like to thank you all for attending practice, and giving each match your best effort. It has truly been a great season!"

Bradley then sat down, and Annie gave out two more awards, "Best and fairest" to Bradley's vice-captain, and "Most improved" to the captain of the runners-up. Everyone clapped. They then turned to enjoying their drinks, and having seconds of dessert or ice-cream.

By some co-incidence, the two subjects that had formal essays, Educational Learning Theories and Psychology were both due on Friday.

Kathy had been busy working on hers, and while Stephanie was well ahead on her assignments, she usually gave the final product a quick edit before handing it in. Both girls were ready by the three o'clock deadline and dropped their papers into the box.

They met Bradley down in the Education Department, as he had just dropped his essay into the box too. He asked them to walk them up to the cafeteria, where he wanted to grab some fruit.

"I have been thinking," Bradley said. "That is everything except our journals for Community Outreach handed up."

I cannot believe there is only one more week of classes before study vacation," Stephanie said.

Bradley held Stephanie by the hands and spun her around in a small circle. "I am so happy," he said.

"So am I," Stephanie replied somewhat breathlessly.

"I sometimes think about Garry though," Bradley said. "I want to go and see him, and make sure things are all square between us."

"Okay Brads," Stephanie said.

"Do you want to go to Wollongong this weekend?" Bradley asked. "We both have our studies pretty much under control. A few exams and we are out of here for the long holidays."

"Oh I can't Brads," Stephanie cried. "I have one Biology practical left to write up this weekend."

"I will go without you then," Bradley said. "And when I get back – I have something special to ask you!"

"Oh all right," Stephanie said. "If you must go, take the New England Highway, it is safer than the coast road."

"And it has all those cool corners!" Bradley agreed.

"You can stay with my parents in Armidale tonight," Kathy suggested. "I will give them a call and tell them to expect you."

"Thanks Kathy," Bradley said. "I would arrive well after mid-night however."

"They will leave a key out," Kathy said. "I know my parents. They would rather my friends be safe."

Bradley kissed Stephanie goodbye and hurried away in the direction of the student car park. He didn't have much in the way of luggage, but that was Bradley, when he was feeling impulsive.

Kathy never knew what made her accompany Stephanie to the foyer that evening. It was possibly because tea was just commencing, and there was no good reason, for her room-mate's name to be called over the public address system. Bradley would barely have passed Brisbane, and would certainly not be pausing to use a telephone. Garry would not be calling at that moment, because subscriber trunk dialing did not commence until six o'clock.

As they were descending the stairs, the girls could see two police in blue uniforms. The girls clung together as they crossed the landing because words were not needed to tell them that something was wrong.

"Are you Stephanie Lowood?" The Policeman asked, stepping over the space between the front door and entry to the hallway.

Stephanie nodded wordlessly.

"Bradley Parker had you listed on his license as his next of kin," the Policeman continued. "I regret to tell you that his motor-bike appeared to have broken down, just before he reached Brisbane. He appears to have stopped to try to get it going again, and a passing truck veered off the road and ran over his bike."

"Just the bike?" Stephanie stammered in vain hope.

The accompanying Police Woman shook her head. "I am afraid your boyfriend or fiancé, whichever is correct, is dead."

Stephanie nodded numbly. "He has parents – they are in Melbourne."

"If you will come with us now miss, we will organize notifying them," the Policeman said.

The police took Stephanie to Brisbane to identify what was left of the body or the bike, Kathy never understood which. Stephanie did not return till the next morning, and then was too incoherent to explain. It was incontrovertible however, Bradley was deceased.

Stephanie cried until she developed a migraine headache, whereupon she was forced to take an aspirin and go to sleep. Andrew tried to take Kathy to choir practice, but when the news of Bradley's death was shared, so many students went into shock that the Music Master was forced to reschedule.

When Stephanie awoke, she did not want to look at her Biology practical report, because she blamed it for separating her from Bradley the previous afternoon. Kathy privately thought the report might have saved Stephanie's life, because if she had been on the road-side at that particular point of time yesterday evening, the truck would have hit her too.

Stephanie, however, was full of anger and denial. She harboured dreams of having been there and called, "Look out," in time for Bradley to have jumped out of the way of the oncoming truck. In the end, she threw the draft of her report out of the window to Dylan, who had been her laboratory partner the previous week, and intended to put the report in for both of them.

Kathy spent some hours crying in Andrew's arms. Bradley was her room-mate's boyfriend, but Kathy had gone out with him once or twice herself, and she was also very fond of him. Andrew comforted her, and quoted John 11 verse 25: "Jesus said to her, 'I am the resurrection and the life. He who believes in Me, though he may die, he shall live'," many times.

Although Kathy was a Christian, and believed she would one day see Bradley again at the resurrection, it did very little to help her grief at the time. Bradley might one day be resurrected, thanks to God's grace and Jesus death on the cross, but he would not attend classes with his friends on this earth ever again. He would not graduate with them, and grow old with them. He would never again crack jokes with his lazy drawl, or win another basketball season. Worst of all, he would not be marrying Stephanie, as Kathy was sure he had intended.

Phoebe had spent the weekend at Hank's, under the chaperonage of his middle-aged land-lady. She did not hear the news until Hank dropped her off on campus Sunday afternoon. And when Hank heard the news, he frowned.

"Bradley's bike ought not to have broken down," Hank said.

"We all feel like that," Kathy began patiently, but Hank waved her into silence.

"I am serious," Hank said. "We all think of Bradley as lazy and impulsive, but he really wasn't. He had me check that bike over Thursday afternoon in preparation for the trip – if he decided to make it."

"Really?" Phoebe was wide eyed.

"Yes," Hank insisted. "That bike was in fine working order. It ought to have been able to tour around Australia. This talk of it stopping before he even got to Brisbane is insane."

"Apparently it did," Kathy retorted resignedly.

"Apparently indeed," Hank replied. "Did the police say why – was it just a tyre or something?"

"I don't know," Kathy replied miserably. "What difference does it make?"

Hank appeared to struggle with himself, and Phoebe laid a soothing hand on his arm.

"Don't interfere," Phoebe whispered. "You will only make Stephanie feel worse."

"Of course I won't say anything wild to Stephanie," Hank said, but he continued to look thoughtful.

Monday, Bradley's parents arrived and began organizing the funeral. They had decided to lay him to rest in a plot in Silver Springs Cemetery. That way all his friends could attend the service. They had no family plot back in Melbourne, and knew that Bradley had loved the beautiful forests and mountains of south-east Queensland. Stephanie would also be able to visit the grave regularly during the remainder of her time as a student at Silver Springs University.

Stephanie spent Tuesday morning cloistered with Bradley's parents choosing Bradley's favourite hymns, and Bible text for the funeral. His parents were doing some of the most onerous tasks such as choosing a casket and flowers, and sorting through his clothes to find his best suit for burial.

In the afternoon Kathy reminded Stephanie that their journals for Christian Outreach were due the next day. To her surprise, Stephanie was pleased to work on her journal. Although her tears flowed freely as she wrote, Stephanie expressed herself as happy to document the last few days of Bradley and her volunteer work at the Nursing Home. Kathy caught a glimpse of what her room-mate was writing and much of it concerned how patient and funny Bradley was with the elderly residents, and how Stephanie had enjoyed their joint service to the community.

Wednesday, the students were able to collect their portraits from student services. Kathy was really pleased with the portraits she had taken with Andrew. Stephanie also collected the portraits of Bradley and herself. Stephanie placed the photographs on the bookcase, where Bradley's handsome face made the girls cry once again. She presented the duplicate copies to Bradley's parents, and one individual shot of Bradley was framed to be displayed at the funeral.

Thursday was the day that Bradley's parents had selected for the funeral. (It was also the day that the Biology Master had chosen for the Biology practical exam, but he had rescheduled to show that he was not completely in-human.) The campus meeting hall was crowded to capacity, for Bradley had been popular amongst the students. His relatives and friends from back in Melbourne, who had been able to travel were also in attendance.

Kathy was thrilled to see that Garry had flown up from Wollongong for the funeral. He walked in with Dylan, and sat down alongside Kathy and Andrew, Cara and Kaleb, Tom and Joelle, and a handful of Bradley's other closest friends. Stephanie of course was seated with Bradley's family.

The text for the day was Romans 8 verses 38-39, which Stephanie insisted embodied Bradley's courage and their hopes for the future: "For I am persuaded that neither death nor life, nor angels nor principalities nor powers, nor things present nor things to come, nor height nor depth, nor any other created thing, shall be able to separate us from the love of God which is in Christ Jesus our Lord." (NKJV)

They sang a few of Bradley's favourite songs, and then those of his family and friends least likely to break down and cry, stood up and testified to what a great guy Bradley had been. The lecturers said he had been a brilliant student, Michael announced Bradly had been a great basketball player, coach and mentor; and Joelle testified to his considerate attitude towards women. Andrew stood and delivered a few words from himself and Kathy, on how good a friend Bradley had been.

The formal service complete, those closest to Bradley followed the hearse to the cemetery in a selection of vehicles. Bradley's family had asked that this ceremony be conducted more quietly, so the main student body were asked not to attempt to follow. Instead there was a memorial meal served in the cafeteria.

It was late that afternoon in the cafeteria, when Stephanie and Garry came face to face. Stephanie extended a hand, and shyly thanked Garry for coming to the funeral.

"It was very kind of you to come," Stephanie said. "Bradley's family and I really appreciate it."

"Bradley was my friend too," Garry said firmly. "Please don't ever forget that!"

Stephanie nodded. "I won't," she agreed soberly.

"What is this some people are saying," Garry asked. "That Bradley was on his way to see me when it happened?"

Stephanie nodded. "He said he wanted to be square with you. Over me, I guess."

"We think Bradley was planning to propose to Stephanie when he got back," Kathy said.

"We don't know what Bradley meant for sure Kathy," Stephanie admonished.

However, the ring Bradley had given her had mysteriously travelled from the third finger of her right hand, to the third finger of her left hand. This was the engagement finger, and normally she would say Bradley had bought the ring just a little too large for that finger.

"I'm pretty sure," Kathy said. "I was there when he dropped a hint."

"Two of my best friends getting married," Garry said. "Why would I have minded that?"

"Some people would expect it because of the past," Kathy murmured.

"The past is the past," Garry said thoughtfully. "And the future is no longer the future - now I see. It is a funny old world."

"It is indeed," Stephanie said somewhat bitterly.

"Ironically," Garry said, "Now that it looks like my mother will be all right, I am thinking of returning to Silver Springs University next year."

"It would be nice to have you around again," Stephanie replied somewhat rigidly. "The Biology class has not been the same without you."

"So I heard," Garry said. "Dyls got his heart well and truly stomped on."

"That was farcical," Kathy said. "Annie put the hard word on him to commit, and then dumped him for an exchange student."

"Herman isn't even a bad bloke," Stephanie said. "He tried to apologise to Dylan - said he wouldn't have done it - but that Annie told him Dylan and she had not gone out for very long and were not serious."

"That was true in a way even," Kathy said.

"But not how Dylan saw it," Stephanie said.

"I see I have a lot to catch up on," Garry observed.

"Please don't expect to pick up where you left off," Stephanie said. "I honestly loved Bradley."

"I can see that," Garry said. "The same as I honestly let you go, when I went back to Wollongong. Now we have both lost a friend, let's just leave it like that!"

Friday was technically the first day of study-vacation, but many lecturers had moved their Thursday submission deadlines to Friday in recognition of the funeral. Kathy took advantage of this, submitting her portfolios for Infant Reading and Infant Maths.

Saturday morning the Music Master attempted to bring the choir back into order with a successful practice. He suggested that they dedicate the coming performance of the *Messiah* to Bradley's memory and concentrate on the way it told the message of the Christ's death and resurrection in song. While many students did not yet feel like singing, it did help to focus on Christ's resurrection making it possible to be reunited with lost loved ones such as Bradley. It also helped that the Music majors were now joining practice and singing some of their solo sections.

Sunday Kathy and Andrew attended the Reform Church service. Kathy found the tears pricking her eyes, as she sat in the very building that had hosted the funeral a few days previously. She barely heard a word of the service, and could not have told anyone what the sermon had been about if she had been quizzed later, but Andrew said it was important she was going through the motions of a normal routine.

Stephanie had not got out of bed since Friday morning. It seemed that depression had struck when Bradley's parents left after the funeral. She was barely eating or drinking, surviving on fruit and other portable snacks that Kathy brought back from the cafeteria. At first, people said it was alright to leave her like that. After a couple of days, however, the friends got worried and suggested Kathy rouse her room-mate. Sunday afternoon Kathy persuaded Stephanie to rise and shower.

The lecturers had offered Stephanie the option of deferring her examinations, but she had elected to complete them along with the other students. Her reasoning, she explained to Kathy, was that she had studied all semester and the material ought to be in her head, just waiting to come out. Also during the long break, she expected to go through all the stages of grief and denial, rendering her pretty much as emotional later, as she was at the present time.

Monday would have been Stephanie and Bradley's three month anniversary. This brought fresh torrents of tears from Stephanie. Unexpectedly, it was Dylan who rose to the occasion, and became the sustaining hero. As he shared most of her classes, except English, he demanded that Stephanie help him study, and she agreed to descend to one of the common areas to share text books and notes. Dylan also offered to come to the foyer and collect Stephanie to walk her down to their exam venues. He said he would even walk her to English, which he did not have to attend himself.

Kathy had no exam for Infant Reading, Infant Maths, Community Outreach or Art, all of which were assessed by portfolio or journal. However, Tuesday morning she and Stephanie had Educational Theories, and Wednesday afternoon they had Psychology. Kathy was then finished with exams, and began to relax and slowly pack her things.

Kathy avoided disrupting the room too badly while Stephanie still had exams. She consulted the exam timetable and subtlety kept an eye on her room-mates' progress. Stephanie had English on Thursday morning and Biology on Friday morning. The Biology practical exam, which had been moved from the funeral day, had to be made up on Friday afternoon.

Dylan was true to his word, reviewing notes with Stephanie and walking her across campus for each of her exams. Kathy overheard Stephanie attempt to thank him, and he said something like that he was the only guy from their original Biology group left, and he felt it was his place to do what Garry would have done for her, if he had still been on campus. He also added that as Cara was so occupied with Kaleb nowadays, and Annie was with Herman, Stephanie's company was a comfort to him. Revising their notes together was beneficial to them both, and could be perceived as a two way street.

As soon as the majority of students had completed their exams, the Music Master scheduled the choir's first full length practice of the *Messiah*. This meant that the students who were involved, were over at the Music Department for most of the day. A straight performance of the *Messiah* would take about three hours. However, with pieces being repeated for practice, and sung again until the Music Master was satisfied, the rehearsal took all day. Luckily the choir members got to sit back and relax, while the Music majors performed their solos and duets. These pieces were generally well polished, as the students had learned them in private lessons and as part of their semester studies.

The Music Master called a break around twelve o'clock for lunch and requested that choir members return around one o'clock to resume practice. After lunch, the Music Master explained that while he had originally envisioned the *Messiah* as a balanced performance for graduation, he had decided to place the emphasis on *Parts II & III* because these sections dealt with the death and resurrection.

It was more common, the Music Master explained, especially this time of year, to present the *Messiah* as a Christmas opera with the longer performance being material from *Part I*. As this presentation was for educational purposes, he had always intended the choir to present the full operetta. However, now that the performance was designed to honour Bradley, the Music Master had decided to trim *Part I* slightly and present more material from *Part III* in particular, which dealt with the resurrection.

This style of performance was occasionally presented around Easter time as an Easter opera.

The Music Master promised that the changes would not involve extra work for the choir, as they had already learned the required movements. It was more a matter of selection and presentation, which would be fine-tuned in the final week of practices. He assured them that for anyone who loved Music or performing, this was an exciting opportunity and well worth the time and effort they would be dedicating over the next week.

Kathy, Andrew and Stephanie were surprised when Dylan told them at Sunday lunch, that he was all packed and leaving campus that afternoon. He confided that he had applied for, and successfully acquired paid work for the long holiday period. Now that examinations were over, the following week of social activities and graduation festivities held no appeal for him. He had rallied his spirits enough to support Stephanie through the exam period, but now felt that he had little purpose on campus.

Dylan expressed the belief that nobody wanted him around, with a resurgence of the bitterness he had initially displayed when Annie dropped him. While Kathy, Andrew and Stephanie assured Dylan that they valued his company, they could not help agreeing that if he could be home spending time with his family, and making money from gainful employment, he might as well exercise his option to do so, and commence as soon as possible.

Stephanie elected to accompany Dylan in the university car to Northcoast station, and see him off on the train to Newcastle. At the last minute Kathy decided to go with them, while Andrew did something with his Theology student friends. The three friends met the college car at two o'clock and Luke dropped them off at Northcoast Station. Dylan and Luke took the heaviest pieces of luggage, then Stephanie and Kathy took the small backpack and hand items.

Dylan 'checked' his large luggage, so that the porters would shift it across from the Brisbane train to the Newcastle train when he changed at Brisbane, and unload it automatically, when he reached Newcastle station. Then he would only have his hand luggage to manage on the train.

Dylan turned to the girls. "I can't thank you enough for seeing me off," he said. "Usually Cara is a sport, but she's got so much on with Kaleb at the moment."

"You are welcome Dyls," Stephanie said. Her forehead wrinkled in concern. "You are coming back to Silver Springs next year?"

"Of course I am," Dylan said. "Don't start worrying your pretty little head about that. You will be coming back too won't you?"

"Oh yes," Stephanie said. "Dropping my studies would not fix anything."

"And with Annie and Herman graduated, and Garry back at Silver Springs, the old Life Science gang will be back together," Dylan exclaimed.

"We will be at that," Stephanie said. "But that was before Garry and I..."

"We were a team before Garry and you got together or broke up!" Dylan said firmly. "And we will be a team again whatever happens. I don't really mind Kaleb either, as he is considerate enough to include me most times."

"We were all friends last year before we started coupling up," Kathy said. She had been feeling slightly superfluous during this conversation, but now saw her chance to join in.

"Yes, we were," Stephanie said. "You are so right Kathy!"

A Brisbane-bound train came rumbling into Northcoast Station just then. The girls hugged Dylan and he climbed into the carriage.

"Goodbye Dyls," Stephanie cried.

"Good luck with the job Dylan," Kathy called.

Dylan gave them a sad-looking grin, which revealed a shadow of his former cheeky self. "I will see you next year girls," he cried, and waved until he was out of sight.

Stephanie turned her back on the train, and walked to the wooden seat that was usually their rendezvous point with the university car. "Bradley is gone forever," she said. "But it seems life goes on for the rest of us."

"Life has to go on," Kathy said. "It doesn't make Bradley's memory any less precious."

"Or any less sad," Stephanie said.

A thought struck Kathy. "Stephanie, what are you going to do while the rest of us are occupied in rehearsal for the *Messiah*?" she inquired.

"Pack the room, go for walks to all our old places, hang with friends who are not involved in the performance," Stephanie said. "Bradley's parents left me on box of his things, and I haven't visited the grave yet."

"Don't get too sad and lonely," Kathy cautioned.

"A little crying is a good thing," Stephanie said. "I have to grieve, or I don't think I will ever be able to love again."

CHAPTER FIFTEEN: THE END OF THE YEAR

Sunday morning brought a welcome freedom of choice. Andrew attended both the Inter-denominational praise service and Reform Church service, simply because he could. Kathy slept through both services because she could, and they each allowed the other to do different things, because they were supremely confident of their relationship.

Lunch time they both wanted to eat, however, so Andrew collected Kathy at the girl's dormitory and walked her across to the cafeteria. Stephanie, who had been very slowly working on packing their room, because so many things reminded her of Bradley, for instance, the dress she wore to some special worship or event, the jeans she had worn on the bike, and the poetry book they had shared, agreed to accompany them to the cafeteria.

They were half way through lunch when Phoebe entered, holding hands with Hank. Of course, Phoebe and Hank holding hands was not unusual, but the couple being on campus on the weekend when they had Hank's boarding house to retreat to, was slightly more unusual. Kathy waved and Phoebe led Hank across to their table.

"You two look happy," Kathy said.

Phoebe glanced nervously at Stephane. "We are happy," she said. "And I know the time is not quite right for you Stephanie, but please try to be happy for us."

"Of course Phoebe," Stephanie said. "I don't need you to be unhappy for me."

"Well," Phoebe said, putting her tray down and sliding into her seat.

"You know Hank has been working at the garage in Northcoast? And what with paying low rent, where he has been boarding - he has managed to save the deposit for a house."

"Well, with the first home-owners grant being reduced each year, it makes sense to buy now before it is phased out completely or anything," Hank added modestly.

"The house is tiny," Phoebe said. "It is one bedroom really, and outside Silver Springs, on the way to the state forest."

"It is one bedroom," Hank confirmed, "But there is a kitchen, lounge and laundry. The back verandah has been enclosed and I have been told that approval to turn that area into proper rooms, would be fairly easy to obtain."

"Does it have a garage?" Andrew asked, knowing that was always very important to a guy like Hank.

Hank nodded. "There is a small garage and a rundown shed at the back I can repair," he said.

"That is great news," Stephanie said.

"I sense there is something more," Kathy guessed.

Phoebe extended her left hand and the girls could see a gold band. Set into the band were a small diamond, emerald, amethyst, ruby, emerald, sapphire and topaz.

"It spells D.E.A.R.E.S.T.," Phoebe explained. "And the stones are all set in nice and deep for when I do housework."

"I'm a little confused," Stephanie said. "Is it a friendship of engagement ring?"

"It's a bit of both," Hank replied. "Most of my money has gone into the house."

"When do you plan on getting married?" Kathy inquired.

"At Easter," Phoebe said. "I checked. Easter is early next year, only the thirtieth of March. I have set the wedding date for Holy Wednesday which is March 25. That should be before you all go home for the holidays!"

"Oh wow," Kathy exclaimed.

"My mother will stay at the house a couple of weeks to chaperone and help me organize the wedding," Phoebe said. "I don't plan to take a room in the dormitory, and I'm not letting the Reform Church expel me for living with my fiancé either."

"Of course not," Andrew said. "Many Christians take an engagement as seriously as a marriage."

"It's amazing," Kathy exclaimed. "Oh I am so happy for you Phoebe!"

Stephanie brushed a couple of tiny tears aside. "It is so good to know some things can go right!" she said.

Monday to Wednesday Kathy was booked all day at rehearsals for the *Messiah*. Whenever she was not busy with rehearsal, she was occupied boxing up her possessions. Some of her clothes would be taken home, to be discarded or exchanged for other clothing. However, the textbooks, linen and clothing she relied on to get her through the university year, would all be stored in the basement, and waiting for her return.

Joelle was busy practicing for the *Messiah* with Kathy, Andrew and most of the other Theology and Music students. However her boyfriend Tom, who had also been Bradley's good friend, was not involved in the performance. He dropped by and watched occasionally, but also took the time to walk Stephanie out to Bradley's grave, so that the grieving girl could lay some flowers.

Wednesday evening, the girls gathered in Debbie's room to work out their rooming arrangements for the coming year. Kathy, who was doing a three year Primary Teaching course, was exercising her prerogative as a graduand to claim a single room. She glanced nervously in Stephanie's direction as she announced this, because she feared she was abandoning Stephanie in her time of need. However, Stephanie appeared pleased.

"Cara and I thought, that as we had so many classes together, we might share a room," Stephanie said. "We took the liberty of booking one of the basement rooms, which are absolutely huge!"

"And good for sneaking in and out of the back door," Kathy remarked slyly.

"Well that might be handy for Cara," Stephanie returned primly. "But not so useful for me at the moment."

Your time will come again," Debbie murmured.

"Phoebe is not planning to live in the dorms at all," Joelle observed. "Just fancy that!"

"We will miss her," Stephanie murmured. "What about you and Joelle, Debbie? Do you two plan to room together again?"

"No offense to Joelle," Debbie said. "But I'm planning to room with Tess. Both our boyfriends are Theology students, so we feel we have a lot in common."

"I could room with Elisabet from your English class," Joelle said, "But she may have other plans."

"There is Anita," Debbie suggested, but Joelle shook her head.

"No way," Joelle cried, "I still haven't got fully over the way she and Larry fooled me first semester."

"I don't blame you," Kathy said. "You are going out with Tom now, of course, but there is the basic issue of honesty."

"I might ask Danielle," Joelle mused, "Unless she is already rooming with Elisabet." Joelle was the least popular of the friends, as she spent long hours practicing her music, and could occasionally be insensitive to relationship cues. However no one wanted to see her completely left out.

"Well that's sorted then!" Cara said. "How many of you want to choose the basement to be near Steph and me?"

Thursday was a full dress rehearsal for the *Messiah*, which was actually fun! The members of the choir were all wearing their black and white robes, but the soloists were wearing real costumes. The choruses and movements were all falling into place, and the operetta was beginning to feel like a finished product. It was also exciting to be backed by the whole university orchestra, rather than just the piano or organ as they had been in rehearsal and on trips.

"Are you nervous about tomorrow?" Andrew whispered as the rehearsal finished.

"Not a bit!" Kathy said. "There are so many other singers and instruments, no one is going to notice me at all! I would not like to be one of the soloists however."

"I should say not!" Andrew said. "Just imagine missing a line in a huge production like that!"

"Which bits do you like the best?" Kathy asked.

"To be strictly honest," Andrew said. "I like our choruses. They have rhythm, and I know what I am saying."

"Some of the solos are a bit highbrow," Kathy admitted.

"I think the audience will have programmes with words printed in them," Joelle said. "I'm sorry, I couldn't help overhear your conversation."

"That's all right Joelle," Kathy said. "Your part on the piano is much more important than ours. Are you nervous at all?"

"A little," Joelle admitted. "But a good accompanist blends into the background. I am also pleased to be part of such an excellent arrangement."

"What do you mean?" Kathy inquired.

"I think the Music Master has done a really good job of directing this particular production," Joelle said. "I listened to a few others on tape when I was learning the pieces. Some are too heavy with the singers being drowned out by the orchestra. In others, it is hard to recognize the famous choruses when they commence."

"I see," Andrew murmured.

"Of course, music is a matter of personal taste," Joelle shrugged. "I like this, however, because the choir has been well trained and the parts are used very well. It almost has a touch of the Mormon Tabernacle Choir about the styling."

"Thanks," Kathy said. "That was a compliment to us, I think!"

"It sure was!" Joelle said. She turned and walked off with Craig, who was a music major and sung some of the solo pieces, as well as play the violin.

The families began arriving Friday morning. Some were connected to the graduands, and looked forward to seeing their loved ones walk down the aisle Sunday afternoon, to receive their degree parchments. Others, like Kathy, Andrew and Cara's respective parents, had been invited especially to hear the *Messiah*.

The graduation celebrations usually placed a strain on accommodation in the Silver Springs area, and this year, with the *Messiah* performance thrown in, the caravan parks were also full in Northcoast and even the next town over.

Kathy hugged and kissed her parents, and made sure that they were comfortable in the guest rooms of girl's dormitory. Then she hurried out to meet Andrew's parents, with her heart thumping a little. However, they turned out to be lovely kind people, who had brought up the honest and caring young man she was dating. Andrew's father was a spry, brown haired man with a sense of humour, and his mother had a lovely warm personality. Andrew's parents were staying in guest rooms in the boys' dormitory.

The cafeteria began serving tea early, so that the performers could eat, and then return to the dorms to get dressed. Once attired in their gowns or costumes, the singers discretely made their way to the private door at the back of the gymnasium.

Inside the gymnasium, the stage was filled with seats for the choir, and the area just before the stage had been set up for the orchestral accompaniment. The grand piano had been dragged out, for Joelle to play, and an organ answered her notes from the opposite side of the stage.

The singers sat down, and it seemed like mere minutes before the audience filed in, and sat on the rows of chairs which had been set up across the basketball courts. Kathy had wondered how she would feel, being able to look into the audience as she had on some of their earlier performances, but it turned out that was not a problem, because the spotlights were shining on the singers and the audience was seated in the dark.

The instruments struck up the stirring first notes. Movement flowed into movement, and soon their choruses were sung. The choir had a breather while several soloists sang their parts, and then they had a chorus or two more to sing. True to the Music Master's intention, some of the prophetic movements had been trimmed, and a slight emphasis had been placed upon the dramatic elements.

Some people say that *Handel's Messiah* does not narrate, and is more correctly described as an oratorio than an opera. However, the Music

Master had emphasised the narrative elements, and the music clearly spoke to the audience that day. During rehearsal he had justified this to the performers as reflecting the historical roots of opera that led up to the Messiah. Indeed, attendees at the first ever performance had even feared the show might be bawdy like the secular operas, or controversial like Handel's *Esther*.

The entire operetta was too long to be sung without an interval, so *Part I* and *Part II,* Scenes 1 - 3 were sung together. *Part I* dealt with the prophecies surrounding the coming of the Messiah and Jesus birth, with the very last scene hinting at his earthly ministry. *Part II,* Scene 1 dealt with Jesus' death on the cross, while Scene 2 hinted at his resurrection. The first half of the program concluded with the choir singing the rousing chorus, "*Lift up your heads*" based on Psalm 24.

There was a drink break of about half an hour, and the choir were encouraged to get up and walk around for a few minutes before returning to the stage. Then they sat down again, and the second half of the performance commenced with the recital in *Part II*, Scene 4, followed by the choir chorus. The Music Master had removed Scenes 5, 6 & 7, which generally dealt with earthly events, and transitioned straight into *Part III* with "*I know that my Redeemer Liveth*".

Part III was also full of beautiful recitals and choruses about the availability of resurrection to all Christians. The performance concluded with the rousing anthems of the "*Hallelujah Chorus*", which had been moved to the end, and placed just before the "Amen".

It was late when the concert finished, and all the excited families made their ways to their various accommodations. The front door of girls' dormitory even had to be blocked open using a brick, to prevent the electronic locking mechanism taking over and locking the door!

Saturday morning most people slept in, and the cafeteria offered extended breakfast hours, to accommodate the crowd. Kathy's Mother came into her room, to help box up the items which were scheduled for storage, and her Father carried several of the cases Kathy was taking home for the holidays, to their car. Then her father went across to the boy's dormitory to socialize with Andrew's father because he said he felt strange hanging around a girl's dormitory, even in the guest area.

Kathy's Mother extended her sympathy to Stephanie and the women shed a few tears together over Bradley.

"What a pity you did not get Bradley to buy a car earlier," Mrs. Shipton ventured to say. "That lovely young man might still have been with us today."

To Kathy's Mother's surprise, Stephanie shook her head. "I spoke to the Police at some length," Stephanie said. "The bike did not kill Bradley. The truck did. They say, 'allegedly' but that's what they mean. If a car had been broken down at that spot, the truck would have gone straight over it too."

"What exactly was wrong with the bike?" Mrs. Shipton inquired. "If you don't mind me asking."

Stephanie shrugged. "I don't mind," she said. "Most people are too frightened to talk to me about it. Some sort of fuel problem. The engine appeared to have just cut out. The Police won't say anything more."

"I guess it is best not to dwell upon it," Mrs. Shipton concluded.

"I try not to," Stephanie said. "But there is a grieving process I must go through."

"Of course dear," Mrs. Shipton said.

Saturday afternoon incorporated the formal graduation address, and the second years were not too interested in that programme. A few had attended the previous year, as everything had been new to them, however, this year they were of the opinion that the preliminary graduation festivities primarily concerned those senior students, who were due to receive their degrees. Kathy and her friends therefore continued with their own end of year chores.

Sunday afternoon, however, following the various church services and lunch in the cafeteria, the formal graduation celebration was held in the gymnasium. A number of their friends were involved, so Kathy, Andrew and Stephanie attended.

They saw Annie receive her Bachelor of Education in Physical Education, Lionel receive his degree in Science and Herman receive his Honours. Damaris received her Hospitality Certificate and Hank received recognition of his Pilot's License. Several others from Hank's class, including Rob's friend Dennis, returned to accept their Testamurs in person, but Rob did not. Somehow Kathy was not surprised.

The next morning Kathy's parents waited discretely for Kathy in the student's car park, as she returned her room key, reclaimed her deposit, and said farewell to all her female friends. Andrew and his family came over and said goodbye as well. They had decided to drive back to Canberra via the coast road, which was about an hour-and-a-half quicker than following the New England highway, although it had the reputation of being far more dangerous.

"Please take care," Kathy said, her heart skipping a beat at thoughts of Bradley.

"My father is a very safe driver," Andrew said with some amusement.

Andrew kissed Kathy full on the mouth, even though his parents were watching.

Andrew's father and Mother hugged Kathy too and made it clear they had accepted her as a potential daughter-in-law. "We want our son to ourselves until Christmas," Andrew's Mother said. "There are many family members planning to visit, and we will have a proper Grosvy reunion this year. But it's only nine hours on the bus, so you can come to us, or Andrew could go to Armidale for New Years. We will let you young ones work it out yourselves."

"Thank you Mrs. Grosvy," Kathy said. She kissed Andrew again and then walked down to the student car park to join her parents who were waiting for her.

Kathy had just reached the car, when she felt a touch on her shoulder. It was Andrew, who had run after her.

"I just had to say goodbye once again," Andrew said. "I look forward to seeing you again sometime during the holidays and then all next year."

"I can wait," Kathy said. "I am sure I've found the right guy this time. Isn't there a text somewhere which can be paraphrased 'love is patient and kind'? That is so you Andrew."

They kissed again, this time in full view of Kathy's parents.

1 Corinthians 13:4-6, 13 (New King James Version)

"Love suffers long and is kind; love does not envy; love does not parade itself, is not puffed up; does not behave rudely, does not seek its own, is not provoked, thinks no evil; does not rejoice in iniquity, but rejoices in the truth; bears all things, believes all things, hopes all things, endures all things.... And now abide faith, hope, love, these three; but the greatest of these is love."

ABOUT THE AUTHOR

Cecelia spent some years volunteering as a counsellor. She hopes that sharing her insights (in fictional form) can help empower modern youth. Life is all about being true to yourself – and maintaining your deepest beliefs.

Cecelia is also the author of:

Special Pictures to Talk About (ISBN: 978-0-646-97235-0), which developed out of her work on language delay and speech development in Kindergartens.

Silver Springtime (ISBN-13: 978-0-6481160-1-1), the first of a series of period romances following the developmental struggles of a group of teenagers attending a Christian university in the 1980s.

All for Love (ISBN: 978-0-6481160-2-8), the first of a reality television spin-off romance series.

Mystic Evermore (ISBN: 978-0-6481160-0-4), the first of the vampire series "Nevermore Parables".

Saints and Sinners (ISBN: 978-0-6481160-4-2), the second of the vampire series "Nevermore Parables".

www.ingramcontent.com/pod-product-compliance
Lightning Source LLC
Chambersburg PA
CBHW071447110726
47908CB00003B/539